BROKEN WOMEN FIGHT BACK

TALES OF THE UNDEAD & DEPRAVED

ADRIAN J. SMITH

EREKA PRESS

BROKEN WOMEN
FIGHT BACK

CHAPTER 1

Do you trust me?" Arloa's voice was sweet and tender—as if she really cared.

Jerry squinted against the bright lights she was so unused to after being in Joab, that steel-blue gaze still meeting hers. Jerry knew what she wanted to say. She equally knew what she *should* say.

"Where am I?" Jerry croaked out, going hoarse when she least expected it, but she couldn't remember the last time she had water, or the last time she used her voice for something other than screaming.

"Supply ship." Arloa brushed her fingers against Jerry's cheek, caressing her skin as though nothing had marred it.

Jerry nodded slowly and sank into the floorboards. Did she *trust* Arloa? That question had too many answers to possibly give. Yet as soon as she'd known she was in Arloa's presence, that her escape from Joab had all been arranged, an easiness spread over her. She could relax for the first time in so long, she wasn't even sure. Joab was a mindless pit of dark and torture and lessons that were forced down her throat, and she really truly had no idea how much time had passed.

Pushing her tongue against her lips, trying to wet her mouth without any water, Jerry asked, "How long?"

"Four months. I…I couldn't get to you any sooner. I tried." Again that hand against her cheek, the soft caress—Jerry couldn't tell if it was meant to soothe her or remind Arloa that she really was alive.

Her heart hammered, uncharacteristically. She couldn't get it to stop either, and she felt as though she was running a marathon, a race for her life, but she lay completely still, her hands and ankles still tied with rope, the sack that had been over her head right next to her cheek, and she couldn't move if her life depended on it—which it very well might. Jerry tried to slow her breathing, but she wasn't hyperventilating. Arloa's fingers, gentle, soft—she focused on those. Closing her swollen eyes, Jerry waited for whatever was next because at this rate she couldn't control anything.

She couldn't control herself.

"You're crying." Concern filtered through Arloa's tone.

Jerry wondered how she even managed to make tears before clenching her eyes tightly and attempting to ignore the embarrassment that hit her hard. "I tried to kill myself."

"I know," Arloa murmured. "I read the reports."

"Reports?" Jerry hurt, everywhere, but this hurt in her heart, the pain that Arloa had known everything going on while she was in Joab—everything that happened to everyone there—and just accepted it, was too much.

"Yes. My family…"

"*Is* Joab, I know." Jerry swallowed hard. "Is there any water?"

"Yes." Arloa reached into a pocket sewn into her skirts and pulled out a small vial of water. "The healer advised me not to give you too much at once, that it might make it worse in the long run."

Jerry didn't care. All she saw was the clear liquid that sat in the vial Arloa opened and handed over to her, except she couldn't move to sit upright. Her hands were still tied behind her back, making it next to impossible to move and drink, and

Arloa had yet to untie her. Arloa shifted, her knees pressing into the wood of the ship as she put the small vial against Jerry's lips.

Jerry tasted the water, the cool flavor hitting her tongue, the liquid wetting her mouth and her throat in an instant. It felt amazing. She desperately wanted more. Putting her lips around the edge of the small vial, Jerry sucked and swallowed. It was pure and heavenly. Arloa held it still, though Jerry was sure she was debating whether or not to move it.

She finished the vial before Arloa pocketed it again. Bending down, Arloa pressed their mouths together softly. Jerry tensed. She hadn't expected that, hadn't thought it would ever happen again. In fact, her entire goal had been to die and not suffer through the torments of Joab. Moving away as best as she could, Jerry murmured, "Stop."

Arloa listened, sliding away, but a pained expression filled her face. Jerry didn't have time to deal with it, or energy for that matter. She rested on the floor and wondered not for the first time when Arloa was going to release her wrists and ankles so she could stretch her muscles in a way they hadn't been used in months. *Four months.*

She still couldn't believe it had been that long. She'd never been stuck on the third-floor east wing for that long before. Jerry sighed and willed her body to fall back into a slumber, perhaps one where she might feel rested. Arloa didn't touch her again, but she did shift to lean against the wall by Jerry's head. She stretched out her legs, crossing her ankles, and Jerry frowned before clenching her eyes shut and ignoring the rest of Penum.

"I'm going to have to keep you bound," Arloa stated. "When we return to Raegina, they'll take you to a safe place for you to heal, and there I can release you."

Jerry waited in the silence, wondering if Arloa had more to say or if she was trying to keep information from her. Finally, she asked, "Why keep me bound? I'm not exactly fit to run."

"So no one can see you. I'll need to put the cover back on."

"Am I your prisoner now?"

Jerry could feel Arloa's stare even though her eyes were still closed, that intense look that meant business. She'd received it many times before and now was no different, except she'd meant her comment as a jab, as a reminder of who held all the power, which wasn't her. Staying absolutely still, her shoulder and hip dug into the floor to the point that pain seared its way into her joints.

"How could you think that?" Arloa whispered. "You're anything but my prisoner."

"You're a Kauket. It was your name that got me out of there."

Arloa blew out a breath. "It was the only way to get you out. Trust me, I tried other ways, but my family has built that place like a fortress. There is no escaping without my name."

"Then I really am still a Kauket prisoner."

"Jer, that's hardly true or fair."

Jerry remained frozen in her spot. She wasn't going to give Arloa anything to work with. She was tired of being tossed around as if her life didn't matter to anyone, of being the one who reaped the consequences of so many other's actions.

"I used my family's name to free you."

"And what about everyone else who's there? Hmm? Are they not worth your name?"

"They are." Arloa scooted down, lying alongside Jerry and hovering her fingers over Jerry's shoulder. "May I?"

"No, you may not." Jerry bit the words hard, her tone brusque as anger finally hit her. "You may not touch me, you may not kiss me, you may not do anything to me."

Arloa looked surprised, her eyes widening slightly as she lay half poised next to Jerry. Eventually, she rested her head against the floor, her gaze still locked on Jerry's. Damn the woman for having so much fucking control. "Jer, I know you're mad."

"You don't know what the hell I'm thinking or feeling, Arloa Kauket, and you won't ever understand it."

"I want to."

"You can't." Jerry wished she could turn over. She wished

she could walk out of the damn room and be done with talking to this aristocratic woman in front of her, a woman who came from a world of privilege and would never understand what it was like to grow up the daughter of a whore. Jerry just wanted to hide in a corner and never see her again.

"But I want to. Jer, let me touch you."

"No." Jerry glared with everything she had left in her. "No, you can't touch me."

"I'll have to when it's time to take you out of here."

"Find someone else to do it."

Arloa frowned. "Do you really hate me that much?"

"At the moment? Yes."

Jerry swore she saw a tear in the corner of Arloa's eye, but it vanished quickly. Arloa was slow to move, but she stood up, pushing herself to stand. She left the room without another word, and Jerry relaxed completely.

Did she trust Arloa Kauket?

Absolutely not. No Kauket was worth any trust. She had learned that from an early age when fear of Joab had hit her and she knew she'd likely end up there one day. The Kaukets fostered a sense of security and entitlement for their family that couldn't be undone by anything. They had their hands in the government, in the systems that kept the classes divided, in everything that would keep them in power and others not.

But did she trust Arloa?

Fuck, she wanted to. Jerry would give anything to go back to that first day in the bar when they'd met, those first few months of a relationship that was building, pure and without expectations or complications. Pure lust and love were all it was, and both had fallen headfirst into it, willingly. She wanted to trust this woman who kept rescuing her, who kept pulling her out of the pits of hell that oddly enough Jerry landed in because of her.

But right now, while she lay on the floor of a supply ship, a ship that would keep Joab running smoothly, her hands still bound, her body still weak, a small amount of water in her system, she couldn't. She wouldn't allow herself to trust someone who hid behind smoke and mirrors, who held secrets so close to her heart that she wouldn't let Jerry all the way in, a woman who willingly used a name she claimed she abhorred in order to get what she wanted.

If Arloa wanted to divorce herself from her family, she would. She wouldn't use that to her advantage. But time and time again, she did. She used her family name to get what she wanted and needed. Jerry would never be able to do that because the fucking name Adelric was so unknown that it meant absolutely nothing. Cringing, Jerry closed her eyes and calmed herself. If she was going to be stuck there while they flew back to Raegina, she might as well rest while she could. Because the first opportunity she got to escape Arloa's clutches was one she would take.

Jerry woke up when the ship settled. She assumed it was in harbor, but knowing Arloa, she couldn't actually make that conjecture. Frowning, Jerry looked at the door to the small room she had been shoved into and waited for it to open. She waited for Arloa to come through and talk to her, because as much as she was angry, she wanted to see those steel-blue eyes again, the blonde curls in a mess down her back.

The creak of the door alerted Jerry to the fact someone was about to join her. She was still somewhat surprised when Arloa stepped inside. She frowned. "I need to put the sack on. They don't know who you are."

"I...what?" Jerry's eyes widened. "They don't know?"

Arloa shook her head. "I didn't want anyone else to know."

"But the guard who took me—"

"He knows, but he's been taken care of. No one else is aware." Arloa knelt down, her skirts fluttering around her. She grabbed the burlap sack and frowned at it. "I'm so sorry to have to do this."

"Just do it already. I don't need apologies."

Arloa sighed and pulled her full lower lip between her teeth. "I think you deserve apologies from more than just me, but unfortunately, I can't make the world bow at your feet as much as I would like to."

Without any further preamble, Arloa pulled the sack over Jerry's head and tied it loosely around her neck.

"Please know, Jer, I do genuinely love you."

Jerry bit the side of her cheek to keep from saying anything. Whether it was stupid or stubborn she wasn't sure, but she wasn't going to say a damn thing to Arloa that she didn't have to. Eventually, she heard Arloa stand up and leave the room. It seemed to take forever, but the door opened again and Jerry was wrenched from her place on the floor. She was shoved into the wall, a hand around her neck to the point she sputtered for air.

A heavy body pressed against her, hot breath pushing through the burlap and into her face. Jerry cringed at the scent, which was enough to tell her the rest and water had done wonders for her already. She held still, hands groping her breasts, her hips, her crotch. They stopped in an instant before dragging her out and shoving her forward.

She couldn't see to step over the doorway, so her boot hit it hard and caused her to almost fall forward. She was dragged back by the collar of her shirt and the burlap bag, strangling her sharply. Jerry held back the grunt and growl, straightening her shoulders as best as she could. At least she could walk out this time, mostly.

Large hands on her shoulders shoved her down into something. She found it odd she was going deeper into the ship rather than toward the deck. Finally, she breached the door and the cool breeze off the harbor brushed against her skin. Immediately, she was dragged down and shoved into a small vessel. A hand on her head forced her to lie down against the curved bottom of the transport. Jerry frowned, wondering where she was being taken, but she played along with it.

They flew for at least twenty minutes before they set down. She was rolled out of the transport and dropped onto the hard dirt. The transport flew off. Confused, Jerry tried to wiggle free from the ropes so she could see where she was, fend for herself, but she was greeted with nothing other than silence and the inability to do anything she damn well wanted to.

"Fuck this," Jerry muttered as she tried again to wiggle her legs through the loop of her hands to at least get them in front of her body so she could move more freely.

"Hold still." Arloa's tone shook her.

The sound of rope cutting halted every movement Jerry made, and she lay still. With her wrists free first, she flopped onto her back and pulled them around her front to grab at the sack on her head while Arloa cut the ropes at her feet. Finally seeing this woman in the blessed daylight stunned her. She was gorgeous. Jerry's stomach twisted with the desire to thank her and hate her at the same time, so she kept absolutely silent, trying to judge what she was really feeling.

It was simply a gut reaction to being freed, wasn't it?

Arloa sat back on her haunches, the knife still held loosely in her hand. "Happy now?"

"Thank you," Jerry murmured with a slight pout to her voice.

"We have to walk to the edge of town before we can get you into a carriage."

"Where are you taking me?"

"To a safe place." Arloa sighed and stared down at the ground between them. "Somewhere you can heal before we figure out what to do with you."

"Is *Yarrow*..." Jerry couldn't even finish the question, her voice breaking. Did they make it? Did they evade the authorities? Was her crew still alive and well?

Arloa nodded sharply. "Yes, *Yarrow* is safe. She's been under Yafe's command since you've been gone."

Arloa said it as though Jerry had taken a trip instead of having been locked inside Penum's most notorious prison system disguised as rehabilitation. Jerry sighed in relief, closing her eyes and rubbing her wrists.

"We have to get moving. We're not safe here." Arloa went to grab Jerry's arm to help her up, but Jerry jerked back.

"I told you not to touch me."

Arloa held her hands up. "I was going to assist you in standing, since you haven't exactly had a good track record at doing that since we found you."

"Found me? You knew exactly where I was. There was no finding."

"You're right. Since I was able to secure your freedom."

"What freedom? I'm a fugitive now."

"For now," Arloa corrected. "Come along. I have a healer who's going to look you over."

Jerry said nothing to that, not wanting to add to the tension before she was someplace she could relax and rest. As soon as they got wherever they were going, she would find a way to get hold of Yafe or Azar and find her way home. She wasn't going to stay in Arloa's presence any longer than necessary.

Hating to admit it, Jerry had to hold onto Arloa's hand to stand. Her legs were far weaker than she anticipated, and as soon as she was fully upright, a wave of dizziness hit her head and nearly took her back down. Arloa wrapped an arm around her back and held tightly so she wouldn't fall. She waited for it to pass before nodding her affirmation to Arloa that they could move forward.

The walk to the edge of Raegina's city borders was slow. Jerry was exhausted by the time they were halfway there, but she'd forgotten the beauty of this part of the country. The trees were tall, high into the sky as they protected the ground from the onslaught of the sun. The ground was covered in life, crops that harvesters would come out and gather in order to feed those in town and create the food packets they all abhorred.

Squash grew wild, climbing the trunks of the trees in order to find the sun and grow faster and better. Arloa glanced around before leaving Jerry and bending down to a tomato. She grabbed a small one, barely bigger than Jerry's thumb, then another. She plopped one between her teeth before putting the other up to Jerry's lips. Instinctually, Jerry took it, and groaned as the flavor hit her. She'd never tasted food like this before. Arloa smiled at her.

"My father used to take me here when I was young to learn how our food stores were created."

Jerry remained silent.

"I had never tasted food like this until then, and never again. Food packets, while nutritious and filled with what we need, lose something of the essence of flavor. And the *fresh* fruit you can buy in the city is old."

Jerry pursed her lips and took a step toward Raegina. She wasn't going to respond, anger still burning in the pit of her belly. Arloa said nothing else as she wrapped her arm around Jerry's back, and they continued their long walk to the edge of town.

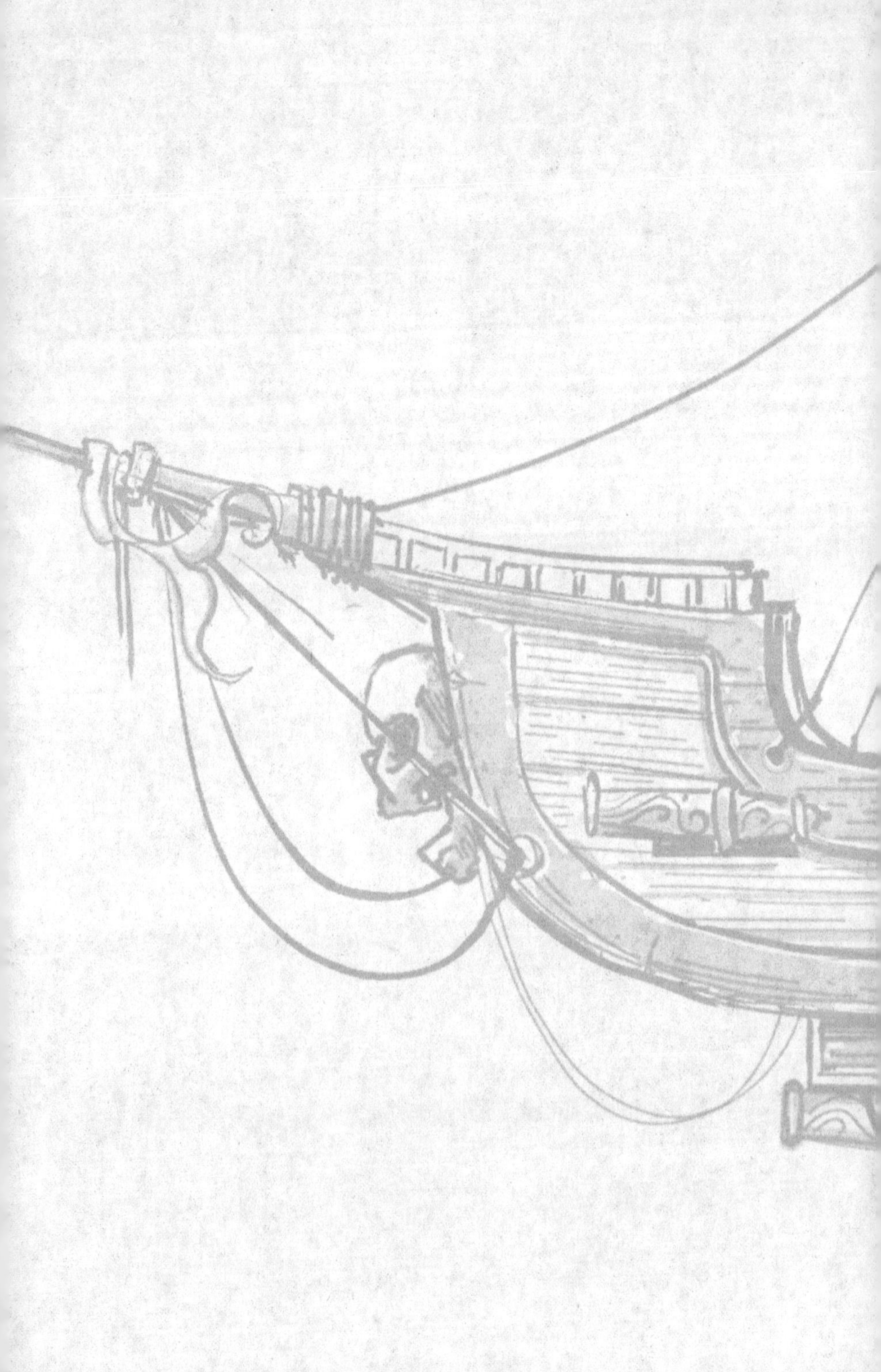

CHAPTER 2

The little hidey-hole Arloa took her to was not what she had expected. It wasn't done up with extravagant things, although that would be odd considering they were on the edge of the inner city. Jerry had collapsed onto the small cot in the corner of the basement room when they'd arrived and had slept blissfully all night. Arloa had said she wasn't going to leave her alone just yet, and as much as it pained Jerry to admit, that was a welcome relief.

When she pried her eyes open, Arloa was right there with a vial of water and a food packet. Jerry had each of them slowly. It had been so long since she'd been given more than scraps to keep herself alive. She stared at Arloa as she ate, the way her crooked nose seemed to stand out a little more now than before.

Wetting her lips, Jerry asked, "How did you break your nose?"

"What? Oh." Arloa blushed, her cheeks tingeing a beautiful pink as she glanced down at the floor and back up. "Schoolyard fight."

"I want the whole story." Jerry wasn't going to let her off easy. This woman had once proclaimed love for her, and if that was true, then Jerry wanted to know every facet of who she was. "How'd you get it?"

Arloa sighed heavily and dropped her hands to her lap as she leaned against the far wall, sitting on the floor. "Mind if I sit with you? This floor isn't the easiest on my old bones."

"Because you're so old."

Arloa frowned, but Jerry nodded her agreement and scooted over to give Arloa the room to sit. She stayed half-propped on the cot and wall while Arloa sat with her back rigid, probably the way she had been taught. "I am old compared to you."

"Hardly."

"I was sixteen when you were born, the same age as your mother."

Jerry stilled, raising her gaze up. "How do you know about that?"

"I'm in the government, Jer. I did my research when I discovered who you were, and as I said, I read your files while I was plotting your escape."

Cold washed through her. If Arloa knew everything about her already, they were on uneven footing by far. Jerry clenched her jaw tightly, not sure what to say or do next. Luckily, she didn't have to because Arloa continued.

"I am much older than you, all things considered. However, I didn't break my nose in a schoolyard fight. That's simply the story I was told to share when I was a child and it became too much of a habit for me to break."

"Then how did you break it?" Jerry took another small bite of her food packet, savoring the tar flavor in a way she never thought she would. Compared to the fresh tomato, it was nothing, but compared to what she had been given in Joab this time around, it was everything.

"My father broke it." Arloa paled. "In one of his rages when I accidentally said something I shouldn't have. I had a question about my homework for school and found him in his study. He was in a meeting of some sort, I don't really remember, but I pushed back when he said my homework could wait. Later that night, I received my punishment for embarrassing him in front of his colleague."

Jerry gave her a hard stare. Nothing that Arloa had shared about how she was raised had given any hint that she had grown up with an abusive father. Jerry had never been hit like that, not by her mother or Miriam. "That's awful."

"I know." Arloa gave her a sad look. "That's honestly not the worst of it, just the most visible."

"Arloa," Jerry crooned, sitting up as best as she could and leaning forward to touch Arloa's arm. She realized too late she was breaking the rules she had set in place, touching without permission, a societal rule she upheld frequently. But something about this moment felt right to break down those walls. "It's not your fault, you know that, right?"

"Some days." Arloa's eyes were filled with tears when she glanced into Jerry's. "Others that's difficult to believe." Arloa swiped her hands against her cheeks and swallowed to clear her throat. "The healer will come tomorrow."

"Maisie?"

"No, someone else. Maisie's no longer alive."

"What happened?"

"It's a long story."

There Arloa went again with hiding things. Jerry hated when she did that, and it made her all the more determined to unravel the truth from her. "I'll be here awhile."

"You will. But not today. You'll have to stay here until we can sort out your identity or clear your name."

Jerry snorted. "No one gets their name cleared in Raegina. Not after six stints in Joab."

Arloa's look echoed Jerry's truth.

"What will my new name be?"

"I don't know. I suppose we should speak with Miriam, but that can wait."

"It can," Jerry agreed.

Jerry coughed into her shoulder, the need for blood resurfacing rapidly. She shuddered at the sensations roiling around her, as if the beast within her was awakening for the first time in months. She frowned at the thought, suddenly realizing the entire time she'd been in Joab these cravings had been muted. Swallowing hard, Jerry debated whether or not to say anything to Arloa. At one point she had shared everything she could with her, trusting that Arloa would hold the truth sacred. But now? She realized how much she truly didn't know about her, and what a risk it was to do that. And yet, Jerry was going to need some kind of sustenance to tide her over.

"What are we going to do about my other need?"

"I can bring something tomorrow."

Jerry took the flying risk because she honestly saw no other way to do this. She was stuck there until she found her way out, and at that point, she wouldn't be able to walk down to the harbor on her own. "Do you know what they gave me in Joab?"

"What do you mean?"

"I haven't…" Jerry paused, starting again when she had more gumption. "I haven't had any cravings."

Arloa raised her thin blonde eyebrow before her forehead wrinkled in concentration. "What do you mean?"

"Meaning I don't remember them giving me any kind of drug or…brain…and I don't remember craving anything or needing anything to survive." Jerry crossed her arms against her chest, as if to protect herself from the outside world that saw her as the enemy. "What did they give me? Or what did they do to me while I was there?"

"I don't know. I do know they gave strict orders that they couldn't kill anyone else because of the virus."

"But if they're facing the lack of vestigen like we are out here, then how—"

"I don't know," Arloa cut her off. "I'll have to do more research."

Jerry held herself tightly, closing her eyes as she tried to remember again if she'd felt anything like she was feeling now while she'd been locked away. They had to be giving her something, somehow. It would be impossible for her to survive into sanity without it. But what on Penum were they giving inmates?

"I can speak with my father—"

"No," Jerry stated firmly. "You won't. There's no risk or answer that'll be worth that."

Arloa nodded a slow agreement. "I'll see what I can find."

Jerry pushed herself up more, grimacing at the pain in her back. She remembered the lashings suddenly, regretting the move in an instant. It was as though all the injuries she'd sustained in the last few months were coming back slowly, as if a drug was leaving her system. As much as she didn't want a healer, perhaps they would be able to resolve that as well.

"Arloa?"

"Hmm?"

"Will you look at my back? I...I don't know how bad it is."

"How bad what is?"

"The cuts."

At Arloa's confused look, Jerry shifted again to pull at her tunic. She pulled it over her head and dropped it onto the floor. Not that she wanted to wear the thing again, but Arloa hadn't brought her any clean clothes and so she would have to put it on. Arloa stood up and moved to the top of the cot, hissing as she got the first glance at Jerry's back.

"What did they do to you?"

Jerry looked over her shoulder. "Standard whipping. Everyone gets whipped in Joab. I thought you said you read the reports."

"This wasn't in them." Arloa put her hand on the side of Jerry's shoulder, likely to avoid any open wounds. "This looks... Jer, I've never seen injuries this bad before."

"I've had them before. The last time I was in Joab."

"You didn't have any scars."

"I found a healer."

Arloa locked their gazes together. "I'm going to see if Issa can come sooner."

"It won't matter."

"You'll be in less pain." Arloa lifted her hand as if the mere touch hurt. "If I had known..."

"What exactly was in the reports?"

"Psychological evaluations, medical evaluations, a strict routine of behavior modifications and education."

Jerry pursed her lips. "Well, it's not exactly wrong on that front, just the depth and specificity of what they do was left out it seems."

"They whip you?"

"On the cross."

"What do you mean?" Arloa moved around to sit in front of Jerry again.

Jerry dragged her knees up to hide her small breasts, still never quite comfortable with her own awkward body, especially with the image of perfection in front of her. She rested her chin on her knees and looked Arloa over. "The cross. They shackle your wrists and ankles to it and whip you until you tell them the correct answers to their questions."

Arloa's gaze hardened. "They torture you."

"Well, yes. What did you think they did?"

"Rehabilitation."

Jerry laughed. "Hardly. The goal of Joab is survival. They do release most inmates, so long as they're not there for a grievous crime or so long as they're not back too many times, like me."

"You don't think they were going to release you?"

"No. I know they wouldn't. In order for me to escape Joab, I would have to die, and unfortunately, the virus makes it far more difficult to kill me."

"But you did escape." Arloa leaned forward and hovered her hand over Jerry's on her arm. "May I?"

"Yes."

"I should have known," Arloa confessed. "I know what my

family is like, and I should have suspected there was far more going on than they said, but I never honestly looked into it. I had other things to worry about."

"Like becoming a senator?"

"Yes. Fulfilling my duties as a daughter and as a Kauket."

"I thought you had escaped your family." Jerry flipped her hand so she grasped onto Arloa's, curling their fingers together. "Seems neither of us has managed to escape our past."

"Seems so," Arloa whispered. Silence fell between them until Arloa broke it. "I'm so sorry, Jer. I'm so very sorry."

"You didn't know."

"But I should have."

"But you *didn't*, so stop letting guilt eat away at you. There's nothing that could be done about it except exactly what you did."

Arloa lifted her eyes up to meet Jerry's in a long look. It seemed as though they had found an impasse, as much as Jerry had wanted to be mad at Arloa still, she couldn't. Not with that look, not with the soft touches and words and apologies.

"I want to know what's going on."

"What do you mean?" Arloa seemed taken aback, and Jerry realized how forceful her question had come out.

"I want to know what's going on with this virus. Why did it suddenly reappear after seven hundred years, why is there a new strain, why didn't I suffer any of the symptoms while in Joab. There has to be another treatment out there."

Arloa nodded. "Yes, we need answers. I would love someone to blame, but sometimes these are freak things that happen."

Jerry furrowed her brow. She didn't think this was a "freak thing" that had just happened. This felt far too calculated, and she'd been so caught up in surviving that she hadn't paid attention, but with returning from Joab where she had in one way been tortured and in another found the best reprieve ever, she wanted answers. At the very least, she wanted to know what kind of treatment they had that she didn't. It would ease her discomfort immensely.

"Why are only the lower-class citizens affected by the virus? Hmm?"

Arloa shook her head. "That's not true."

"It's largely true, and you know it. Stop arguing like a politician and look at the trends." Jerry straightened her back and instantly regretted the move. She slouched again when the pain receded. A healer would be welcome, as much as she hated to admit it. She didn't want to see another person go through the pain she had experienced in order to heal her own body of its mutilations.

"I'll look to see what I can find," Arloa muttered. "But Jer, you need to rest."

"I know, and I will. I have nothing to do here anyway, no devices to toy with, no name to leave with. If I sneak out now, I'll never be able to return."

"Good, I'm glad we're in agreement on that at least."

Jerry was about to say they agreed about one other thing— love—but she kept that to herself, still settling in with the idea in her own heart. She didn't need to bring much more attention to it. "How long can you stay today?"

"I do need to leave soon, but I wanted to make sure you were fed—" Arloa looked pointed at the half-eaten food packet "— and well enough that I could."

"You need to show face in the government so they don't suspect you."

"What will they suspect? That I've taken a few days' rest?"

"Which coincides with the escape of a prisoner from Joab?" Jerry knew what that would look like to anyone, and she knew the coincidence wouldn't be overlooked so easily by Arloa's enemies.

Arloa parted her lips as if she was about to speak, shook her head, and then relaxed back. "I should be going. I'll come back tonight."

"I don't need watching over."

"You do." Arloa touched her hand lightly. "And I want to. Call it fear, but I don't want you out of my sight for very long, at least not right away. When you're stronger, then I'll trust more."

Jerry couldn't fault her logic there. If there was a fight, or if Jerry did have to escape for any reason, then she would be hard pressed to take care of herself. She had barely managed to stand long enough to relieve herself in the chamber pot, and had nearly toppled the thing over while she tried to get back onto the cot. It was something she didn't want a repeat of.

"Would you mind bringing some fresh clothing for me? The thought of getting back into that," Jerry indicated the tunic still on the ground "is stressful."

"I'll do that."

"Thank you." Jerry bowed her head slightly.

"May I kiss you this time?"

"Yes."

Jerry lifted her chin to receive a delicate kiss from Arloa. There was nothing meant to incite, but everything about it was comfort and, dare she admit, nearly home to her. She lingered in the touch until Arloa pulled back and curled her fingers around Jerry's ear with her hair in tow.

"We'll have to do something about your hair."

"Is it that bad?"

"We'll likely need to cut a good amount of it off."

"Perfect." Jerry grimaced. "I'll mess with it while you're gone and see what I can salvage."

Arloa nodded but said nothing as she stepped away from the cot and toward the steel door. She opened it and left without another word. Cast into silence, Jerry sighed and relaxed every single muscle that was still tense. She knew she was on the edge of the inner-city limits, but her brain had been so fuzzy when they'd arrived that she barely remembered how to get out—not that she couldn't figure it out should she need to. Arloa had certainly not locked the door.

With nothing but her memory of the last four months, which was scant and difficult to bring to the forefront of her mind, and the longing to find her family and home again, Jerry stayed put. She was in no shape to go on an adventure or to make her presence known. Both she and Arloa had known that when she'd arrived there. Until then, Jerry would have to wait for her body to heal, and pry more into Arloa's personal life and past.

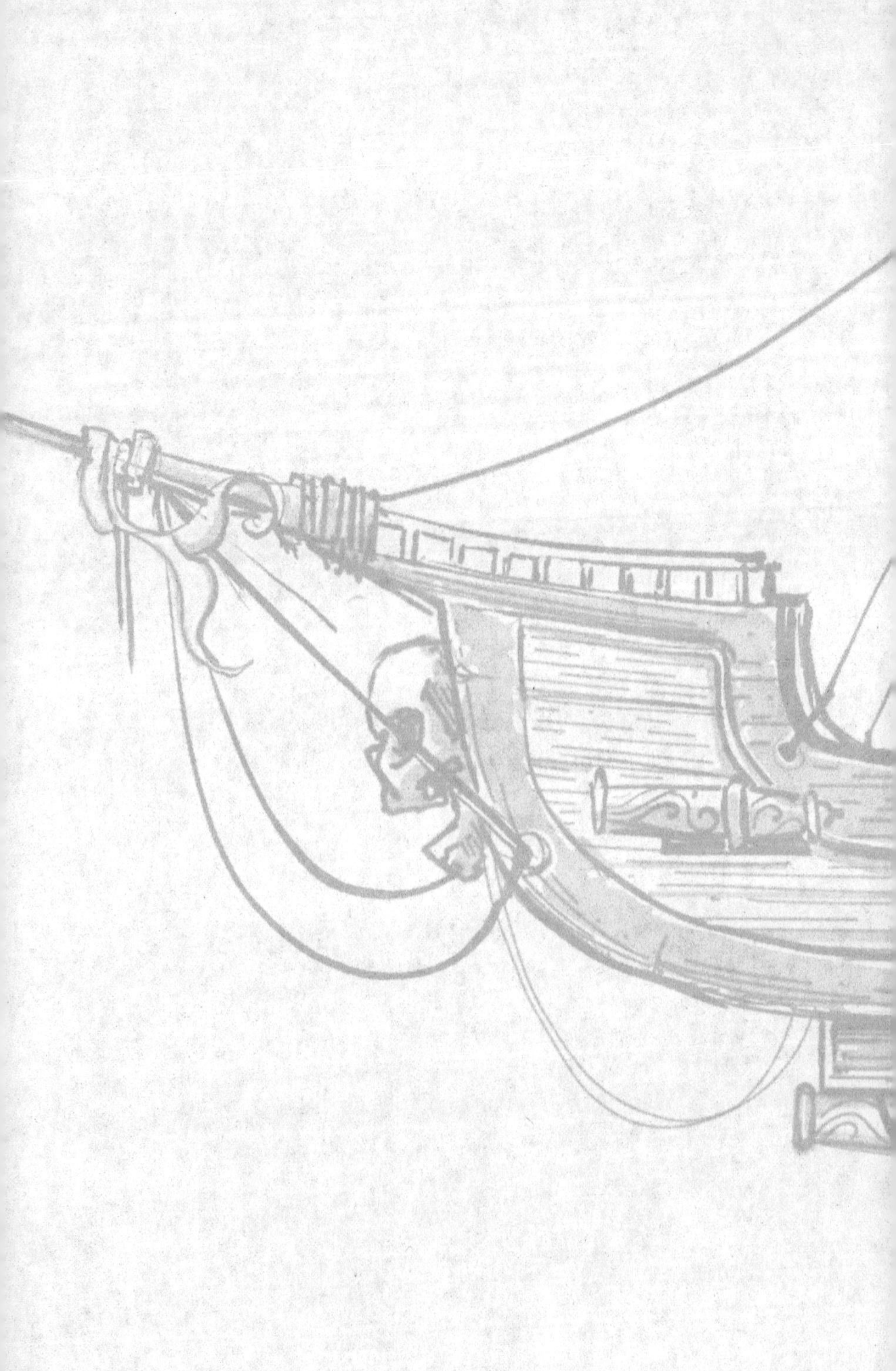

CHAPTER 3

Over the days Jerry had taken to sleeping when Arloa was gone and staying up late to talk with her when she returned. Surely at some point Arloa would have to stop. Someone would notice that she was coming there frequently, a woman of money, and it would be out of place. Surely someone would follow her.

Jerry sat against the wall on the cot, staring at Arloa's profile as she worked on a device she had brought with her. Jerry still hadn't been allowed technology, not that she had the energy to deal with it in the first place. Sighing, Jerry rested her cheek on her knees again, watching as Arloa worked on something she had little desire to know about.

"Why did you rescue me?" Jerry asked, out of the blue.

Arloa jerked her head upright, eyes wide, as they stared at each other. The small room had yet to become confining, and Jerry was pretty sure that was because of the excessive amount of time she had spent in Joab.

"What?" There was accusation in her tone, and Jerry wasn't sure what caused it.

"Why did you rescue me?" Jerry repeated.

"What else was I supposed to do? Leave you there to die?"

Her eyes bored straight into Jerry's soul, the offense at Jerry's question unmistakable.

"If you truly thought those reports were reliable, why would I need rescuing?" She was picking a fight, but she couldn't seem to stop herself. Anything would be better than the depression she couldn't escape.

Arloa sighed. "You were there unjustly. Legal means to release you were fruitless."

"Unjust?" Jerry furrowed her brow. "I stole your ship, killed a pirate and his crew, stole his ship, then killed my own captain when she usurped my ship. I'd hardly call that unjust. And that's just the month before I was arrested. We're not even talking about stealing from Potelia."

It was the first time Jerry had admitted just how much maiming she had done in the past year, and she shuddered through the memory of the faces she'd killed before bolstering herself. Killing was all part of pirating, and that was something she was going to have to continue to get used to. Glancing up at Arloa, Jerry seemed to catch her off-guard. Arloa looked as though she had no answer to give.

"Truly…why did you rescue me? If you thought it was reha-bilitation, then why would you come for me?"

"Because I didn't want you there." Arloa sighed, her cheeks pinking as the argument calmed.

That was at least a somewhat satisfactory answer, but Jerry wanted more. She needed a better reason in order to give all of herself over to Arloa. "Where did you want me?"

"Where *I* could have you," Arloa mumbled, glancing down at her device as if she was going to go back to work. It was no doubt a distraction technique, but Arloa had never been someone who needed to be distracted from these types of conversations before.

Jerry leaned forward and covered Arloa's hand to still her fingers. It took a long time, but Arloa raised her gaze up to

Jerry's eyes and sighed, her entire face softening as if she was giving in to the inevitable.

"I always want to help, Jer, but when it comes to you, I am compelled to."

"Compelled?" Jerry gave a light laugh. "You make it seem as though you're a machine and I'm pulling the levers."

"Some days it feels like that." Arloa settled the device next to her on the cot and lowered her gaze to their connected hands. "I started looking for a way to reverse engineer vestigen because after you became ill and vestigen was discovered I realized the stores were limited."

"Limited?"

"Yes, there wouldn't be enough. I lobbied to convince the government to make more, but they were adamant they couldn't. When I had exhausted all those possibilities, I moved on to creating it myself."

"Helps to have money, doesn't it?" Jerry hadn't meant the comment to come off as a jab at how Arloa had grown up and the family she was born into, but it did have a sting in it.

"It does some days," Arloa answered on a sigh. "It also helps to have connections with the underground, which you have."

Jerry frowned. "But if I'm to remain hidden…"

Arloa lifted a shoulder in a shrug. "It'll take some people knowing, unfortunately. Can you trust Miriam to keep that secret?"

Jerry wanted to be able to say yes, but at the same time, she worried that Miriam would sell her out for the right amount. But Jerry couldn't imagine who might be interested in who she used to be for any reason except her connection to the woman in front of her. Jerry kept her mouth shut, not answering that question when she realized Arloa had neatly evaded the simple question she had asked.

"Why did you rescue me?" she repeated again, really wanting to know.

Arloa's lower lip trembled. "I have spent most of my life

building walls around me to protect me, and in one simple night, you managed to shatter some of them."

"Not all."

Arloa let out a light chuckle. "No, not all of them. That night when I met you something happened for me, and suddenly there was more to my life than aspirations and dreams."

"Are you calling it love at first sight?" Jerry wrinkled her nose.

Laughing, Arloa shook her head. "Hardly. Lust for sure, but love came later. However, sitting with you, meeting with you on *Yarrow*, learning about your life caused me to realize how insulated I had continued to stay despite my attempts to break through those barriers."

"You're still not answering my question," Jerry prodded.

"I am, bear with me." Arloa pulled her feet up under her, smoothing out her skirts around her legs and ankles to cover any skin like a proper woman would. Jerry wondered if she even realized what she was doing, if she knew how modest she was despite the desire not to be.

"I rescued you because you were in need, because I couldn't find any other way to release you from Joab. However, I rescued you because I knew you needed it."

Jerry raised her gaze, meeting those steel-blue eyes in a firm stare. "Needed it?"

"I knew you had been in Joab before, and when I discovered you'd returned, I...I couldn't let you stay there. Call it a compulsion to have what I want, but I wanted you with me. I still want you with me."

Jerry frowned, not sure if that was as good an explanation as she wanted to get, but it would have to do for now. "Are you still working on reverse engineering the vestigen?"

Sighing, Arloa grabbed the device again and pulled something up on it before handing it over to Jerry. "Yes, but not as heavily. With the recent discovery of an alternative—"

"You mean brains."

"Yes." Arloa rubbed her thumb over her fingertips. "Brains. With that alternative in the cycle and with the majority of individuals dead rather than attempting to live, there hasn't been as pressing a need."

Jerry wrinkled her nose. "Were you able to look and see what they were giving me in Joab?"

"I looked, but I haven't found anything. I'm still looking, however." Arloa took the device back and set it next to her. "The longer you remain hidden, the more time you'll have to heal properly. I'm sorry the healer hasn't been able to come."

Jerry shook her head. It wasn't anything she hadn't dealt with before, and she would continue to deal with it until she had an alternative. She'd been slowly garnering her strength back, walking laps in the small room. "Arloa?"

"Yes?"

"This virus...you can't tell me it's natural."

Arloa sighed heavily, pushing herself to stand and gather the supplies she had brought. "I'm not entirely sure I agree with that."

Jerry barked out a laugh. "What news outlets have you been trusting? You really think this virus lay dormant for seven hundred years and suddenly it comes back to bite us all in the ass? It's never been seen before."

Arloa leaned against the small table that was in the room, sitting against the edge of it. "I think we don't know where it came from. Could be someone unearthed something that still had the live virus in it."

"Horseshit!" Jerry moved to the edge of the cot, debating whether she could stand to argue or not. She wanted to. She wanted to be able to push herself up and use her body to win this argument, but at the same time, her knees still felt weak and her back ached something mad. Instead, she pleaded. "Think about it."

"I have thought about it." Arloa pinned her with a hard stare. "And I just don't see it."

"You've been drinking the tea." Jerry shook her head in disappointment. "I thought you were better than that."

"I haven't." Arloa shot her a dirty look. "I simply believe it can happen."

"And what about aristocrats not becoming ill? Hmm? You said yourself you were immune."

"I am. I've tested my blood."

"How? No one else I know from my part of Raegina—you know, the poor part—is immune."

Arloa's lips parted, but she had no argument.

"No aristocrat who wasn't already sick has fallen ill, no one who has—"

"A place in society?" Arloa raised an eyebrow at her. "If I take this as fact, let's make that assumption for a moment, that this virus was manufactured. To what end?"

"You really are one of them, aren't you?" Jerry's heart shattered, the devastation that they had been through so much and Arloa still wouldn't believe her.

Arloa snapped her eyes up at that, anger and hurt flashing through her gaze. "I beg your pardon."

"No one wants us here, Arloa. We're the scourge of the earth, the ones who can't be bothered for anything, the ones who carry the load of this world on our shoulders, but no one seems to blink and see."

"What you're talking about is genocide."

"A slow one, yes!" Jerry's eyes lit as if Arloa finally understood. "That's exactly what I'm talking about. A slow death for those of us who are so unsightly we can't be allowed to exist anymore. It's the perfect way to take over the world."

"It would break Penum to lose that amount of people."

"We're not broken yet, are we?"

"That's in debate." Arloa crossed her arms, her breasts pushing against the fine deep blue corset she wore, the creamy skin rising and falling with her breaths. Jerry snapped her eyes up to her face as Arloa continued, "Penum is failing, miserably.

It's not just Raegina. Some countries are faring better, but Raegina is one of the worst."

"Because the government never cared about *our* people!" The way Jerry said it was meant to imply that Arloa was not considered one of Jerry's people. The shadow that fell across Arloa's face told her enough. She understood the implicitly spoken comment, and she understood that Jerry was correct. "It makes perfect sense they would try to reduce our population enough that we were less of a burden on society but still able to carry the burden of making society run."

"But so many have died."

"But what if that wasn't the intention? I've looked at history. It's clear as day. There are dozens of stories where some virus sweeps through the poor and kills us off. Population control."

"That's asinine."

"It's true! Look at the historical records."

Arloa shook her head slowly, but suddenly she stopped, as if the realization had hit her. "Who would do something like this?"

"Anyone. I always assumed the government as a whole planned it."

Arloa scowled. "I've not been part of any conversation like that."

"You wouldn't. You've shown your true colors before you even entered the governmental ranks. They know not to talk to you about it." Was Arloa honestly considering this? Was she giving Jerry's insane idea credence?

"They wouldn't do something like this."

"Think about it, please. Because most of us in the pits of Raegina and Penum agree. They want us for what we can provide and nothing more. We're strong in masses, and if they can control our population, they will. Why do you think they made it legal for relationships like ours? It reduces the population."

"This is ridiculous."

"How can you be so blind!" Jerry's voice rose, and she

worried she was going to cause someone beyond the safety of the door to find her. Biting her tongue, she brought her frustration down to a reasonable level. "Why can't you see this?"

"Because I haven't wanted to. I like to think the best of people when I can. That much should be obvious by now."

"And when they shatter that image?" Jerry was pushing it, but she wanted to. They needed to have this out already.

Arloa's look said revenge, and Jerry was glad to find it lingering in the abhorrent expression. She had never thought about attempting to turn the government in on itself in order to succeed in getting her point across. To be fair, though, she had been too busy trying to survive in the world she'd been born into than to save it from itself.

"What are you going to do?" Jerry whispered.

"First I'm going to research this and confirm whether your insane thoughts are accurate or not. Secondly..." Arloa trailed off, her hands clenched into tight fists at her sides. She scoffed and rolled her eyes.

Jerry felt awful for her. Standing, she moved carefully to Arloa's position against the table and brushed fingers across her shoulder before threading their fingers together in a tight grasp. "I'm so sorry."

"No." Arloa shook her head. "I'm sorry. I should have paid closer attention."

"You were raised on the inside, and you were taught not to look."

"But I have looked, Jer. I have. I swear I have."

"But how deep?" Jerry reached behind Arloa's head and pulled her tight against her in an embrace. She rubbed the tense muscles of Arloa's neck and eased them as they stood together. She breathed in Arloa's scent, remembering what it had been like to fuck her, to kiss her, to be in her presence each and every time they had managed to meet. Jerry sighed into that memory, one of those good times she didn't want to lose. "Do your research. We can discuss more later."

Arloa nodded, and Jerry pulled back slightly.

"When did you say the healer was coming again?"

Frowning, Arloa put her hands on Jerry's hips and stayed leaning against the desk. "There's been a delay."

"How long?"

"I don't know." Arloa swallowed. Her breathing increased. Her gaze was locked on Jerry's chest, as if she could forget the conversation they'd been having simply by focusing on something else, something far more pleasant. Jerry curled her fingers in Arloa's hair and tugged slightly until Arloa's chin was raised so their lips could meet.

The kiss was meant to soothe ruffled feathers, to ease Arloa's emotional discomfort, and that was solely what it was, nothing more, since Jerry was still recovering physically and neither of them was ready to push those boundaries since the turmoil they had both faced.

"I would like to tell Yafe and Azar I'm alive and out. They'll be worried."

"I wish you would wait a little longer."

"They're my family," Jerry argued. "They deserve to know what's happened to me."

"But if you tell them you escaped, there will be rumors of it in Joab."

"Why would that be such an awful thing?" Jerry kept her fingers locked in Arloa's long curls, the mass of hair she had never ending, and Jerry loved to play with it when she could. "To give a prisoner hope of escape? It might help."

Arloa raised an eyebrow and cocked her head to the side. "True. I didn't think of it like that."

"If I'd had hope…"

"You wouldn't have tried to kill yourself?"

"While there. The first time? Absolutely. I had zero desire to return to Joab." Jerry's lips pulled into a smile, the first genuine one she had given since her rescue. "Thank you for that, by the way."

"For what?"

"Coming to find me. Again. It seems as though you have a knack of saving me. And here I thought you were the damsel."

Arloa grinned broadly, her eyes crinkling in the corners. "I've always defied expectations and prescribed roles."

"Hence this?" Jerry pressed a single finger to Arloa's once-broken nose.

"Yes. Plus all the other broken bones he gave me."

Jerry sighed, hurt settling into her heart at just the thought of everything Arloa had to endure as a child. "I'm so sorry he was your father."

"I'm not." Arloa gave a wry smile. "Without him, I wouldn't be who I am today, and without him, I wouldn't have the resources to correct his beliefs and actions."

"Makes sense." Jerry felt the same way about her own mother. She had worked as a whore in order to provide the best life possible for Jerry, but living in a whore house, listening to her mother fuck sailors as she slept under the cot beneath them, hearing what they would do and say to her had not been an ideal environment to grow up in. But would Jerry have taken life any other way if given the option? She wasn't sure. Her mother loved her, that much she knew was true, and she had given her many tools in life to survive.

"I need to return to my apartment soon. Someone will get suspicious if I'm not there."

"Don't worry about me. I have what I need here."

"Are you sure you'll be all right?"

"Yes." Jerry trailed a finger across the tops of Arloa's breasts, unable to resist the urge to do so. "I'll be right here when you return."

"All right." Arloa kissed her again before shifting to gather the items she had brought for work. Jerry watched every move she made with rapt attention.

As soon as Arloa reached the door to the small room, Jerry asked the one question that had been clawing away at her mind since their conversation had gotten heated. "What will you do if you find out the government is behind all this?"

Arloa paused, staring at her from the doorway with her satchel clutched in her hand. Her gaze was true when she answered. "Seek vengeance."

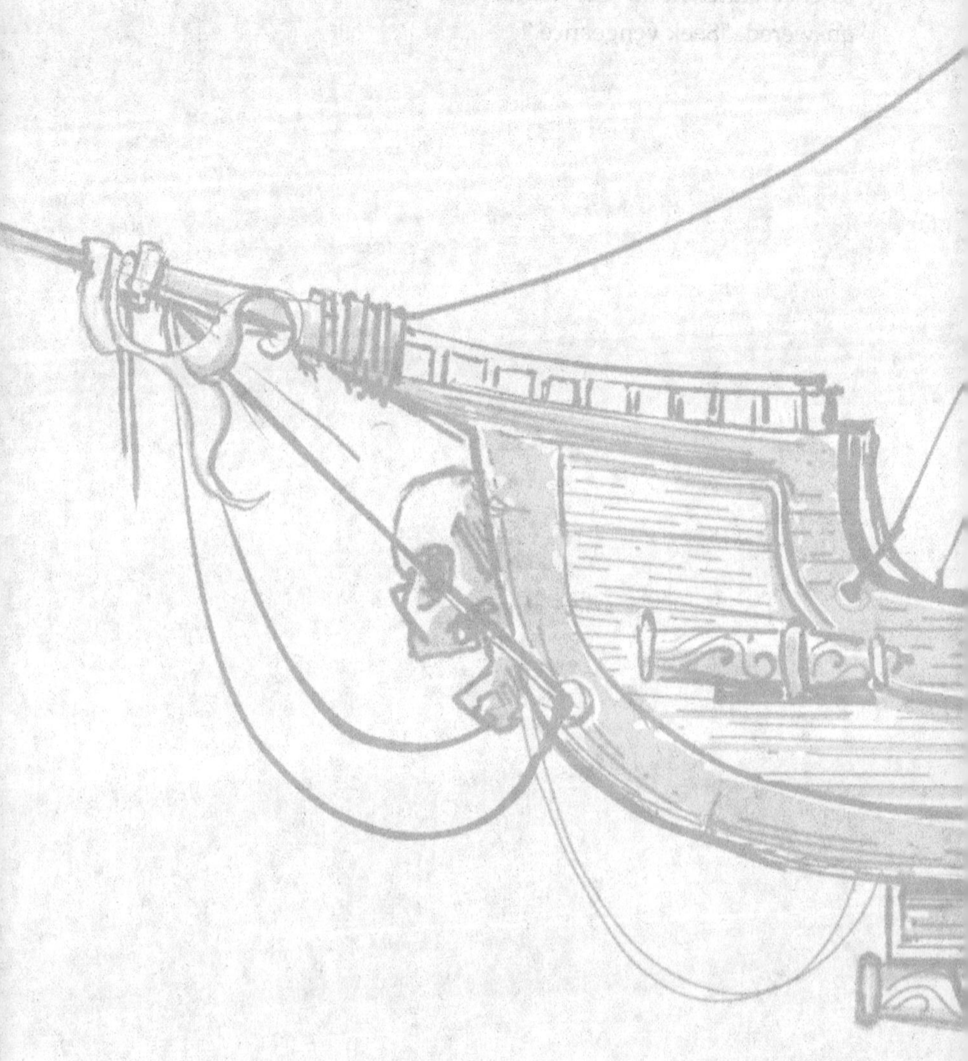

CHAPTER 4

Jerry wrapped herself in the jacket Arloa had brought along with the new clothes she'd purchased. She shivered as she stepped out into the misty, humid evening. It had been so long since she'd freely walked these streets and even longer since she'd done it in hiding. Never had she been an exile like this before.

The air was thick with smog and pollution, which was so normal to most folk there that they didn't even think of it. Jerry, however, had breathed fresh air more times than she could count and longed for it again. Taking shallow breaths, she moved down the cobblestone street toward the gate that would lead to the outer parts of the city.

Miriam's newest residence was right on the edge of that area, and it was closer for her to get there from here than from her ship when she'd been in harbor. Fuck, she missed *Yarrow*. That ship had been her home, and to her credit, it was the entire reason she had ended up back in Joab. She just hadn't been able to give *Yarrow* up to the pirate who had stolen her.

Moving quietly and keeping her head down to hide her face and the hideous haircut that Arloa had given her, Jerry walked right to the last building she knew Miriam had been at. She paused, biting her lower lip when she realized far too late that it had been four months since she'd spoken to or seen the woman and that she could have easily found a new lair.

She would just have to try. Sliding into the basement entrance in the alleyway, Jerry picked her steps carefully. Her body still wasn't ready for anything arduous, and the mysterious healer Arloa had promised had yet to show up. Not that Jerry minded —in some ways she preferred it—but it would have been nice to heal up faster than her malnourished body could manage.

Walking the thin corridor, Jerry found the stairs and started to climb them. The noises and scents around her told her this was definitely still Miriam's place, which was a good thing. She wouldn't be able to go on two adventures that day to try and find her. The walk up the stairs to the topmost level of the building was harder than she'd anticipated.

By the time she reached the top, she was out of breath and every single one of her muscles ached. She was going to need a lot more time before she boarded a ship again. Two men stood at the door, hands to their sides as they watched her stumble the last few steps. They likely had heard her ascent and knew she was coming from the way Miriam ran the place, but everyone had refused to help.

"Hey boys," Jerry stated firmly through heavy breaths, knocking her chin up a level or two. "I'm here to see Miriam."

"She doesn't see ghosts."

Jerry frowned at that. She supposed they would think she was dead since there was never a moment where she thought she would live to see Joab again herself, but still that didn't mean they had to ignore her request or be so callous. Especially when she was struggling just to stand—though she'd never let them know that.

"Tell her an old friend is here."

The one on the left shook his head and crossed his arms. "Miriam doesn't take unexpected guests."

"She'll take me," Jerry insisted. Never had Miriam denied seeing her when she wasn't already doing something else, and with two guards, she was definitely in her small office. Jerry wasn't going to climb down the stairs with nothing in hand. "Tell her."

"No."

Jerry furrowed her brow, absolutely confused as to the audacity of this man. Miriam had practically raised her as soon as her mother had died when Jerry was a teenager, and she'd never been denied access to her mentor. Not in this capacity. Normally she would browbeat them, but she didn't have the energy or the stamina to even consider it this time around.

Clearing her throat, Jerry stepped in closer to the door, making sure to keep her eyes on both of them. "I'm an old friend, and Miriam will very likely kill you both if you don't tell her that I'm standing on the other side of the door."

The one on the right sent the other one a curious look. Perhaps they'd never had someone be so insistent before. He slid his hand backward and hit a small brass bell. The sound echoed loudly but shortly. Jerry glanced at him and nodded.

"Thank you."

Neither of them said anything else as they all stared at each other in awkward silence and waited. When the door finally opened, a mousy man with a shaved head exited the office and Miriam stood at the door. She leaned against the frame, her hand raising up above her head as she eyed Jerry over from top to bottom in an assessing look.

"You look like death."

"Can we go in?" Jerry asked, indicating the room behind the door. She really didn't want to have this conversation with the two guards right next to her where they could hear everything.

Miriam frowned slightly but nodded and shifted so Jerry could enter the room first. Miriam's sheer skirts rustled from the movement, hitting just above her ankles in a dance before she shut the door. Jerry dragged her bad foot toward the desk and sat on the edge of it, unable to keep herself upright on her own any longer. She sighed as soon as the weight was off and she could focus on the head of the underground in front of her.

"I thought you were dead." Miriam's voice had softened since they were alone, concern filtering through every word.

"I was, multiple times." Jerry wasn't going to sugarcoat anything that had happened to her.

"Pity. And they let you out?"

Jerry clenched her jaw tightly as Miriam came closer. She wouldn't spill that secret if she could avoid it. Her silence would be enough of an answer for Miriam, though she would also likely want to know how Jerry escaped since they all had friends and family who ended up there.

"I need new cards."

Miriam sucked the back of her teeth. "That's a hard ask."

"I know, but I'm supposed to be in Joab, so I need new cards in order to be out there. I took quite a risk coming up here with none."

Miriam settled next to Jerry on the desk, putting a hand on her thigh in a gentle gesture. "You look like shit."

Jerry snorted. "I feel like shit."

"What did they do to you this time?"

"More than they ever have before," Jerry confessed in a whisper. She'd never been tortured quite so much, but she also supposed since they knew she was infected and that it was far harder to kill her permanently that they could toy with her even more than before. "I don't want to talk about it."

"You'll have to eventually."

"Not today."

"I've seen Yafe and Azar around. I've helped them out a few times."

"Good. I haven't told them yet." Jerry clenched her fingers around the edge of the desk, missing her friends more in that moment than she had since Arloa had rescued her. She had never felt so isolated or alone before, even when she was in Joab. This was all by her choice, to protect them and find physical healing herself, but it was her decision. She hadn't been forced away with no means of contact.

"I'll keep your secret," Miriam stated firmly.

"Thank you." Jerry believed her, and that put her at ease.

Jerry lifted her chin when Miriam put her finger under it, looking deep into her eyes. They gazed at each other, Miriam's brown eyes with hints of amber like gazing into a window of her past. Jerry wished she had that kind of wisdom and knowledge, but she knew she didn't. She was far too young for it, and far too inexperienced in the depths of the chaos in Penum.

"I like that cute little girl they've got with them."

"Which one?" Jerry pushed, hoping to ease away from the emotional turmoil that Miriam was sending her.

"Vivian. Sacha isn't bad either."

"I didn't realize you knew my whole crew."

Miriam's lips twitched upward. "Only those four."

"Good." Jerry tried to ease away from Miriam's grasp, but she held tightly, not letting go. "Miriam?"

"I worried you were dead, but I hoped you weren't. How did you escape?"

"That's a story for another day," Jerry answered. "I tried to end it before they took me, but I didn't manage it."

Miriam's eyes watered, the droplets gathering along the lower lashes, threatening to spill over the dam. It was the one small tell of emotion Miriam allowed herself to have, something Jerry knew she needed to pay attention to because Miriam was making her do that. Finally, Miriam blinked away the tears and lowered her hand so Jerry could be released into a far more comfortable position.

"I can get you new cards, but it'll cost."

"I don't think credits are an issue, but do let me know how many before you give them to me."

Miriam nodded. "When will you come out?"

"I have no idea. I need to heal first." Jerry's lips pulled

upward as she indicated her still very broken and bruised body. "I'm not well enough to do anything yet."

"A healer?"

"One's been called, but I hear they are few and far between lately."

Miriam hummed her agreement before standing and moving around the desk. "They are. I'm struggling to find one who can help me."

"Help you?" Jerry furrowed her brow, twisting to look over her shoulder at Miriam who was now behind her. "Help you with what?"

"To stay young, my dear girl. Did you think I came by this naturally?" she indicated her face.

Jerry grinned broadly. "Yes, actually."

"Hardly," Miriam barked out. She pulled out a device from her desk and settled it onto the top. Jerry watched as she did some things on it and then stopped. "Was there anything else you needed in your great escape?"

"One of those, actually." Jerry pointed at the device. "A hand-held, preferably. I have some research I need to get done, and I'd rather no one be able to trace it."

Miriam wrinkled her nose but nodded.

"How is the supply chain going?"

"Are you here to reclaim your income from it? Yafe—"

"No," Jerry answered quickly. "If they're using it, let them keep it. I was curious how it was going, if the market turned profitable yet."

"It did. Rather quickly, actually."

Jerry frowned. The buying and selling of brains on the underground hadn't been something she ever wanted to be involved in, but having given Miriam the idea of the market, she damn well knew she was also going to profit from it. She was glad it was funding her ships still, and her family.

"Anything else you need?"

"Someone to fix this." Jerry raised her hand toward her hair. "It's…well, it's awful."

Miriam chuckled lightly and stood. She moved to the door and murmured something to the guards before coming back in. "We'll take care of it. It's nothing I haven't done before."

"You?"

Miriam's nod was filled with something akin to love, though Jerry wasn't quite sure. She had always relied on this woman. Growing up in the underground with her mother had given her a special opportunity to meet and see Miriam up close, though she hadn't quite been in charge when Jerry had been young, like she was now.

They had spent countless hours together while Jerry's mother had worked and when she needed to be out from underfoot. She had been one of the few children allowed to remain there and grow up. The rest had left, although their mothers had left as well.

The knock on the door broke Jerry from her reverie, and Miriam was handed a small leather pouch. "Sit in the chair."

Jerry forced her body upward and moved around the desk to sit where Miriam had once been. She'd always dreamed about being here, about being in charge, but she had never dared to think that dream would come true. Just sitting in the chair felt odd.

"How much length do you want left?"

"I don't care," Jerry answered. "So long as it doesn't look awful."

Miriam hummed an answer as she checked out what Jerry had been left with. She sat in silence while Miriam assessed what to do with the strands that had been left after Arloa hacked her way through the nests that had been created in four months of not washing or brushing. Jerry waited for the first sound of the clippers sliding through her hair, but it took some time until Miriam got started.

"You are so like her, you know," Miriam muttered as she made that first cut.

"Like who?"

"Your mother. What no one saw in her, except from me, was her tenacity. She wasn't someone who was going to be put down."

"She died when I was a teenager."

Miriam agreed with a click of her tongue against the roof of her mouth. "But the number of times she could have died before then is extraordinary. Like you, she had a tenacity for life."

"There's not much living in life these days."

"I'll agree with you there." Miriam made a few more cuts, the hair falling onto the floorboards below.

Jerry held as still as she possibly could, not wanting Miriam to make any cuts that would damage the look of her hair any farther. It would be hard to masquerade as an upper class, well-to-do woman now with short hair, but it was a necessity. It would grow back eventually—at least Jerry kept telling herself that.

"My mother was a whore."

"Yes, and she loved her work. She was one of my best."

Of course she was, Jerry thought but didn't dare voice the words out loud. Her mother had been trapped in the same hell Jerry was. She'd tried to divorce herself from the underground but found it was impossible and had landed right back in her clutches.

"I took her in because I saw that light of life in her."

Jerry said nothing, letting Miriam take the conversation whatever direction she wanted. But getting nostalgic for a woman who was long dead was not what Jerry wanted for the next hour while she sat there getting her hair hacked away.

"I wish she had been able to step into a different role."

That caught Jerry's attention. She'd never heard Miriam talk about this before. "What role is that?"

"My second, but I suppose you can do that now."

Jerry tensed. Miriam had never made any overtones about Jerry's role in the underground aside from doing Miriam's bidding when they could both come to an agreement about it. She frowned, tightening her hands together on her lap as she waited for more information.

"I would like it if you did."

"I'm a dead woman," Jerry answered.

Miriam made one more cut before leaning in with her hands on Jerry's shoulders. "So am I."

A shiver ran up Jerry's spine and not in a good way.

"You're all done, love."

Instinctively, she reached back to touch her hair. It felt much cleaner than what Arloa had left her with. Miriam came around the chair to look Jerry right in the eye. "Please consider it. I'll have your new cards as soon as possible, and yes, I'll let you know how much it'll cost you before I send them your way."

"Thank you." Pushing herself to stand hurt, but Jerry ignored the aches as she stepped around the desk. "I can clean that up."

"Don't worry about it. I have people for that." Miriam waved her away. "Go back to your hideout, Jeraldine. I'll see you soon, I'm sure of it."

Jerry left, walking down the stairs and holding on to the wall to keep herself steady. Her knees were weak, but it wasn't because of her physical ailments. It was because of the odd turn of conversation Miriam had taken with her. She had been born to fly ships, that much she knew, and to be confined to land for so long wouldn't do any good.

Then again, Miriam frequently moved her operation in order to hide from the authorities. What better way to do that than to be on a vessel that consistently moved. Jerry put a stop to that line of thinking. She didn't want to be in charge of the underground. The responsibility was immense, and she would never be able to surface with Arloa if that was the case. She would have to hide permanently if she were to make that decision.

It took her twice as long to get back, not only because her

body was weary but because she couldn't stop thinking about the conversation with Miriam. As soon as she reached her cot, Jerry collapsed onto it with a grunt of pain. She hadn't managed to get a device from Miriam, so she would have to go back, and she knew that was deliberate on Miriam's part. It could wait a few days easily enough because it was going to take her that long to want to walk up those stairs again.

Sliding beneath the rough wool fabric, Jerry closed her eyes and begged for sleep to take her. But she couldn't stop thinking about her crew—her family. That's truly what they were to her, and she missed them dearly. She needed to see them again, to tell them that she was alive and mostly-well. To figure out exactly what she was going to do now that she was a fugitive. Sighing, she relaxed her muscles and hoped the pain would ease as sleep consumed her.

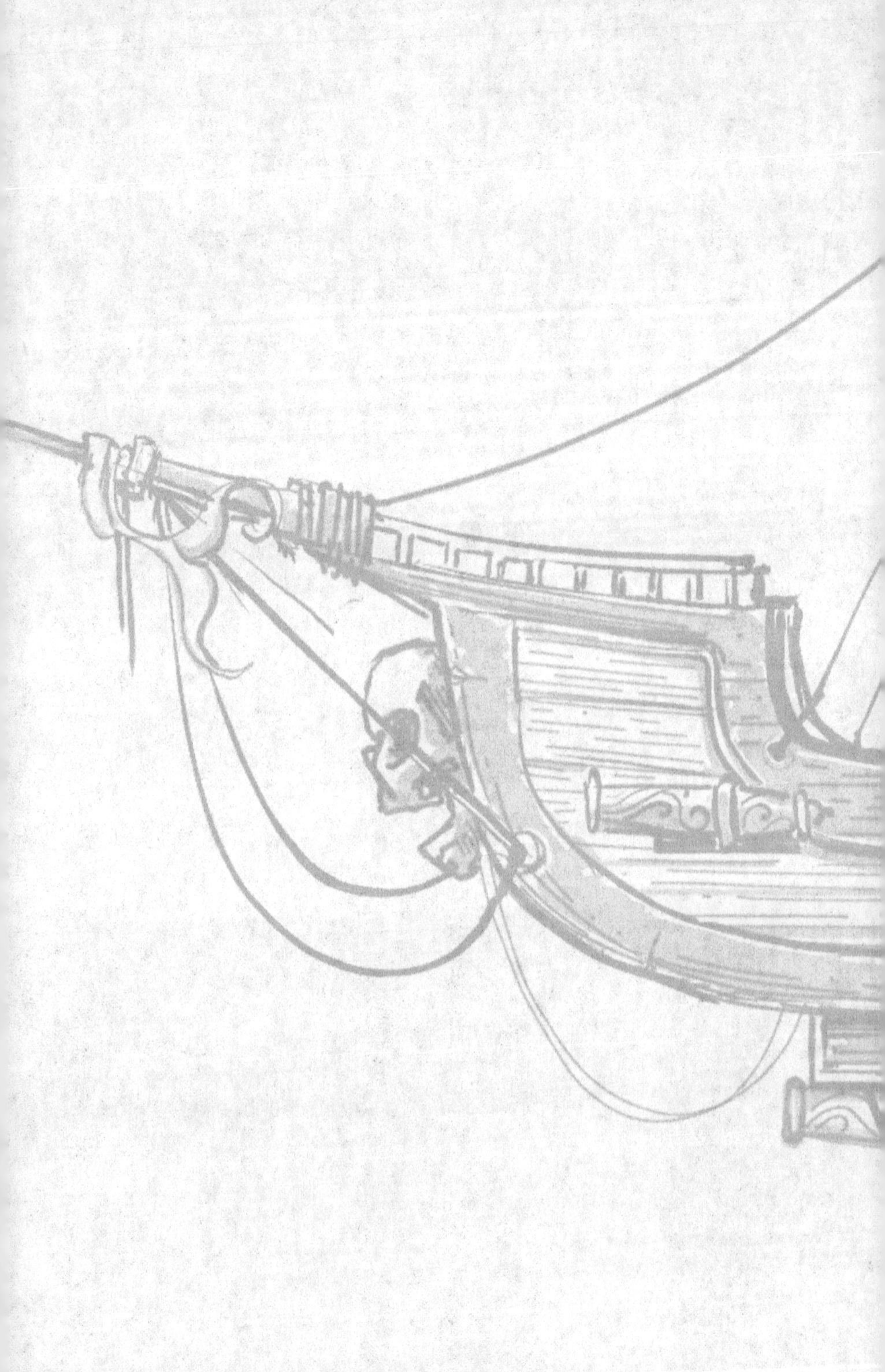

CHAPTER 5

By the start of the second week of her confinement, Jerry was feeling much better. Still no sign of the mysterious healer Arloa had promised, even though that promise was reiterated multiple times. Arloa had been spending less time in the hideout as well, which Jerry was comfortable with, but after having grown up and lived in the tight vicinity of so many others, the silence was deafening.

She missed being able to think, the background noise of voices echoing in her mind while she worked to solve a problem. Still there had been no solution to the problem she faced, and the current prospect of trying to solve a mystery she wasn't even sure was a mystery was hell on her feeble mind. She wanted to give it up and had thought about it on more than one occasion.

She was officially back to where she had been before Arloa had thrown her the bone of cirax, the substitute to vestigen. A pill that might save them all from insanity and zombie-ism if only she could prove it was real and find it. Which she had, but then she'd lost it, and it had put her right back where she had been, the bottomless pit of despair that always seemed to find her.

How did someone like Miriam manage it? They had never

truly talked about it, but throughout the years of her life, Jerry had seen Miriam go through losses and blows that would knock anyone else off their feet, and yet she had managed to stay standing. Jerry would be a piss-poor substitute for that woman and no match to take over when she was gone.

Dragging herself to her feet, Jerry dressed in the clothes Arloa had brought her. Thankfully they were largely masculine, something she was grateful for. She hated corsets with a passion and found very little use for them except to fit into society better and perhaps make fewer arguments when she wanted something.

Jerry stepped out of the small room and followed the corridor toward the door to the back of the building. She'd only walked that way a few times since she'd come to live there. She walked toward a building that was only vaguely familiar to her. Getting in was easy, which was a good thing because where she was going was someplace she wouldn't be allowed in without proper cards, which she still didn't have.

The shop was small, and it clearly catered to the rich. Jerry could easily see Arloa shopping here, or anyone from the government, which was probably why it was located right where it was. The glassware they had were beautiful, and even with the virus they had managed to maintain their presence. Which again was a testament to who was affected by the virus and who wasn't. Most of the shops by the harbor had been shut down for over a year. Only the necessary ones had managed to stay open and that was with governmental handouts.

Jerry kept her chin tilted down, but she took off her top hat and held it under her arm. The woman behind the counter eyed her suspiciously—probably because she'd never seen Jerry before.

"Hello there, ma'am." Jerry lowered her voice so it was deep and husky, and she drew out a southern accent, one that she was quite familiar with. It would make her seem like a foreigner.

"Hello," she answered, her eyes lighting up.

The clothes Arloa had purchased were expensive, something Jerry never would have been able to afford on her own, so she was glad that it had happened this way. It would be easier to hide in plain sight. "I'm visiting–a meeting with Senator Lukatt. I was strolling by and saw these. Thought I'd see if there's something to bring home for the missus."

Jerry pointed to some fine carved glass bowls with lids. She had no idea what they were used for, but they were pretty.

"Oh, certainly, Mr..." the woman trailed off, obviously fishing for information.

Jerry clenched her jaw and drew in the one name that popped in her mind, the one person she had been close to from that particular region—Matty. "Mr. Laurier."

"Yes." Her eyes widened, and she reached for the glass bowl to pull it out of the case.

Jerry conversed with her for several minutes, talking over the cost and history of the piece. Eventually she decided she didn't want to buy it and wandered toward the back of the shop. Another customer came in, thankfully, and as soon as the shopkeeper was preoccupied, Jerry opened and shut the front door but stayed inside. She then walked around the store to keep out of the sight of the shopkeeper and found herself at the back door.

Sliding into it was far too easy. There wasn't even a creak as she opened it. Shutting it, Jerry let out a nervous breath. Vivian had told her about this place months before when they'd been on Arloa's stolen vessel and trying to steal back *Yarrow*. There should be a passageway somewhere down here.

Jerry took the wooden steps, holding her breath and tightening her muscles as she went, hoping to keep as quiet as humanly possible. She made her way down to the bottom of the cellar. Crates were stashed in every corner, labels on them, some faded, some not. Jerry wandered around, looking for a door, anything that might lead to a passageway.

It was on her second trip around the cellar that she found it.

A small door, with a half circle on the top. She would have to crawl through it. Jerry got onto her knees and found an ancient lock on it. Frowning, she pulled out a small knife she'd stashed by her ankle and opened it in a heartbeat. She wouldn't be able to re-lock it from the inside, which was unfortunate because anyone could see where she'd gone, but also fortunate because if she needed to get out, it would be quick.

The door opened with a loud groan. Jerry cursed and crawled inside, shutting it swiftly and praying the shopkeeper hadn't heard a single thing and was thoroughly distracted by the other patron. Jerry leaned back against the wall, catching her breath and letting her eyes adjust to the lack of light. She'd been in these situations before—when she couldn't see. It wasn't something she preferred, but if Vivian was right, this passageway would lead right to the government building in the center of town.

Finally ready, Jerry used her hands to feel up the wall and see just how high the passage was. She was in luck that she could stand, although the ceiling was very close to her head. Gripping her knife and her top hat, Jerry moved forward one step at a time. Her boots echoed, which told her that if anyone was down there with her, she would hear them unless they were completely still.

With the side of her palm against the wall, Jerry moved forward. There was only one way to go from there, and she was going to have to make sure that she took it all the way. She was going to have to make sure that she wasn't caught, because she would have no explanation as to who she was or what the hell she was doing down there.

When she reached the end of the passage, Jerry slowed her heart rate, eased her body, and concentrated on what she could hear. Voices echoed into the small narrow corridor, but she couldn't quite make out what they were saying. Leaning against the door, she pushed her ear to the small crack and focused everything on listening.

"There's no more vestigen." The voice was deep, masculine for sure, and someone who spoke with authority and purpose.

Jerry winced, if the government was talking about how there was none left, then there really must be none left. None of the news outlets had told her that though.

"What are we going to do?" The other voice was much higher in pitch, although also masculine from what Jerry would guess. There weren't many women in the government, and she could only assume Vivian had been right about where the passage led, since she'd thus far been right about everything else.

"Nothing." A hint of menacing anger echoed through. "With Potelia making cirax, we might have a problem."

"I thought you'd solved that."

The first man snorted. "No. But there has been a rapid increase in deaths lately. Something that others are bound to notice."

A pause in the conversation increased the tension. Jerry pushed harder against the door. Who the hell was she listening to? And where the fuck did the other door lead to? She kept as quiet as she possibly could, wanting to hear absolutely everything.

"How many?"

"The streets on the outskirts are like a ghost town."

Jerry frowned. It had been like that before she'd gone back into Joab, so to hear someone say that about how it currently was meant it must be bad.

"The workers aren't cutting it anymore."

"There's too many deaths to sustain our country."

The first man said nothing, but there was a rustling around. Jerry closed her eyes to focus her mind on what was happening in the room beyond. What could she actually find out being able to hide in here? If only it were easier to access than through a glasswares shop when she had to sneak around there.

"We've been long past that for a while now, Kent."

Well, she had a name for one of them, but it wasn't ringing any bells in her memory. Jerry leaned in closer, the entire length of her body pushing into the door. If it cracked or broke, there would be no hiding she was the reason behind it. She had no idea how old the door itself was, but she was willing to bet centuries.

"We've been farming out work to other countries for close to a year now."

Jerry clenched her jaw. That had to be one of the few perks of the great unification. It was the only thing that really came of it since all the countries still functioned separately. Trade was easier, and apparently trade in labor was equally as easy.

Kent cleared his throat. "We could start manufacturing vestigen again."

The other man barked out a laugh, his voice reverberating down the thin corridor. Even if Jerry had been on the other side of it she would have heard it, although the sound would have likely been super muffled. "We can't do that. It costs too much, and we're broke."

Raegina was broke? That was something Arloa hadn't mentioned, nor the news outlets that were on in every establishment every moment of the day. If they were out of funds, then the government must be in a tizzy, especially if they were having to farm out work to other countries in order to function as a country.

"Not to mention the formula was lost."

"Lost?" Kent questioned. "How can it be lost?"

"No one can find it. We've had researchers on it since the virus hit shores, but no one has been able to find it."

"What about reverse engineering it?"

The first man sighed heavily. "Why are we rehashing this? You have to have vestigen in order to make it."

"But, sir, Potelia was able to make some."

Sir? Jerry furrowed her brow. Was the first man a senator?

Someone who had power and knowledge and command? Fuck she wished she knew who he was. Jerry shifted her boot against the ground, scuffing it.

"We aren't Potelia. That should be obvious."

Jerry had to agree with him there, as much as she didn't want to. He seemed so damn arrogant.

"What are we going to do then?"

Damn this Kent guy was stupid, wasn't he? Then again, if he was a runner like Arloa had been at one point, then she could understand why a senator might want someone who couldn't rival him.

"Nothing we can do, Kent."

"But Senator Riley, if we don't—"

"Stop. We have done as much as we can at this point. People are dying in the streets, and there is nothing we can do about it."

Riley? Jerry's heart thudded wildly. This corridor must end right into Riley's offices, which would make sense because Vivian had said she'd heard him, but that was also stupid. If he was the only one with a secret escape, what would happen to the rest of them? *Damn that was probably what he intended.*

Jerry had never liked Riley, hadn't voted for him either. She bit her lip as she held perfectly still, her muscles protesting because it hurt so much to stand for that length of time after being so sedentary for so long. Arloa had issues with Riley too, if she remembered correctly.

"Our world is dying, Kent. This is the end of it."

It wasn't the end. Jerry knew that. Seven hundred years ago they had managed to find enough of a treatment to get through and the next generation born was immune, but they would have to survive long enough to get to that point, which if Riley was correct wasn't likely to happen. She would have to look and see if the numbers truly reflected that.

Jerry's boot slipped, hitting the door loudly. Wincing, Jerry stayed put, not moving. Sweat trickled down her back as suddenly Kent and Riley stopped talking and they shuffled around the room. She hated not being able to see in there and know where they were going or what they were doing. Someone stepped close to the door. She heard the rustle of his clothes, the depth of his breathing, but nothing else.

He didn't open it. He didn't check to see if anyone was in there. He did absolutely nothing other than stand by it. Jerry held her breath tightly in her chest, not wanting to give away any hint that she might be standing right there, that she might be listening in on a conversation that she shouldn't be, that she had found the damn secret passageway.

"Kent, I need those files for the summit tonight. You should have gotten them for me already."

"Oh, yes, sir."

This was it. Riley was going to send Kent away, and he was going to open the damn door, and Jerry was going to tumble through it to her death, because it would be her damn death this time. She still held still as possible, even though her fate was already sealed and she wouldn't be able to escape it again.

Riley moved away from the door. He moved some things on the desk, the slide of metal against wood loud to her ears as she tuned into everything happening on the other side of the door.

"Idiots," Riley muttered. "They don't know anything."

Again, Jerry found herself agreeing. She hated that she agreed with someone so despicable. But they were all idiots. No one saw the patterns, no one saw the deaths. All they saw was the shops closed, the convenience of getting what they wanted was gone, and it was impossible to get what they needed in order to survive—mostly. It seemed they had found a way around that so far.

"Kent!" Riley bellowed.

"I have it right here, sir."

They mumbled quietly, and Jerry struggled to hear the words. Footsteps echoed, a door shut, and suddenly she was plunged into silence. Jerry's heart thudded wildly as she dared herself to open the door and see what was on the other side. After it had been quiet for at least a minute, Jerry reached down and found the small handle.

It would be a fucking miracle if there wasn't a lock on this side like there wasn't on the other one. She pulled upward, unlatching it. The door popped open. Jerry bit her lip as she crouched down and pushed through the thick fabric on the wall. No wonder everything had sounded so muted. Jerry stood up in his office, the dim lights indicating he certainly wasn't planning on returning soon. The fabric was part of a wall hanging, a nice disguise for the passageway if she'd ever seen one.

Jerry put her hands on her hips as she closed up the door and covered it again so she wouldn't be discovered. She debated whether or not to go through his desk, but she had no way to break the code on his devices and find something salacious. With a cursory glance, Jerry knocked her chin up and walked toward the door.

Riley clearly knew the escape route was there. He had gone looking for her when she'd made too loud a noise, but since he hadn't been alone in the room, he hadn't done anything about it. That had been pure luck for her, and the fact he hadn't rechecked? Also luck. Never before had she been one to have luck on her side. Jerry rolled her shoulders and put on the facade that she belonged there.

She could find Arloa's offices easily enough and hide out there until she could sneak back to her hideout. However, Arloa would probably yell at her for coming right into the center of a place she could easily be caught—that would be an argument for another day, or at least another time when they wouldn't so easily be interrupted.

Jerry moved swiftly toward the door to the office and wrenched it open, glad to see the outer offices were empty. Kent must have gone with him. Within seconds, Jerry was out the door and in the corridor, trying to get her bearings. Just where were Arloa's offices in comparison to Riley's? It had been so long that she barely remembered where they were. But she certainly remembered what they had done in them.

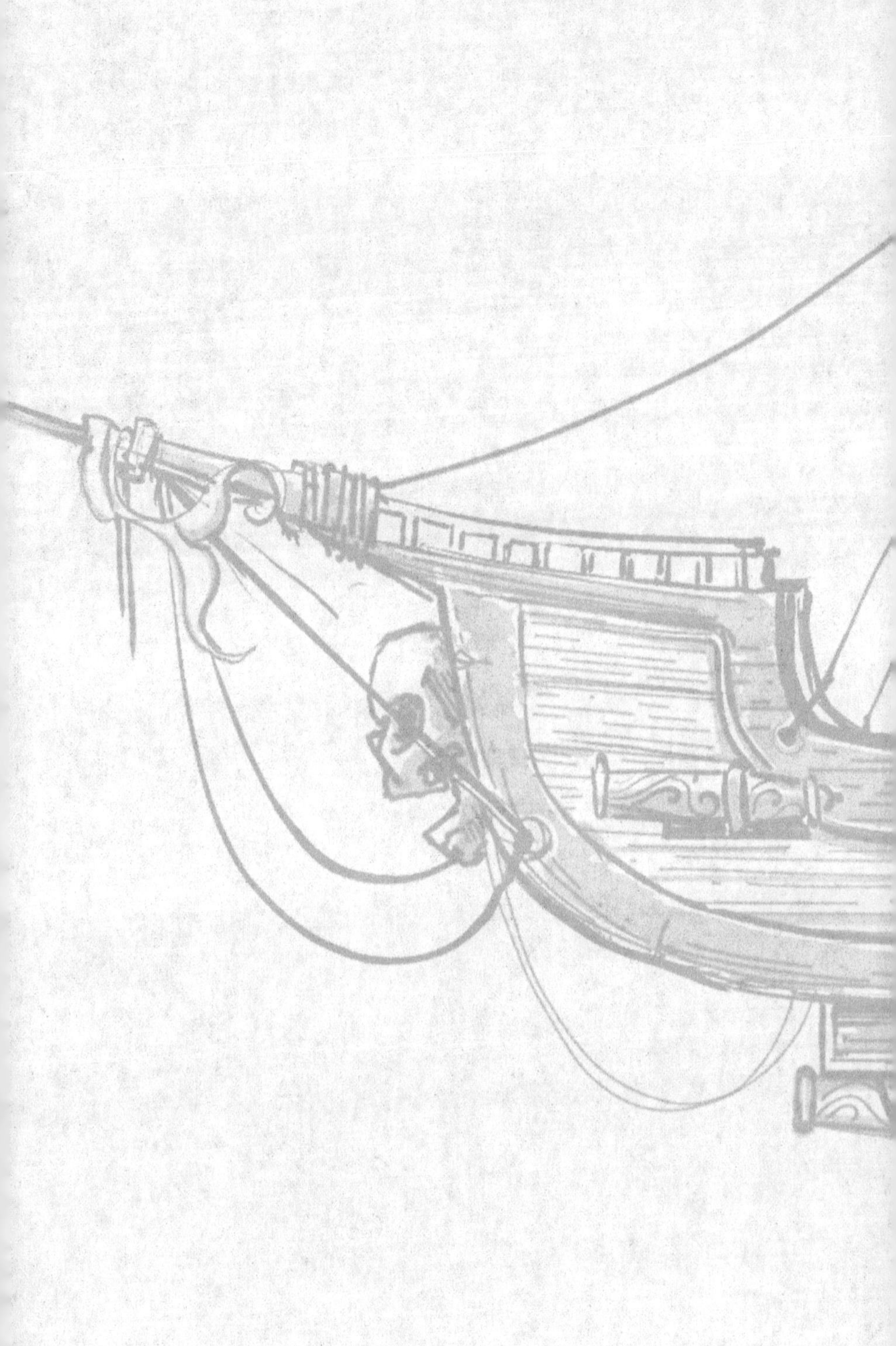

CHAPTER 6

Jerry walked the halls of the government building, keeping her shoulders square and her back rigid. Instead of tilting her chin down to hide as was her norm, she looked straight ahead as if she knew exactly where she was going. That was what would keep them away from her here—cockiness, and an air of entitlement.

It took her at least ten minutes to find Arloa's offices. They were stashed away in the back corner of the government building, and Jerry had almost forgotten how out of the way she was compared to the other senators. It showed truly how much they thought of women in that position. They were not equal.

As much as the world had fought for equality, and on paper women did have it, the reality was they didn't. Women were seen as lesser than others. Arloa was one of two women elected to the Senate, and neither had an easy route to get there. Jerry had watched Arloa's election with rapt attention during the year they had been separated. While she'd remained silent in her support of Arloa during that time, she had voted for her.

Knocking swiftly, Jerry let herself into the outer offices and was met with a busty short woman with a sharp demeanor. Her hair was poofed up into some dated style, with a small hat pinned onto the top of it. Her skirts were immaculately pressed, the jacket she wore tight around her waist to show off her bosom and her hips, which no doubt had a bit of extra padding around them.

"And you are?" She raised a single red eyebrow in Jerry's direction.

"A visitor to Senator Kauket." Jerry kept her voice low in the same manner she had in the shop, hoping she could pass for a man. It would honestly be a saving grace if she could, and one that she was debating on taking full advantage of. She'd always thought that the only thing defining her as a woman was the length of her hair.

"And you are…?" the woman repeated.

Jerry pressed her lips together hard, giving her a sharp and demanding look. "I'm here to see Senator Kauket. You will kindly tell her I'm here."

She narrowed her eyes, and Jerry wasn't sure if her faux confidence was going to win her any favors in this situation. She was determined to get away without using a name, since she had yet to find out what her new name was going to be for the foreseeable future.

"I will when you give me your name."

Jerry clenched her jaw, hoping Arloa would hear her outside and come to investigate what was going on, but it seemed she wasn't in luck. "My name is not of interest to you."

The woman scoffed. "Actually, it is. You see, that is my job here, to keep *pests* away from the Senator."

Jerry bristled at the accusation. She was in a relationship with Arloa despite the time they hadn't spent together, but she was drawn to her in a way she had never been drawn to someone before, and she knew that the feeling was mutual. They had a lot to learn about each other and each other's pasts in the upcoming months, but that was something Jerry was willing to tackle, for the first time since she'd met Arloa.

"I'm hardly a pest," Jerry retorted, making her tone so indignant the woman would have to agree that she was of some upper class. "I'm one of Senator Kauket's constituents, and I have a right to speak with her."

The woman rubbed a circle into her temple. "I'm afraid you're not hearing what I'm saying. Without your name—"

"You're not hearing what *I'm* saying," Jerry corrected. "I'll speak with Senator Kauket. Immediately."

Her tone was so harsh that she thought she'd overdone it, but then she remembered how men usually talked about Arloa, how they treated women. She would have to bring that out, as much as it pained her to do so, in order to pass as one. The woman shivered, the movement so minuscule Jerry almost missed it, and she nodded sharply. She stepped around the desk and toward the interior office, knocking slightly before stepping inside and shutting it behind her.

Jerry could have either won the argument or lost it. She wasn't quite sure which it was yet. Mumbling echoed through the wall, so at least Jerry had confirmation that Arloa was there and she wasn't going to be completely left in the dark trying to hide from Bert Riley while also trying to figure out how to get out of the damn building without being seen.

She kept her back rigid in case anyone else came in or saw her, or in case the woman came back out to try and shoo her away. Jerry sincerely wished that wouldn't happen. This was her first true outing since she'd been broken out of Joab, and it felt delicious to be on the streets again, even if she had to keep a low profile through it all.

Leaning over the desk, Jerry glanced at the paperwork on it. Oddly, the papers were old, their corners torn, burned, or severely worn. There were books that looked as though if she were to flip a page that they would completely fall apart or melt into dust between her fingertips. She didn't dare touch them, even though she wanted to see what they were.

Sliding in a little closer, Jerry looked at what she could see. The paper had crude drawings on it, ones she remembered from growing up. The drawings were similar to what she had found in the bottom of ships, the corridors where sailors rarely went. She'd taken to sneaking out when her mother had a sailor in the room so she didn't have to listen in, and she'd wander the ship unattended.

These drawings had been painted on the interior hulls of several of the vessels they had lived on for short periods of time. There were no words with them, and when she'd described them to her mother, her mother didn't believe her. "What in the world?"

Jerry brushed her fingers over the drawings, still not quite believing her eyes at what she was seeing. Could these really be the same drawings? The same results that she had long searched for? When the door clicked, signaling it was about to open, Jerry straightened and kept her hands at her sides, fists unclenched. She needed to come off as sophisticated as possible.

The woman came out, clearly upset by something, and Arloa started to shut the door before she stopped suddenly. The door widened, revealing her full form, the beautiful sky-blue dress with gold embroidery all along the edges and on the bodice of the tight corset. Jerry hadn't seen her dress that morning, but fuck she wished she had.

"I didn't realize it was you," Arloa stated simply, glancing from Jerry to the woman. "Katlin, this is my friend. He's allowed in at any time, do you understand?"

"Yes, ma'am."

Katlin sat in her chair behind the desk, immediately going back to work. Jerry followed Arloa's hand as she was beckoned inside the inner offices. The door shut and Arloa pushed Jerry's shoulder. "She thought you were a man."

"Well, seems my plan worked then." Jerry grinned broadly.

"How the hell did you get in here without cards?"

"That's a story for another day." Jerry pointed to her ears, indicating she wanted to make sure that she wasn't overheard by anyone. "But for now, I'm here until I can find a way back out, or until I can have an escort that will deprive me of the need for cards."

Arloa sighed and pursed her lips, looking down at their joined hands. "I wish you would have told me you were planning this."

"I honestly didn't know I was until I left."

"How did you—"

Arloa stopped suddenly, the exterior door to the offices opening. A loud booming voice greeted them. Arloa tensed. She grabbed Jerry's hand and shoved her toward the closet, pushing her inside it and closing the door, locking it in place with a finger to her lips. She'd barely managed to turn around when the interior office door burst open.

"Sorry, ma'am. I tried to tell him—"

"It's quite all right, Katlin," Arloa interrupted. "As you can see, I'm free."

Jerry peeked through the slots in the closet door, wanting to see everything going on, but at the same time knowing she needed to remain hidden. Arloa wouldn't so imperiously hide her if it wasn't important. The man standing in the way of the door blocked Katlin from entering any farther into the room.

Katlin huffed, but she left. The tension in the room increased. Jerry could feel it through the closet doors. Whoever this was, it wasn't someone Arloa liked. Jerry was willing to bet that she tolerated him because she had to.

"Miss Arloa, I thought we had a meeting scheduled." His voice moved from booming and angry to smooth and seductive. The hairs on Jerry's arms stood straight up, and she was ready to bust through the door at the slightest provocation.

"Mr. Lukatt, I told your secretary there was no need for us to meet, so I canceled the appointment."

"There's always a need to meet with a lovely lady like you."

Jerry ground her teeth. Did Arloa have to deal with this every day? Jerry had never heard a single word about it, but it seemed as though this was a common problem Arloa faced. Jerry pressed her hand against the closet door, ready to step out should Arloa need her—even as only a distraction—but she would let her have some more time before she gave herself up to the senator.

"Was there something I could help you with, Senator Lukatt?" Arloa's voice was low, it had a dangerous edge to it. Jerry had heard that tone before, but it was always in reserve and rare that she did. She wasn't sure what Arloa was going to do next, but Lukatt was going to bear the full brunt of it.

"I need your help with understanding the contract with Potelia."

Jerry frowned slightly. She was so out of the loop, and while she did pay attention to what was happening in the government, fully understanding the ins and outs of it all still confused her. She'd never had a head for such studies, preferring to learn by her hands instead. Arloa, however, had a much better head for these things than Jerry could ever dream of having.

"What's wrong with the contract?" Arloa's tone dipped, as if she didn't quite believe there was something wrong.

Jerry pressed her lips together hard, staying as still as possible, once again confined to hiding behind a door that she really wasn't sure she wanted to be behind. She couldn't move, otherwise he would see her shifting. This door, unlike the one in Riley's office, was slatted, so she could easily be seen moving if she so much as slid too quickly.

"There seems to be a problem with the cost associated with some of the workers."

"Which ones?" Arloa pried.

"The ships' transports." He seemed so damned pleased with himself, and Jerry couldn't figure out why. There must be something else going on with the conversation that she wasn't privy to. But she was damn sure she was going to ask as soon as they were alone and away from any prying ears.

"I'll look them over again." Arloa had a tone of finality. "If you'll excuse me, Senator, I have another meeting I must get to."

Arloa opened the door and held her hand out, waiting for

him to leave. Jerry bit her lip as she watched him stand there, unmoving. They had a long stare down before he finally stepped toward the door. Arloa shut it and pressed her forehead against the door itself, sighing. Jerry waited patiently, not able to get out of the closet without breaking it or Arloa unlocking it.

"I don't want to talk about it," Arloa murmured, her voice quiet enough that Jerry knew the words were meant for her. It wasn't much longer until she opened the door again and said, "Katlin, I don't want any other interruptions for the next hour. Do you understand?"

"Yes, ma'am."

Arloa shut the door again and locked it. This time, she leaned against it with her back. Jerry watched from her hideout in the closet, the way her breasts fell and rose with her breaths, the sharpness of her breathing even though the rest of her seemed absolutely calm. Jerry wanted to wrap her up in her arms and hold on tight, not let her go until Arloa was settled and unhurt.

"Does he do this often?" Jerry asked.

Arloa raised her gaze instantly. "I said I don't want to talk about it."

"You're going to need to talk about it at some point."

"Hardly." Arloa stalked forward and wrenched open the closet doors. "And I expect you to respect my boundaries."

"If you love me like you say you do, you'll share when something is bothering you."

Arloa's cheeks tinged pink, and Jerry knew she'd caught her. It seemed as though Arloa, as forward as she was with what she wanted or needed, preferred to keep her unpleasant feelings under the surface where no one could see them.

"You do love me, right?"

"Yes, Jer. I love you," Arloa whispered, stepping in close and resting the side of her face against Jerry's chest. She closed her eyes and drew in steady breaths. "Why are you here?"

"That's a bit of a story for later, remember? But I do need an escort out of the government building because if you'll remember, I have no cards to prove who I am."

"So you thought you could drag me down with you? Hmm?"

"I believe you're the one who committed a crime when you broke me out of Joab."

"Rescued," Arloa corrected, sending Jerry a serious and firm look. "I rescued you."

"Two words, same thing."

"Not quite." Arloa brushed her fingers along Jerry's cheeks. "I'm sorry I haven't seen you in a few days."

"You have a life, Arloa. I don't expect you to be around me every waking moment. You're an elected authority. I know that."

"Doesn't mean I can neglect you."

"It also doesn't mean you can avoid direct questions like what was that about with Lukatt."

Arloa wrinkled her nose, and it was the cutest thing on Penum. Jerry bent down and kissed it gently. "He fancies me and has since we were children."

"Children?"

"I may have gone with him when we were younger."

"Arloa Kauket, how dare you!" Jerry teased.

She frowned. "He's never quite given it up, and this is one of the ways he proves he hasn't. It's more annoying than anything. Katlin can usually keep him out."

"I'm glad it was a quick conversation, then. I almost came out and beat the fuck out of him."

Arloa's lips curled into a small smile, which Jerry was glad to see. "I'm glad you didn't. I don't need to try to explain you any more than I'll already have to."

"Yes, but to think I passed for a man."

"I thought you were one when I heard you through the door."

"Did you?" Jerry teased, curling one of those long blonde strands around her finger and tugging it. "That could be fun to play with."

"It could, but not tonight, Jer. I've got a lot of work to get done."

"When will I see you again? We have a lot we need to discuss."

"Tomorrow, I promise. I'll be there early in the evening, and I'll bring some fresh fruit for us." Arloa squeezed Jerry's hand and stepped away as though she were breaking contact. "Let's get you out of here."

"Arloa…" Jerry trailed off, not quite sure how to ask her question or if there was even an appropriate time to ask it.

"What is it?" Arloa prodded.

"It can wait, so long as you promise to come tomorrow."

"I promise." Arloa gripped Jerry's hands tightly. "Ready to make your first debut as my boyfriend?"

"Yes," Jerry answered, nearly gleeful.

The thought thrilled Jerry more than she wanted to admit, and for the first time ever, she found herself wanting to walk with Arloa out of the building and down the streets, hand in hand in a way they never had done before. It was odd in some ways. Their relationship was anything but normal. They had met at a bar by the harbor, a place where aristocratic women certainly weren't supposed to go, and they had founded their relationship on sex.

Since then, they had come to rely on each other in different ways, using each other for what they needed, and sharing with each other to fulfill their needs. It was an odd little relationship, but moments like this spoke true to it. Jerry had never felt comfortable in her body, and Arloa had always made her feel perfect just as she was.

Offering Arloa her arm, she held still as they went out the back door into the corridor. This was the perfect way to walk out of a building she had no business being in. Perhaps one day she would.

Arloa's shoulders were still filled with tension when she came into the small room that had become Jerry's home. Immediately, Jerry wanted to walk to her, massage out the tension, and make sure that Arloa was taken care of in whatever way she needed, but instead she stayed put. It had been over a day since they had seen each other last on the street right in front of the government building. Arloa had sent her off with a quick kiss on the lips, sealing their relationship in the eyes of the world.

Jerry had heard nothing since then, waiting in anticipation for this moment, when they could talk freely. Arloa locked the door behind her and leaned against it, closing her eyes and letting out a sigh that seemed to wash all that tension through her. Jerry did stand then, coming forward and running her hands up and down Arloa's arms.

"Are you all right?"

"It's been a long few months, Jer." When Arloa opened her eyes, her steel-blue gaze locked on Jerry's, a wave of sadness filling them. "I thought I'd lost you."

Jerry shattered. In all the weeks of recovery, she hadn't truly thought about what Arloa was going through while she'd been in Joab. She'd been selfish in her recovery, in the time that she had spent in Joab and away from everyone else, not fully thinking about what they were all feeling. It rekindled her desire to find her crew and let them know she was well.

"Again," Arloa's voice broke on the word. "I never thought… I thought the last time was it, that I wouldn't have to go through something like that again, but Jer, you were gone for months, and I couldn't find you. I knew where you had gone, but that was it. It took me months to even get word that you were still alive."

"Your family funds Joab."

"I know." Arloa tilted her chin down, embarrassment filling her gaze. "I know they do, and I've never agreed with them on it, but what can I do? Father is a proud man, and he believes in these things I so vastly disagree with."

Jerry lifted her hand, cupping Arloa's cheek while trying to offer what comfort she could. "It's nothing I haven't been through before."

It was a small white lie. Everything about Joab this time around had been unexpectedly different. The formula was still the same, but the torture had been worse, the death she had endured was seared into her memory.

"Hardly." Arloa frowned. "I read the reports, remember?"

"They tortured you." She said it in a whisper, as if admitting out loud what had happened in Joab would be too much for either of them to handle. Squeezing Arloa's shoulders, Jerry tried to lead her to the cot, but Arloa dug her heels in.

Jerry furrowed her brow. "They torture everyone who's sent there."

Arloa's eyes widened, and her lips parted in surprise.

"Didn't you know that?"

"No, I didn't." A single tear fell down Arloa's cheek to her chin.

Jerry reached up and wiped it away, this time cupping the side of Arloa's neck. She bent down and pressed their mouths together sweetly, tenderly, taking all the time and softness she had left in her at that moment to make sure that Arloa felt every-thing. "I don't know what you thought they were doing there, but it's why I said I would never go back there."

"I understand now." Arloa closed her eyes, her face becoming lax. "I understand."

"I'm sorry you didn't know."

Arloa's lips pulled tight, and when she looked into Jerry's eyes, she shook her head slowly. "I realize this might become normal for you, especially if you go back to pirating. In some ways, I hope you never do. I love you, and I want you safe, but I also realize that the underground is a part of your world. It's not something you can so readily give up."

The opportunity Miriam had hinted at came back into her mind. Jerry clenched her back teeth tightly, wanting to be able to tell Arloa about it, but at the same time, if she were to take Miriam up on the offer, secrecy would be imperative to keep everyone safe. She wasn't sure how to even begin to speak about it.

"I don't know what I'm doing yet other than continuing to heal."

"Yes," Arloa murmured. "I'm still trying to find another healer. Issa has gotten delayed in Teedo, unfortunately."

Jerry nodded, not sure if this Issa character really existed, but she wasn't going to argue about it either. Her injuries were rela-tively healed for the most part, and the most a healer could do was rid her of the physical scars. Taking Arloa's hand, Jerry led her to the cot, and they sat down together. She placed her fingers high on Arloa's thigh, keeping the physical connection as a reminder that she was no longer in Joab, and she didn't need to think about that place any longer. Still, they had a lot they needed to talk about, and it was Jerry's turn to speak.

"I followed a rumor today, which is how I ended up in your offices."

"What rumor is that?"

"That there was a secret passageway from a glasswares shop

nearby into the government building, one that is unwatched aside from the shopkeeper, and that it leads to a particular senator's office."

Arloa's lower lip quivered, her eyes narrowed as she no doubt tried to determine if Jerry was telling the truth or not. "What?"

"When I was with my crew still, there was a rumor circulating the lower decks about a tunnel, a passageway, that leads from that glassware shop nearby straight into a senator's office. I went to see if the rumors were true."

"And I suppose since you landed yourself in my office that it is true."

"Yes." Jerry raised an eyebrow, squeezing her fingers on Arloa's thigh. She rolled her shoulders and debated what to share of what she'd found. Surely Arloa would have more insight into Bert Riley than she did. "Have you given more thought about this virus being manufactured?"

"I have. In fact, it's been almost impossible not to think about." Arloa covered Jerry's hand, threading their fingers together. "I wish I could, but if you're right, if that theory is correct, then this was mass genocide."

"It was." Jerry watched the gears click in Arloa's mind, the thoughts flash through her eyes as she put multiple ideas together.

"How did I not see it before?"

"Because you were too busy putting out fires, which I suspect was intentional. You're smart, Arloa, and you care for all the people in Raegina, which would make you the enemy to someone like this."

"I suppose."

"No *I suppose* about it. You would be the enemy, because I can see you tanking your career in order to expose whoever was doing it."

Arloa pulled her lip between her teeth and shook her head slowly. "No, I would find some other way to do it. To end my career would end my ability to stop this from happening again, which is something I can't live with."

"Fine, then something else, but you would be the last person they would want to find out about this."

"Perhaps."

Jerry sighed in frustration. "So do you believe it happened? That this really could be planned genocide?"

"Yes," Arloa whispered, still not fully committing to the belief. "Yes, I think it's possible. But who?"

"There are so many people I can think of, but it's going to have to be someone who had the means and money in order to do it. Someone who can hide their participation, so that means someone with power."

"Someone like me, you mean."

"Well, yes." But Jerry hadn't wanted to say that out loud. Arloa had been hiding things from the government for years, namely her desire and attempts to reverse engineer vestigen when no one else was working on it, which now Jerry had a little more information about. "What about Bert Riley?"

Arloa's face pinched in concentration. "I don't suppose anyone should be left out of the list."

"But what do you think about him?"

"He's an even-keeled man. I've never had any major issues with him." Arloa stopped, clearly mulling through something in her mind. Jerry gave her the time to think, wanting to make sure that she was able to process everything that had happened in the past few years.

"Arloa?"

"Hmm?" Arloa lifted her chin up.

"May I kiss you?" Confusion crossed Arloa's features, but Jerry was determined. Not only would a kiss serve to connect them again, but it would help to distract Arloa from thinking too hard about Riley, perhaps clear her mind for the truth to needle its way through. "Will you trust me?"

"I suppose since I asked you to trust me it's only fair."

Jerry's mouth pulled upward at the corner. "I would hope so. But may I?"

"Yes. I've longed for your touch." Wispiness filled Arloa's tone as she leaned in toward Jerry almost imperceptibly.

Jerry wasn't quite ready to jump straight to fucking, especially with the amount of new scars she had on her back, legs, and arms, but this could at least be a gentle transition in that direction. They hadn't kissed since Jerry had been here, not really. Everything had been about her healing, and she still had a long way to go, physically and mentally. She was nowhere near her previous strength.

"I won't say that I've longed for it. Most of my time in Joab was spent trying to survive so I could properly die."

Arloa's smile faltered. "I'm not sure I'll ever fully understand what happened to you there, but I'd like to try."

Warmth flooded Jerry. She'd never had someone tell her so forthrightly that they would be there with her through thick and thin, that they would take care of her, wanted to take care of her. But Jerry had never let another soul into her heart quite this way before. She'd never wanted to.

"Weren't you going to kiss me?"

"Yeah." Jerry's cheeks heated unexpectedly. "When we met—it feels like years ago, but it's only a couple—everything was fire."

Arloa chuckled lightly. "A fire we both fanned until it consumed us."

"Yes." Jerry reached up and brushed her thumb over Arloa's plump lower lip. "I remember thinking that you weren't the most beautiful creature on Penum, or rather others wouldn't find you that way, but I certainly did. It wasn't because of your looks necessarily, but because of what was in here."

Moving her hand down, Jerry covered Arloa's heart with her hand. It thrummed steadily. Curling her fingers, Jerry dragged her dull nails slightly against Arloa's soft flesh, remembering how much she enjoyed a slight bite to her pleasure.

"You were confident in droves." Jerry gave her a free smile. "I believe I used the word intrepid to describe you. Entitled for sure, but soft and curious at the same time, brilliant."

"Jer," Arloa's voice dropped off.

"No, I need to say this." Jerry moved her hand, trailing fingertips over the tops of Arloa's breasts, the edge of her corset, back and forth in a steady rhythm. "That first year we were apart, I was obsessed with you. I think I still am, actually."

Tears filled Arloa's eyes, but she didn't shed them. This time, Jerry knew they were happy tears, rather than the cold ones of exhaustion and frustration she'd refused to let loose before. Jerry said nothing else as she leaned in, holding the tension of space between them. Arloa's breath on her lips, the sigh, the whimper in the back of her throat, every part of it called to her.

Jerry trailed her hands up Arloa's shoulders to her neck, curling them around the back of her neck and into those luscious curls she could never get enough of. This was so different than it had been even six months before. That had still been lust, but an odd combination of lust and love. Jerry had heard from sailors for years that separation made the heart grow fonder, but those were usually the same sailors who would pay to fuck her mother, so she'd never believed it—until now.

Four months away with the inability to focus on Arloa, the constant stress and threat of death told her one thing firmly. She didn't want to lose this woman. She wasn't sure what her life would be without Arloa. Fuck, Jerry wanted to lean in and kiss her, wanted to steal Arloa's breath and maybe give it back, but this moment, this one seemed so pivotal for some reason, something she couldn't quite break yet.

"Thank you, Arloa, for being exactly who you are."

Arloa dragged in a ragged breath, that first tear spilling over the curve of her cheek and leaving a wet trail in its wake. Jerry moved in then, pressing their mouths together. She didn't take. She didn't move to draw on the heat that was between them. Instead, she held the moment, her eyes wide open as she looked straight into Arloa's, going halfway cross-eyed in the process. Parting her lips, her eyelids fluttered closed as she pulled Arloa with her into the abyss that was them.

They moved together in tandem. Arloa slid against Jerry, pressing into her and pushing deeper into the kiss. Jerry sucked lightly on the lower lip she had admired so much, nibbling on it before diving back in. This must be what it felt like to be in love. To have that connection be so strong there was absolutely no way to deny it. Jerry tugged Arloa closer, keeping their bodies as close as possible without lying down.

Arloa whimpered again, the sound moving straight to Jerry's chest and between her legs. She still wasn't ready for that, wasn't ready to move beyond what they were currently doing, but she wanted this connection to last as long as possible.

"I love you, Jer," Arloa whispered, her tongue pressing between Jerry's lips.

Jerry lost herself in that moment. It was perfect in a way nothing between them had ever been before, and exactly the way she'd needed it to be. They stayed together like that until Jerry finally pulled away and pressed their foreheads together. She said nothing as she calmed her breathing and kept her eyes closed, breathing in Arloa's scent, the feel of her body, the tingling still in her lips.

"I think you're right," Arloa stated softly, not giving any information as to what on Penum she was talking about.

Jerry held the silence, having learned early on that Arloa never said anything she didn't mean and that she normally knew what she was going to say before the words even left her beautiful lips. She intuitively knew that whatever Arloa was going to say was going to be heavy.

"Bert Riley is someone to look into."

Jerry smiled. "What did he do?"

"He's always been interested in genetics, ever since we were little, and he's never had very good morals. He comes off as upstanding, but I've seen so many times, especially when we were younger, that he didn't give a shit about ethics."

"I think he still doesn't, but he's very sly in how he talks about it."

"What did you hear?"

"He's not surprised about the shortage of workers, he refuses to even consider reverse engineering vestigen, and he expected this."

Arloa frowned. "Well, we all did, to be fair. Everyone in the government did. We knew how bad the virus was when it first hit, and what the repercussions were going to be when we couldn't find a quick enough solution."

Jerry swallowed hard. "Let's spend some time thinking about who might be behind this. We can weigh all the options, but I don't want to exclude anyone or focus on anyone too soon. All right?"

"Sounds like a good plan, Cap."

Jerry froze at the familiar endearment. Arloa had never been one to call her that, always preferring the personal nickname that she'd chosen, but to hear herself referred to as Captain again? It was far too soon. Her crew didn't even know she'd escaped Joab, let alone had done it weeks ago and was well on her way to healing. And she wasn't sure she would ever be allowed to captain a vessel again.

"I'm sorry. I didn't mean—"

Jerry interrupted her with a shake of her head. "It was unexpected. That's all."

"I'm sorry," Arloa repeated.

"I don't know if I'll ever be captain again." Confessing that out loud was harder than she'd ever anticipated. "I can't imagine what life will be like without that."

"You'll figure it out. I have a feeling you always do."

Jerry gave a wry smile. "Perhaps."

CHAPTER 8

Arloa had fallen asleep in Jerry's arms on the small cot. Jerry had stayed awake most of the night, soothing Arloa when she stirred near waking and staring at the blasted ceiling she couldn't unsee. Going into the government building the day before had been more than a need to search for information—she'd needed to get out.

The hideout that she'd been living in had become too much like the prison rooms in Joab, keeping her confined in ways she couldn't bring herself to think about. Whenever she was in it without Arloa she was tense, ready to fight at any moment, except there was no foe coming. So that tension would sit in the center of her chest, tightening her inside out until she could barely stand without pain.

She needed a plan to get out of there, and thus far, Arloa hadn't mentioned anything yet. They hadn't talked beyond Jerry getting new cards. No conversations about where she would live, or what she would do for credits, or even if she would go back to her ships. Having no idea what time it was, Jerry slipped from the cot without disturbing Arloa and grabbed her overcoat and top hat.

Stepping from the hideout, Jerry closed the door as quietly as possible and prayed Arloa didn't wake up from her lack of presence or heat from her body. Debating one last time whether she should go or stay, Jerry turned on her toes and walked silently out of the building. It took her time to get to the harbor. She took the streets slowly, wanting to make sure that she didn't accidentally stumble upon anyone wanting to harm her in any way.

The scent in the air changed as she got closer to the harbor. It was slightly cleaner, the breeze sharper, and she could take deeper breaths, ones she hadn't been able to manage since that fateful day she'd landed herself back in Joab. Jerry kept her head down, walking by rote memory as she went through the streets toward the piers, toward the one she'd rented for years for *Yarrow*.

What would it be like to see her again? Her ship, her home, the one place she had never longed to be so much as she did now. Tears nearly stung her eyes as she was only a few blocks away. How would she force herself not to run up to *Yarrow* and take her back under her control, to run her fingers over the smooth shellacked hull?

Her heart raced as she broke through the thin street to find the sea in front of her. In the dark early morning, everything was black, nothing more than a few shapes she had to squint to make out. Jerry stepped right up to the railing on the pier, her breath catching in her lungs as she spun her gaze from ship to ship, searching.

There.

Settling her gaze on the small vessel that was half-hidden behind a larger one, she found her home. *Yarrow*. She and that ship had been through so much together, and Jerry was pretty sure she'd never be able to get her out of her heart. She was Jerry's first love, from the day the credits had officially transferred and *Yarrow* was hers. They had gone through so much together.

"Hello, old friend," Jerry murmured, knowing no one was there to hear her, not even her ship. "I miss you."

Her lips quirked upward, and she forced her gaze downward. What was she going to do? She longed to be there again, to be walking the thin corridors inside, to have her hands on the worn wood of the wheels on the bridge. She loved to feel the vibrations under her feet, traveling up into her legs and hands, that would tell her exactly how fast they were moving and to feel the wind as it pulled at them.

Tears prickled at her eyes, stinging as she tried to swallow them back. Seeing *Yarrow* was far more emotional than she had ever dreamed it would be. She had spent countless hours on that ship, refinishing her, fixing her up so that they could work together—legally. Then the virus had hit and all had gone to hell.

Then Arloa had contacted her again, a chance at a new life with a new drug, and her world had been turned upside down when Captain Blaise Lotchski of *Wench's Dream* had boarded and stolen *Yarrow* on their way back to Raegina. She'd spent the next few months of her life with nothing on her mind but revenge and getting her ship back.

And here she was. Safe in the harbor. Floating meters above the seas as she idled in sleep, her crew most likely resting inside until they went back out over the ocean's waters for work. Fuck, how she missed it, not just the vessel herself, but the camaraderie and not being so damn alone.

A single tear escaped her eyes and slid down her cheek. Jerry didn't bother to brush it away. Forcing her gaze to move, she searched for the second and third ships she knew she had. The first being *Calluna*, the second ship she had purchased, and the third being *Astilbe*, formerly known as *Wench's Dream*.

Calluna was nowhere in sight, but she had pretty much been dead in the water when Jerry had been arrested by the authorities, when she had sacrificed herself to save her crew like any good captain would do. *Astilbe*, however, sat on the next dock over, hovering like the perfect vessel she was—stolen, free, and reclaimed. The moonlight hit her just right for the boom from her masts to cast a darker shadow and point right to *Yarrow*. The heart of Jerry's world.

Oh how she longed to walk down onto those docks and see her ships, but if she went any closer, she would never leave again. Forcing herself to walk away was far harder than she anticipated, and as she turned to go, she swore she saw activity on *Yarrow*. Just a slow movement of a person walking across the deck and ducking into the wheelhouse, back inside to safety from the elements.

Ripping herself from that spot on the harbor was difficult. Jerry forced her feet to move, not paying attention to which direction she was going. Sun cracked over the horizon as the dawn bell tolled, and Jerry shuddered, not sure where to go or what to do next. Her heart ached, viscerally, as she left without her family and her home.

She wandered until the first morning bell, finding herself at the alley that led straight to Miriam's current hideout. She never could quite escape the underground, could she? No one was around when Jerry ducked into the alleyway and through the cellar doors. This time, the guard that was at the bottom of the stairs nodded at her and let her continue to walk.

Jerry furrowed her brow, confused as to what was going on. She stopped at the end of the corridor, realizing the time, and walked straight back to the guard. "Is she here?"

"Yes," he answered, his voice clipped.

"Is she sleeping?"

He nodded. Jerry frowned, not exactly sure she wanted to be the reason Miriam was awoken unexpectedly and without urgent news or problems at hand. She had seen throughout her years far too many guards ripped a new one for making that exact mistake.

"You are permitted."

Jerry jerked her head back in confusion. "What?"

"You are permitted to wake her."

"I..." Trailing off, Jerry pointed deeper inside. "Where is she?"

He gruffly grunted at her before pushing his way through

the corridor and leading the way. They didn't go to the very top of the building like she had every other time she'd been there, but stopped only a few floors up. Jerry looked at him, hesitating, when he left her at a door. He went back down the stairs.

Breathing out, Jerry put her hand on the doorknob and then stopped, lifting her hand and knocking instead. She waited, but there was no answer. Knocking again, Jerry was greeted with silence. The third time she knocked, she gripped the cold brass handle and turned it while opening the door.

Odd that Miriam would sleep in a building like this with her door unlocked. Perhaps she really had no fear that she would be discovered, or that her guards knew how to protect her the correct way. Did Miriam trust? The door creaked as Jerry pushed it open, finding the room dark with curtains drawn tightly across the windows.

"Miriam?" Jerry asked, hoping she was already awake and upstairs and the guard had been wrong, even though she intuitively knew he wasn't.

A rustling on the bed startled Jerry, but she held her ground as a young woman with long thin brown hair pushed off and didn't even bother to cover her nakedness. Jerry frowned at her, not the least bit surprised. Miriam had never taken to a relationship unless it was useful for her, preferring sex as an outlet of pent-up stress or emotions or sometimes as payment—which Jerry had done before.

"Miriam," Jerry stated, a bit harsher than before as the young woman walked on her tiptoes around the room, collecting items and cleaning up.

Confused, Jerry moved in and bent down. She found Miriam staring up at her from the bed, a nonplussed look on her face. Miriam sighed but didn't bother to cover her exposed breasts. Jerry knew she wouldn't. They were all too familiar with each other's bodies by that point, and Miriam was too confident in her sexuality, her power, and her dominance in the realm of the underground she had built from the ground up to ever turn over and hide.

"What are you doing here?"

Jerry's lips parted as she was about to answer, then she realized she didn't exactly have one to give. She hadn't meant to go there, hadn't meant to find Miriam like this. She'd been escaping the pain of her past and the fear that she might never have what she once clung to for life.

Miriam must have seen something in her gaze because she immediately sat up and stated harshly to the woman still cleaning. "Get me my robe and get out."

The woman complied, skittering away as soon as her task was done. Miriam moved her feet away from the edge of the bed, allowing Jerry room to sit.

"What's wrong, Jeraldine?"

"Do you have my cards yet?"

"That depends on what you want on them, truthfully."

Jerry didn't raise her gaze up, the words Miriam had spoken barely making a dent in her brain as she folded her hands together, brushing one thumb over top of the other in an attempt to calm her racing heart.

"Who was she?"

"No one," Miriam muttered. "You can have women like her too, if you want."

"I don't."

"Then you don't have to," Miriam answered, pulling the buttons on the sheer robe across her chest to fasten them. It did barely anything to hide her curvy figure underneath. "What's gotten into your head, love?"

"I'm never going to be Jeraldine again, am I?"

"I'm afraid not."

Jerry nodded slowly as the understanding settled into the pit of her chest. She had always been Jeraldine Adelric, daughter of a sailor's whore, adjacent to the underground, and on the outs with the rest of Raegina and Penum. She'd always just fit because she had to, and she made it work because what other option was there? But this would truly be a fresh start.

"Who will I be then?"

"Who do you want to be?" Miriam questioned, and Jerry had known she was going to say that before the words were even out of her lips.

It was something Jerry had been wrestling with since the virus hit. Miriam had asked her that when she'd been released from Joab the last time, and Jerry had told her she wanted to own a ship, she wanted to be captain, and she wanted to do legal work. The slide into the illegal and back into pirating had happened so quickly she'd barely had time to breathe and catch her bearings.

"I want to be me."

"And who are you?"

Jerry drew in a deep breath and let it out slowly, trying to figure out exactly who that was. Frowning, Jerry shook her head. "I don't know anymore."

"Then work on figuring out who you are, and we'll talk about the rest later."

"About the underground, you mean?" Jerry raised her chin.

"Yes. The offer still stands, Jeraldine. I would love for you to be my replacement when the right time comes. I'm not immortal, as much as everyone seems to think I am."

The struggle to think about this woman dying and no longer being present was hard. Jerry had seen so much death throughout her life. Growing up the way she had, death was always a constant companion. Hell, she'd seen her first dead body when she was four, and touched one at eight. But to lose a woman who had been there every step of her way was too much. Miriam had been there long after her own mother had died, and to be in a world without that unwavering support was impossible to think about.

"What would it mean? If I were to become the new you."

Miriam's eyes crinkled in the corners as she smiled. "I would train you, teach you what I've been doing that you don't know about yet, but I would also let you begin your own expeditions. That's the beauty of the underground, isn't it? We can do whatever we want without the oversight of the government, without the judgment of men."

Jerry's lips twitched. She wouldn't lie, that would be nice. She'd always tried to play into the role men wanted for her, but she'd never fit. She wasn't the perfect woman by any means. Her body didn't fit their standards, her small breasts that barely made a bump on her chest, her added height, her awkward gauntness from too few meals, her rough hands from working hard.

"What would you want to do?" Miriam questioned.

"I'd stop whoring out women."

Miriam let out a light laugh. "You never did like that, did you?"

"Who would? It's dirty work."

"It's glorifying work. Especially when working for me. Each whore has complete control over her body."

Jerry frowned, remembering the men who would take it too far, who would beat her mother, rape her, who would kidnap her onto their ships and wouldn't let her go until Miriam came after them. She had to disagree, again. There was no control for those men. They saw women as pawns, as items to be used, as pleasurable and not something to pleasure.

"I know you saw some things—"

"I saw a lot, and I heard a lot, and I nursed my mother back to health more times than you probably realize."

Miriam looked surprised, but she did nod for Jerry to continue.

"So, no, I won't have whores on my books."

"Then you'll have to find some place for them to go so they can continue to earn their living. They will need to be taken care of."

That sounded unpleasant, and already Jerry could feel the

restrictions on what she could do closing in. She wasn't going to be able to do everything she wanted or not do everything she didn't want. Straightening up, Jerry started again, this time focusing on something positive.

"I'd want to live on a ship."

"I think that could be arranged, actually."

"Really?" Jerry raised an eyebrow at her skeptically.

"It would work well. You would need someplace on land to meet with people, but you wouldn't need to spend the majority of your time there. You can have others who do that work for you. It all depends on how you want to structure things."

Jerry wasn't sure she bought Miriam's story. Change and transition were rough for the best of them, and there would be expectations that she maintain some things the same when Miriam was no longer in charge. "I'll think about it. I promise you."

"That's all I can ask for." Miriam leaned forward and pressed a hand to Jerry's arm. "Now, about your cards, what do you want for them?"

Jerry paused, the words on the tip of her tongue. She wanted to say them desperately, see if they were even possible, but she wasn't sure it would be. She'd managed it the other day, but that was only for a very brief moment. Her heart raced, clogging up her throat with anxious fury.

"Can you…" She stopped and started again. "Can you make me a man?"

Miriam's look was brilliant. "I can make you whatever you want, Jeraldine. But again I ask you, who do you want to be?"

Jerry nodded, her confidence slowly edging its way into her as the thoughts and words settled into her chest. She nodded again, this time more forcefully. "I want you to make me a man."

"Then I will do that. I should have your cards ready soon then."

"Thank you."

"I'll give you the contact for next time, all right?"

"Next time?"

Miriam wrinkled her nose. "Do you honestly think my cards say that I'm Miriam Kozawich?"

"I...honestly never thought about it before."

Chuckling, Miriam swung her legs over the edge of the bed. "Hardly. I get new cards every year at least. I need to stay as hidden as possible, you know that."

Jerry did, and she understood why. Dealing with the underground, with the necessary world that was illegal and functioning within the confines of politics, Jerry knew would require precarious line walking—something she was decently good at, actually. She had practiced it while she kept her legal work and illegal work separate but the same throughout the past few years.

"Now, on your way, Jeraldine. I need to get ready for my day."

Dismissal at its finest. Jerry stood up and brushed her hands down the length of her stomach and upper thighs. "Thank you, Miriam. Again."

"Anytime, you know that. You're my favorite."

Jerry genuinely smiled, heat rushing to her cheeks. Miriam had told her that for years, but it had been a good decade since she'd said it. Bowing her head slightly, Jerry slipped from the room and back out onto the streets to head home to Arloa and her hideout.

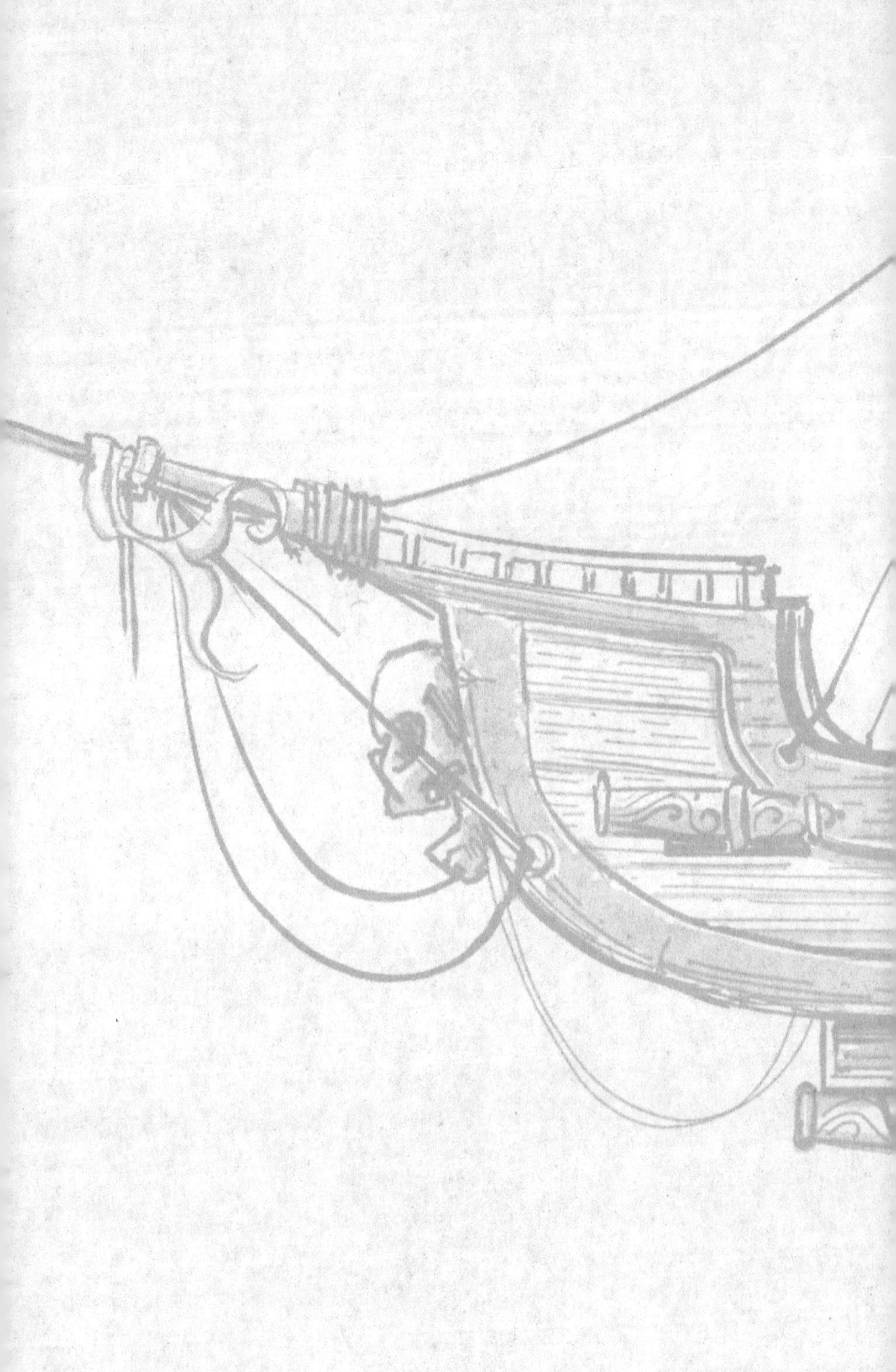

CHAPTER 9

Jerry tinkered with the device Arloa had finally procured for her, sitting on the corner of her cot with her knees pulled up to her chest. She'd done so many hours of research and her brain ached from it. It also ached from lack of the hormone she needed to survive. Arloa had been good about bringing her small pieces of brain when she could, but again she'd been missing for the past few days.

If she didn't come back soon, Jerry was going to have to venture out on her own to find some kind of sustenance to keep her sane. Miriam would no doubt be helpful with that should she need it. She had seen far too many people in the last year deteriorate right in front of her into something that wasn't even human. They would start with anger. It was always anger, though when Jerry examined it more closely, it wasn't so much anger as it was violent impulses.

They couldn't control the need for blood. Jerry couldn't either, though she never wanted to admit that. The call for blood was in her body, singing every time she got a good whiff of it, especially when she hadn't had brain in a day or two. She had worked hard throughout the last two years to control those impulses, but it was next to impossible.

She was forever changed by the virus. There was no coming

out of it. This was her life from there on out. Frowning, Jerry hit the button to send the cryptic message. Now all she had to do was wait, but she wasn't going to do that lying down or in the quiet. She needed to know when her message was received and deciphered so that she could send the next little bit of it.

Dressing quickly, Jerry stepped out of her hideout dressed as the man she was attempting to become. She'd always wondered what it would be like to have that privilege just handed to her, the power and authority she had both craved and despised. She shuddered at the thought. What would they think of her now? Her mother likely wouldn't have accepted it any, but Miriam was so unlike her mother in that regard.

She'd broken from tradition instead of having been shoved out of it unceremoniously. Jerry clenched her jaw as the sunlight hit her cheeks. She hadn't gone out during the day too much, but she wasn't about to let Vivian have all the fun without her. She made her way rapidly down to the docks, following the road-ways and keeping her eye out for any trouble. She saw only one soul on her way there and that was within the main part of town before the gates to the poorer side.

Walking up and down the street following the path of the harbor, Jerry found the perfect lookout. She stepped into the shaded alleyway and found the ladder. Glancing up to the sky, she pressed her lips together hard, debating for a moment whether or not she should climb it. Or rather, could climb it. She'd taken it so easy since she'd been rescued and had been healing. While she could easily find another hideout, being up high where she could follow the path of her target more easily would be ideal for this part.

Jerry reached up, her fingers curling around the bottom rung of the ladder. She counted to three before grimacing just before the pain hit as she pulled her body upward. Fuck she needed to work on that damn strength again. She dropped to the ground, unable to make her body move upward enough to grab the next rung.

It was a damn good thing she wasn't on a ship. She wouldn't be able to make it from deck to deck at the rate she was going. Breathing out heavily to wash her pain away, Jerry glared up at the rung, reaching upward and putting her hand on it again. She wasn't going to let this one go.

Slowing and steadying her breathing, Jerry closed her eyes and focused. She could do this. She could force her body to move like it used to. It may hurt like a bitch, but she could do this. Using her arms, Jerry dragged herself upward. She grunted as she let go with her left hand to jerk her arm upward and clasp onto the next rung of the ladder.

She couldn't stop. If she did, she would lose her momentum and fall back down. The next rung and the next went smoothly, but by the time she got to the fifth one, she started to lose her grip and strength. Crying out, Jerry dropped heavily to the cobblestone alley below, her boots echoing as they hit the ground before her body slumped over and she landed in a heap of misery.

Her heart hurt, physically and emotionally. She'd never been this bad before. Or if she had, there had been healers who had been able to help her out. But it was rare to find a healer who would work with those infected, and according to Arloa, even rarer to find a healer who still worked these days. Whimpering, Jerry pressed her palm against the cold cobblestone and pushed herself over so she lay flat on her back and stared up at the smog-filled sky.

"What the fuck am I doing?"

Glaring at the ladder in question, Jerry dragged herself to sit against the wall of the nearest building defeated. She had no hope anymore. She wasn't a damn pirate and she sure as hell wasn't a captain. What had she even been thinking trying to contact her old crew and drag them into the mess she found herself in? Over half her crew had been in Joab at one point, and if they were discovered associating with a known escapee, they'd be as fucked as she was.

She had nowhere to turn. Even with new cards from Miriam, if she were discovered, everyone around her would be victim to her mistakes—especially Arloa. Jerry hadn't even taken a moment to think of that, but surely that had been some of the fear in Arloa's eyes when she'd snuck into the government building.

She was a parasite, worming her way into people's lives only to bring them devastation. Clenching her jaw, Jerry tightened her hands into fists and dug her nails into the flesh of her palms. She should just let it all go and hide away while she could in order to survive a little bit longer. But then again, what would be the purpose of surviving for that?

Turning her head, Jerry looked out at the sea. The poisoned waters had been her companion for most of her life, and she could so easily run and jump if she wanted to, but she was tethered to the spot, unable to move. She had two options really, watch to see if her hint was discovered and followed, and then see what came of it. New cards would give her a start, but she would have to keep discovery to a minimum in order to protect her family. Her other option was to continue going through the motions of life, the creature created to move with the throngs, but she wasn't sure she wanted to be that person any longer.

With tears in her eyes, Jerry crawled to her knees and tried it one more time. Standing up, she put both hands on the rungs and dropped her entire weight onto her arms. Swinging, Jerry dragged herself up rung by rung until she could reach her foot up to hook her boot on the lowest one. Hissing out a satisfied breath, Jerry skittered her way rapidly to the top of the building, collapsing onto the rooftop as the sun beat down on her.

Sweaty, she dragged her jacket off and stared out at the water. *Yarrow* still sat in port, her sleek lines so familiar that Jerry would never miss her. She kept her head down so she was less likely to be seen, but she made sure that she could see *Yarrow's* main door where hopefully her target would emerge.

Vivian—that's who Jerry waited for. She could have sent the

message to Yafe, and she likely would have recognized it for what it was, but she wouldn't have been able to do anything with it. Azar as well. He was an engineer by trade, but he wouldn't have been able to decipher the clue Jerry had left hidden within it. Vivian was the only one who would figure it out, who would recognize the schematics of the bug Vivian had created months ago when they had gone to steal back *Yarrow* in order to succeed in their heist.

The sun was hot on her head, and she desperately wanted a vial of water to quench her thirst, but she wasn't about to climb down and then have to climb up again. Once was enough. When the large door in *Yarrow*'s side slid open and unfolded down to the ground, Jerry bit her lip and held her breath in anticipation. Who was going to come out?

Squinting to see if she could figure it out, Jerry tried her best to focus her eyes, but she couldn't make out the figure. She was a woman, that was for sure, but beyond the lines of the dress, Jerry struggled to make out who it was.

The woman walked closer. Jerry could intuitively hear the click of the heels of her boots against the wooden dock as she walked, but she was too far away to truly hear it. Leaning over the edge of the roof, Jerry tried to get a closer look, wishing for the first time that she had the telescope that she always kept in the wheelhouse. It would come in perfect for this sort of thing.

As soon as the woman made it to the pier, Jerry grinned broadly. Vivian strolled toward her, head down, hands clasped in front of her, wearing the dress Jerry had purchased for her when they'd first gone to steal Arloa's family vessel in order to steal *Yarrow* back from the asshole pirate who had stolen her in the first place.

Vivian had gotten her message.

Not only had she received it, she had understood it. Scrambling to her feet, Jerry raced to the other side of the roof and climbed down the ladder rapidly. She ignored the aches in her sides as she went, reaching the cobblestone alley with a thump before she straightened her back and then smoothed her clothes. Now for the tricky part. She had to hide in plain sight.

Staying right where she was, Jerry waited to see Vivian pass. The edge of her dress dragged against the road as she walked. They hadn't ever had the time to get it hemmed to her height, and she doubted Vivian had the credits to do it now. Wrinkling her nose, Jerry swiftly walked forward to the edge of the alleyway to see which way Vivian would go.

Just as she predicted, Vivian took a left. She was going exactly where Jerry had sent her. Perfect. Giddy, Jerry waited for her to walk out of sight before following at a slow enough pace that she wouldn't be noticed. She knew where Vivian was going, and that was the point. Once she arrived, she would get the second part of the clue.

Jerry watched as Vivian stepped into the small shop, her skirts rustling as the door shut behind her. She wished she could hear what was being said inside, but she hadn't had time to figure that out and she certainly wasn't about to walk in and risk her cover being blown. She hadn't tested out the looks department, only the voice, so pushing her limits could be an adventure in and of itself.

Squaring her shoulders, Jerry stepped straight toward the small dress shop. She'd go in under the guise of buying something for her daughter. That'd be perfect. With her hat on and low on her head, Jerry opened the door, the jingling of the bell over it echoing through the shop. It was empty inside, which surprised her. She expected to find Vivian and the shopkeeper talking while Vivian attempted to figure out the next clue. Instead the front of the store was abandoned.

"I'll be out in a minute!" Someone shouted from the back. Jerry pressed her lips together hard as she looked around at the different fabrics on display. The options were scarce compared to a few months ago, and none of them were as high quality as the dress that she had purchased for Vivian that fateful day.

Jerry said nothing as she waited, walking the perimeter of the store. Eventually the woman rushed out, brushing her hands against her skirt. She stopped short, almost surprised to find Jerry standing there. "Oh, I'm sorry for the wait, sir."

Jerry shook her head slightly and dropped her voice into the lower register. "Don't worry at all."

"What can I do for you?" The woman's voice held a twinge of the north, her hair in perfect braids down her back and woven together in one large braid that was tied neatly with a bright baby blue ribbon. Jerry remembered this woman fondly, but she had to keep her cover and not let her in on the fact that she'd been inside the store before.

"I was looking for a dress for my daughter. It seems you don't have many to choose from." Raising an eyebrow, Jerry looked down her nose at her, hating the moment she had to do it but still keeping the ruse up. She was dressed in rich clothing, and this woman would no doubt know that.

"Aye, shipments of new fabric have been difficult to get in. I apologize."

"Very well then." Jerry clenched her jaw and resisted the urge to clear her throat. She glanced toward the back where the woman had come from, wondering where the hell Vivian had gone. The pit of her belly twisted at the thought that she could truly be in danger. She was just about to ask, when Vivian stepped through the curtains from a dressing room, looking all sorts of tousled. Smirking, Jerry's eyes lit with humor as she nodded her head toward the seamstress and tilted her hat in her direction. "Good day, ma'am."

"Good day." She looked confused but said nothing as Jerry left the shop.

Vivian up that close would absolutely know who she was. Within a minute, Jerry hid around the corner of the next building over and waited. It took Vivian to the tolling of the next bell to leave, meaning she had been in the shop for the better part of an hour. Jerry frowned, wondering if she'd misread the situation and instead of Vivian finding her clue and deciphering it, she'd instead gone to meet up with a fling.

It would be her luck that it would happen that way. When Vivian finally stepped out into the dimming light, she lifted a parasol she hadn't gone in with over her head. Her eyes were bright with mischief as she walked away from the small shop and toward another row of buildings. Jerry again followed her from a distance, not quite sure which direction she was going this time.

At least five souls passed them as they went, the end of the workday finally hitting. Still the streets were far from full, and if Jerry wasn't careful, she would be spotted. As they rounded a corner, Jerry realized finally where they were going. Her favorite pub, and the second to last stop Jerry had given Vivian. This was the second clue, and the fact Vivian had gone here was exactly what Jerry needed in order to have hope.

She was such a smart woman.

Jerry didn't go inside this time, waiting patiently outside. Vivian didn't take long, obviously not stopping for a drink but only to collect the clue Jerry had hidden in the chair. She remembered every inch of the walls inside, and especially her favorite worn-down chair. She took a risk that it was still there and sent Vivian to find the notch on the fourth leg. The one Jerry had carved when she'd been sixteen and stupid.

As Vivian left the bar, Jerry raced on ahead of her to the place she had planned for them to meet. It would be perfect. Jerry knew where she was going and knew the area well enough to get there first. She would be sitting there waiting when Vivian arrived.

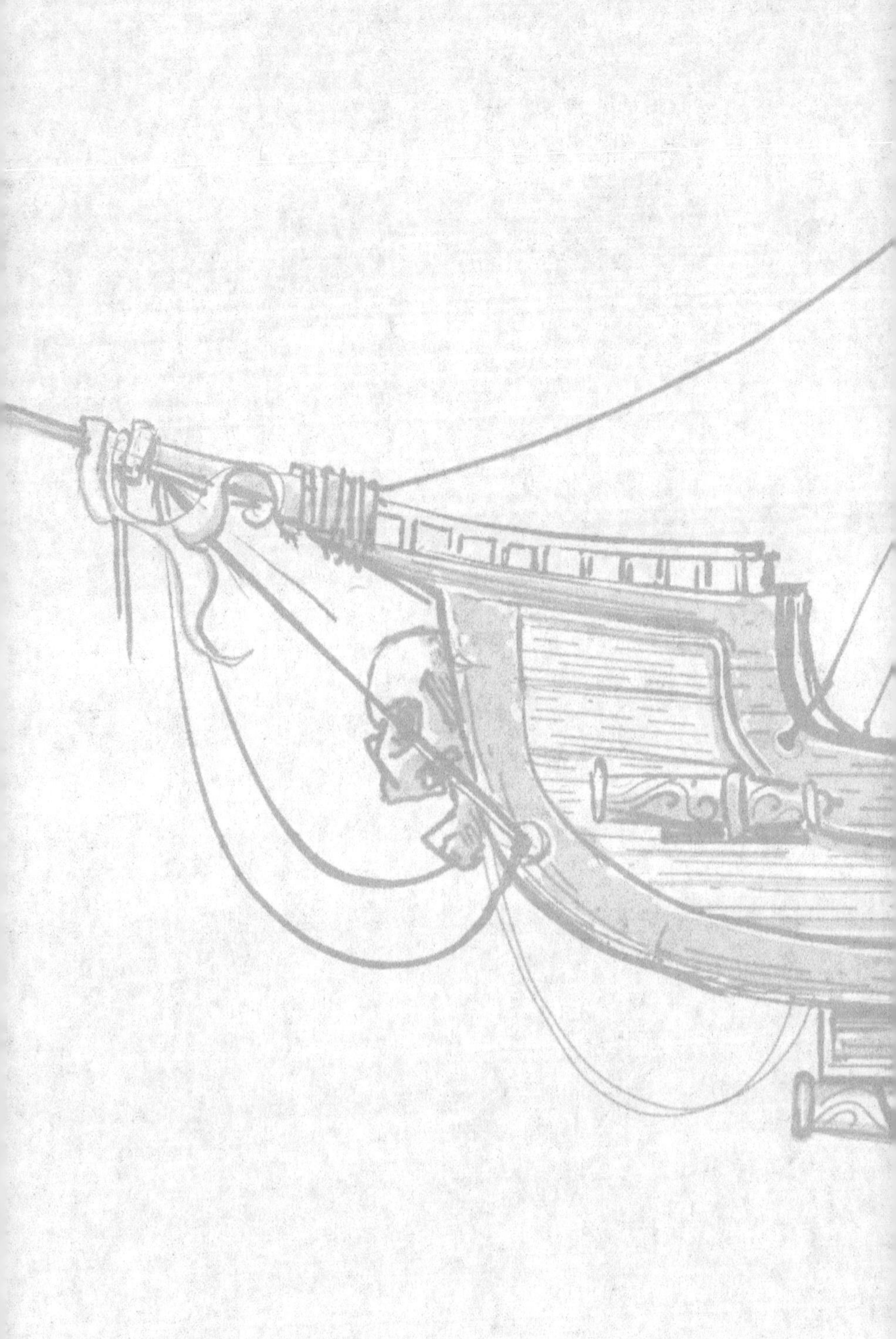

CHAPTER 10

Jerry arrived at the bell tower. Rubbing her thumb against the pads of her fingers, she stood waiting, attempting to look as though she wasn't there for nefarious reasons. She hid in the shadows, waiting a full twenty minutes for Vivian to arrive. She hung in the silence, keeping to herself and watching to make sure Vivian hadn't brought anyone with her on the last part of her hunt.

Vivian climbed to the roof, huffing as she pulled herself over the edge and put her hands on her hips. She tried to catch her breath, although it was rather unsuccessful. Jerry's lips curled upward at the sight. She was a vision, the first person Jerry had seen other than Arloa and Miriam that she knew and cared for.

Jerry had to hold off, however. Vivian walked to the edge of the roof, looking down over the ledge to the ground below before stepping back and putting her hands on her hips again. She blew out a breath and raised her chin to the moon.

"I swear on all things holy, Cap, if this is some trick, I'll kill you myself."

Resisting the urge to laugh, Jerry bit the inside of her cheek. She missed the camaraderie with her crew. She had longed to be with people again, having been so isolated for so long that just the urge to be with other people she knew was immense.

Vivian walked around the edge of the building, and Jerry stayed hidden and quiet in the shadows. She wasn't ready just yet to show her face. The scars were still too new in some ways. But when Vivian stopped and stared at the bell just above Jerry's head, she knew she couldn't wait any longer.

Stepping out from behind the column, Jerry put her hands out to her sides so Vivian wouldn't think she was under attack. She started, her hands going up and her feet planting as if she was ready to defend herself.

"Relax, Viv."

"Fuck, Cap." Vivian relaxed instantly. "You look like shit."

"I know." Jerry moved in even closer, seeing the lines of Vivian's face, the simple rounded curves of her cheeks, the life in her eyes. She'd missed that kind of adventure for too long.

"Where the hell have you been?" Vivian stepped in close, reaching her arms out as if she was going to hug her.

Jerry stepped back, putting her hands up in front of her. She wasn't ready for that. Couldn't even stand to be that close to another person—it was hard enough with Arloa. "Don't come any closer, please."

"All right." Vivian frowned a little, the moonlight touching her skin. "Did you go to Joab?"

"Yeah." Jerry tensed at just the mention of it. "Guess you all didn't get the memo."

"We assumed you were there or you were dead." Vivian put her hands at her sides.

"There's not much difference between the two."

"Right," Vivian mumbled.

Jerry had to get off that topic. She needed to get information, that had been the entire point of the wild chase she'd sent Vivian on in the first place. "I needed to talk to you."

"This sounds like more than just a 'Hey, I'm alive!' conversation."

"It is." Jerry fisted her hands and tried to ease the tension in her chest. "I need to know everything that you know about Bert Riley."

Vivian sucked in a breath through her teeth, causing a whistle. "I don't know much."

"You said once you snuck into the government house and overheard him."

"I did." Vivian raised her gaze toward the sky. "I've continued to do some research on him."

"Why?"

"I don't trust him. Never have, really, but after that day, I really didn't."

Jerry agreed with her, but she wasn't going to let Vivian in fully on her plan. Not yet at least. Using the pull of her title, of the reason they had met in the first place, Jerry started in again. "What did you find out?"

"Other than he's a liar?"

"Yeah, other than that."

Vivian pursed her lips. "How'd you get out?"

"Doesn't matter," Jerry answered, never willing to give up Arloa as the reason she'd broken out. She should have lied and said they'd released her, but then the question as to why she hadn't returned to *Yarrow* would come about.

"It does."

"I've been healing and regaining strength for the last few weeks."

"That isn't what I asked." Vivian knocked her chin up defiantly. "I think I deserve an answer. You vanished on us, Cap, and suddenly you're back?"

"I'm not back," Jerry reiterated. She wasn't sure if she would ever be back as Captain. Her bones still ached from the torture, and she knew she wasn't strong enough to be there for her crew.

"You're here." Vivian stepped in closer, and Jerry moved away. "I'm asking for information. That's all."

"Yafe isn't you."

"She's not supposed to be." Jerry made eye contact with her. "But she's your captain now, not me." Losing that title took everything in her, but it was the right decision to make. She wasn't Captain Jerry Adelric any longer. She was someone who had no name, no place in society, no existence. "What do you know about Bert Riley?"

Vivian sighed heavily and rolled her shoulders, debating and hedging. Jerry had seen her do it so many times since they'd met, and it was almost if no time had passed. But so much had changed since then.

"I know he knew about this virus before anyone else."

Jerry's eyes widened at that. "What do you mean?"

"He was preparing for it before the news outlets even had information on it."

"He's in the government."

"I've hacked into their systems, Cap. No one knew about it then. There weren't any reports or anything in the session notes."

"Are you sure?" Jerry clenched her jaw.

"Positive."

"How the hell did he know?"

"That's the question I haven't been able to answer without speculation."

Jerry raised her chin up to look at the sky. Clouds moved through it, covering the moonlight and making it even darker as they stood on the rooftop. She shouldn't stay there much longer, but she had to know what Vivian knew.

"Yafe won't let me look into it any more than I already have."

"She knows?"

"She knows some of it." Vivian came in closer, and this time Jerry didn't flinch away. She lowered her voice to just above a whisper. "I think he knew about it because he had something to do with it."

Jerry's heart thundered as panic welled in her chest. "You think it was created? It's a virus that's hit us all before."

"Not like this." Vivian shook her head. "It was so different then."

"There's barely any records of it then."

"There's enough."

Jerry frowned and closed her eyes. "You're grasping for connections that don't exist."

"Maybe." Vivian implored. "But don't you think it's odd that he knew before the rest of the world? If anyone is patient zero, it's him."

"He'd be dead like the rest of us."

"Maybe. But not if he had his own personal stash of vestigen."

"It's lunacy," Jerry hissed. "He'd be insane to try something like this."

"Isn't he, though? That's why we all hate him. He doesn't care about us. He doesn't care about Raegina or Penum. He never has, so why would he start now?"

Jerry couldn't fault the logic on that one. They stood in silence, the sound of the poisoned sea lapping against the piers, the wind as it blew through the buildings. Nothing else could be heard. No boisterous sounds from the pubs, no clack of horse hooves, no voices as people walked from one place to the next. They were completely in the dark.

"How do we find out?"

Vivian grinned. "I've been waiting for someone to ask me that."

Jerry moved her hand out in front of her, indicating Vivian should continue.

"I need to hack them again."

"That's dangerous."

"It's the only way I'm going to find anything out."

"Let me see if there's another way, all right?"

"No. There isn't another way." Vivian put her hands on her hips, this time in defiance. "I need to trace back the source of the first report, and if it's him, that's a sure thing as to who is responsible."

"And if it's not?"

"We keep looking for clues."

Jerry scrunched her nose. "This isn't how it works. If someone else is responsible, then we need to be able to look for them."

"It's him. I know it is."

Jerry sighed. She had her own suspicions, but she wasn't going to share that with Vivian—not yet at least. "What do you need from me in order to find out?"

"I can get you a list of supplies, but mostly I'll need time away from *Yarrow*."

"I can't help you with that."

"You can talk to Yafe—"

"No. She can't know that I'm here."

Vivian parted her lips in protest, but she seemed to stop herself. "Why not?"

Jerry swallowed hard. "No one can know I'm alive or where I am."

"Because you weren't released."

Not confirming Vivian's suspicions was easy, although she was resourceful enough that she could easily find record of the escape. Jerry only hoped Arloa had covered her tracks well enough that it couldn't be tied back to her.

Vivian blew out a breath. "What do we do when we confirm it's him?"

"We're not confirming anything. We're looking for answers."

"There's something that brought him to your attention."

Jerry wasn't going to answer that one either. She held her ground, keeping quiet. "We need information before we can decide what we're doing with it."

"We'll have to expose him."

Jerry had her doubts that anyone would listen even if they did. Bert Riley was in line to be the next Senate Leader, and he was so well-liked among the aristocrats that he was a shoo-in for the position. Nothing they did was going to make a lick of difference. "Find out what you can."

"I need time away from the ship."

"You'll have to figure that one out on your own because I can't help you with it. I can get you supplies, but I can't talk to them yet."

"We miss you."

Jerry's heart shattered. She missed each one of them, their companionship, the camaraderie. She had some of that with Arloa, but even their relationship had shifted since she'd come back. Who was she kidding? Everything was because of what she'd experienced in Joab this time. She'd never wanted to go back there. She'd always said she would die first, and she had failed in that one simple mission.

"Azar is in charge of *Astilbe*."

"I'm sure he makes a good captain." Jerry's jaw was tight with emotion, and she struggled to get the words out. She wanted to support him, to be there for all of them, but she couldn't. And the problem was, she wasn't sure if she would ever be in that position again.

"Yafe was unsure of herself at first, but she's gotten a handle on it now."

The update on her crew was welcomed, but it hurt deep within Jerry's soul. It tore at her, ripped her in two. She desperately wanted to be with them, but to be with them would put them in immediate danger. There was no way she had escaped Joab and wasn't a target.

"Vivian," Jerry whispered. "We need to focus on Bert Riley."

"Why's he of interest now?"

"Because I have time now that I didn't before. I'm not running a ship. I'm not a captain."

"So you're what? An investigator?"

Jerry snorted. "Hardly, but I have to do something to keep busy."

Vivian hummed. "And was bringing me up here a part of the game too?"

"No." Jerry looked her directly in the eye. "I needed information and you have it, and the ability to get more."

"You're resourceful. Why not find someone else?"

"There isn't anyone else." Jerry eyed her. "Why the hesitation now? Five minutes ago, you were all for this."

Vivian frowned. "Like you said. You're not my captain anymore."

Jerry blinked away her hurt. "I'm not. And this is a choice you'll have to make. I hope you make the one that'll help me."

"Come home."

"I can't," Jerry whispered. "I'm not going to put all of you in danger."

"Just me?"

Jerry's lips pulled into a smile up on one side. "I've seen you handle danger, and I think you can manage it."

Vivian snorted. "And you? Can you handle it?"

Jerry hesitated. A year ago she would have dived right in to answer with an affirmation, but now, she wasn't so sure. She'd been broken in Joab—again. Only this time they had managed to kill her spirit in a way they'd never done before. The experiences she had were beyond anything she'd had prior, and there was no coming back from that.

"I don't have a choice." Jerry nodded her head down. "Get me the list."

"On it, Cap." Vivian's eyes lit up at the salutation.

Jerry didn't wait. She climbed over the edge of the building and down the ladder. Vivian didn't follow her immediately, which gave her time to vanish behind the corner of a building. Jerry waited for Vivian to find her way down the ladder. She would make sure Vivian returned safely, that no one followed her or hurt her. Jerry might not be captain of *Yarrow* any longer, but Vivian was still her crew, her family, and she'd be damned if she was going to allow her to put herself at risk.

Not that Jerry could do much if something major happened anyway. She was healed, but her strength wasn't back. Jerry followed her silently and in the dark so Vivian didn't see her. As soon as she was back on *Yarrow*, Jerry made her way to her hideaway. Lying down on the small cot in the corner of the room, she covered her eyes with her arm and allowed the emotions she had avoided during that entire interaction to run through her.

Miriam's proposal ran through her mind again. It would be something to do, a new life to live, but Jerry still wasn't sure it was what she wanted. Confusion was all she was met with when it came to her future. She had no idea what it would look like other than it would never be the same. Until then, she could focus everything she had on figuring out where the virus had come from and perhaps finding a solution to it, one that had been in front of them all along.

Turning on her side, Jerry closed her eyes and curled into a ball. This was more her prison than Joab. Vivian had shown her that immediately. Jerry had gone from one form of torture to another, and she needed to decide how she was going to move forward from there. She couldn't wait for Vivian to bring her all the answers. She needed to find some on her own.

But right now all she needed was to lie there and wallow. She needed to find that strength she once had, see if it was still there, and maybe she could even bring it out again. But until then, she was going to be stuck in a hell of her own making.

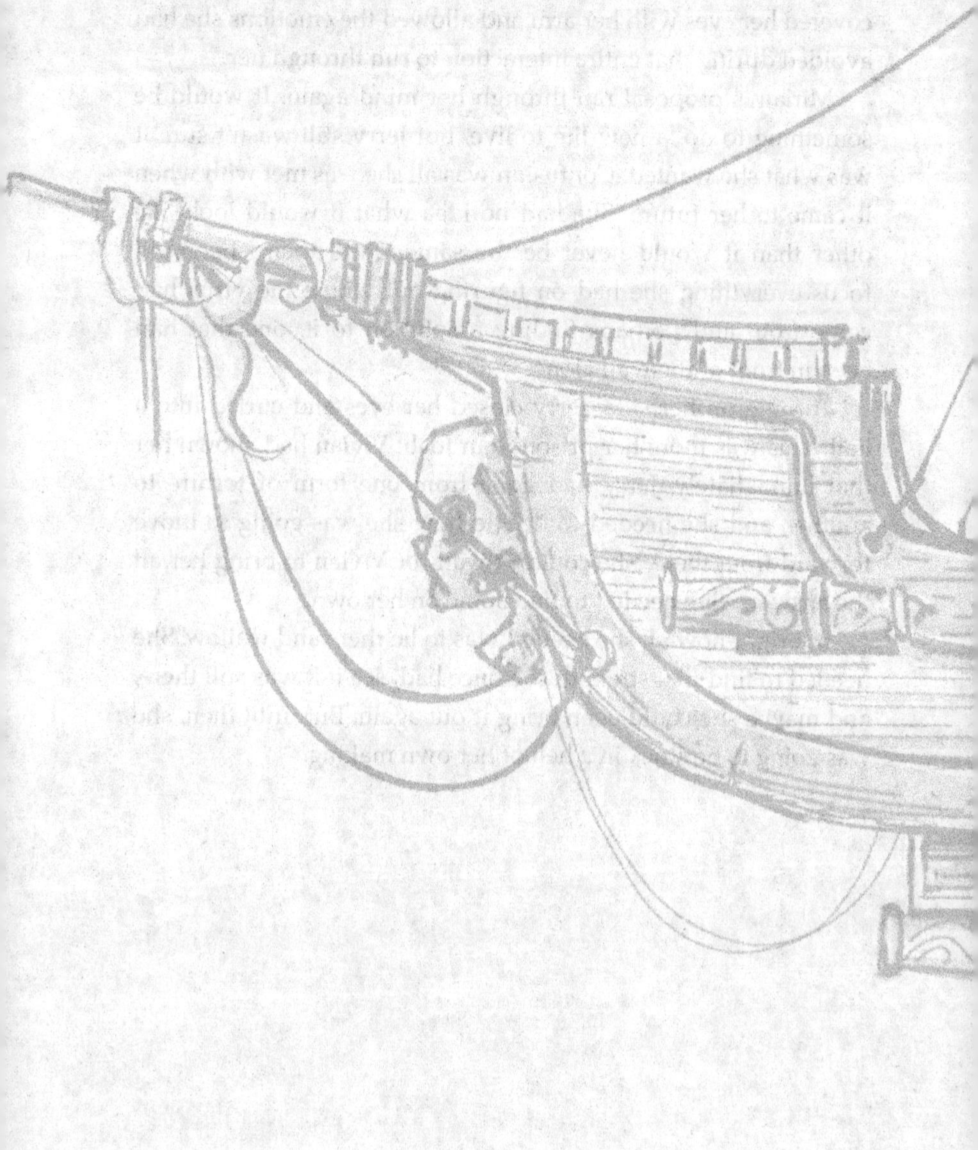

[illegible] I would do later if something might happen. [illegible] Still, she was in bed, but I [illegible] she didn't pass [illegible]

[illegible] going at [illegible] overtaken the [illegible] to turn her to starboard, would have [illegible] her through her mind again, it would be [illegible] to [illegible] the river before she [illegible] was still [illegible]

[illegible] her [illegible] mind he [illegible] when it would [illegible] other than it would never be [illegible] [illegible] depended on [illegible]

[illegible]

[illegible]

CHAPTER 11

Hands on her shoulders startled her. Jerry spun around on the cot, her eyes wide open and her hands up, ready to defend herself. Arloa grabbed her wrists, pinning her down to the bed by using her entire body weight to keep her still. Jerry breathed heavily, staring up at her with wide, fear-ridden eyes.

"It's just me," Arloa murmured, her voice gentle and authoritative.

Jerry didn't relax. She couldn't. After seeing Vivian and reliving Joab during their conversation, after finding herself once again locked into a small room with nowhere to go, she couldn't force herself to drag in a deep breath.

Arloa leaned in, whispering, "Breathe, love."

On command, Jerry's lungs filled with cold air, and she slowly blew it out through her lips. Arloa made her do it three more times before she relaxed her grip and straightened her back so she didn't hover over Jerry.

"Better?" Arloa asked.

Jerry nodded silently, though she wasn't sure how much truth was in it. She didn't want to defend herself, which she supposed was the right direction to go, but she also wasn't comfortable still being cornered on the bed.

"Jer."

Saccharine sweetness floated to her, and Jerry relaxed even more. She trusted Arloa, and she had to keep reminding herself of that. This woman had saved her countless times already, and Jerry had to continue to believe that Arloa had her best interest in mind.

"Talk to me. You have me worried."

Jerry raised her gaze, locking her eyes with those blue orbs above her. "It was a bad dream."

"A nightmare or a memory?"

"Both," Jerry answered. "I'll be fine."

Arloa's hand skated up and down Jerry's arm, the gentle touch centering in a way Jerry hadn't expected. This was the most amount of time the two of them had ever spent together, the closeness but also tension warring with each other. "I wish you would tell me what happened."

"There's nothing to tell that you can't figure out." Jerry shifted so she leaned against the wall, giving herself more space but also a silent barrier between them. "Have you found anything?"

Arloa dragged in a breath and let it go slowly, holding the tension for longer than Jerry was comfortable with. "I have files."

"Files?" Jerry ducked her chin and raised her gaze. "As in you stole government property and brought it here?"

"Don't think I've never done anything illegal before now."

Jerry's cheeks reddened with embarrassment. Finding someone who hadn't done something illegal was difficult, but this was a major breach and could be considered treason if Arloa was caught. This wasn't some simple moment of breaking the law, this would toss her in Joab should she be discovered. Arloa stayed still on the edge of the cot, her shoulders strong in her attitude as she continued to stare at Jerry.

"I don't know if there's anything relevant in it. We'll have to spend time going through the files."

"I didn't think this was the first thing you've done that's illegal. You did break me out of Joab."

Arloa frowned, lines on the side of her mouth. "You didn't deserve to be there."

"I stole a ship, killed people, and that was only within a day or two prior to being arrested. I'm a pirate, of course I deserved to be there. At least according to the law, which you know I disagree with."

"As do I."

"For all intents and purposes, I deserve to rot and die there."

"No one deserves that."

Jerry didn't believe her. Arloa was a Kauket, one of the very people who had created Joab to begin with, the number one financial supporter for the rehabilitation center that more closely resembled a prison built for torture. Her last stint there proved that.

"How did you get the files?"

"It doesn't matter how I got them. What matters is we have them, and we can find the information that we've been searching for."

Jerry pursed her lips. She wanted to take that for an answer but there was so much left unasked about Arloa, so many answers she hadn't gotten, and she needed to know something.

"How did you figure out where to find me?"

"What?" Arloa lifted her chin, looking directly into Jerry's eyes.

"In Joab. How did you know?"

"I went home." Arloa frowned.

"And they just told you?"

"Hardly. I copied my father's entire system, and then parsed through the information until I found it." Arloa was back to working as if it was no big deal that she once again stole information.

An unsettled feeling emerged in Jerry's chest, and instead of easing, it only got worse. "And when I was marooned on that island?"

"That was harder, believe it or not. Finding you in Joab was the easy part. Devising a plan for extraction was difficult. Finding you on an island that wasn't on the maps was far more difficult. But I tracked your projected return flight home and started along that path. You weren't that far off from it, believe it or not."

Jerry hadn't honestly known. She'd wanted to wipe the memory of that island from her mind, and since they'd been so depleted of vestigen and starving, she hadn't paid attention when the ship had arrived to rescue them. The feeling of elation at escaping had been the only thing on her mind.

"And what were you doing in the bar down off the docks?"

Arloa stiffened, her entire body going rigid. Jerry must have hit some sort of nerve, and now she really wanted the answer. Holding on to the silence as she waited, she observed every change in Arloa's demeanor. The muscles in her jawline tightened, her eyes narrowed as she focused on the papers in front of her, and she closed in on herself.

Jerry wanted to reach out and touch her, get some kind of connection going that they once had so maybe she could get an answer to her questions, but she held firm. For nearly two years she had wondered just what Arloa was doing in that bar, what prompted their very first meeting.

"Arloa..." Jerry's voice was near a whisper, tender and imploring at the same time. "Will you answer me?"

"I had an important meeting with a contact." Arloa made eye contact. "That's all I can tell you."

"All right." It was more of an answer than Jerry had expected, although it wasn't exactly what she was looking for.

Arloa pressed her lips together into a thin line, her blue eyes hardening as she held out a file for Jerry to take. Reluctantly, Jerry slid the paper into her fingers. She stared at the blank file before slowly opening it and reading the first line. It was tedious work ahead of them, but if they were going to be spending hours in a room together, at least they would be working instead of talking.

"You're still having nightmares," Arloa commented after Jerry started on her second file.

So much for not talking. Jerry grunted an answer and shifted to snag a third file.

"I know what they did to you in there. They keep fastidious records."

Jerry froze. She dropped the file she'd just grabbed and faced Arloa full on. "They keep records? I always assumed they kept none."

"My parents are ridiculous about recording everything."

"So you *knew*? You knew what's been going on there for years?"

Arloa shook her head. "I didn't. Not until I met you and found out you'd been there. I was curious and so I looked. It's disgusting."

"Then why aren't you doing anything about it? You have power being in the government. You could stop them. It's illegal."

Arloa's face hardened, her lips pursing, her eyes narrowing. "It's not as simple as that. If I want to retain the power I have, then I need to find a balance."

Jerry snorted. "What balance is there? The rich get richer every moment and the poor get poorer. We can't survive in this world that is built solely for the likes of you."

Arloa sighed. "I'm working on that, but Bert Riley is a thorn in my side when it comes to changing policy."

"It's not about changing policy. It's about enacting the policy that already exists!" Jerry stood up sharply, ready for a fight. She'd been wanting something to happen, something to pull her in one direction or the other, something that would mean anything was happening.

Arloa shifted the papers slowly off her lap and stood up. She was so small compared to Jerry, but her demeanor was bigger. She held the power in the room–any room–that she walked into. Jerry envied that. Arloa stayed away from her, hands at her side, fingers loose. She wasn't a threat, as much as Jerry wanted her to be at that moment.

"You've been through something awful."

"It's not anything new," Jerry argued. She wasn't going to put excuses on her life. She pushed through it to the next and kept on carrying on. That was all she could do. "I've been through a lot since the moment I was born to a sixteen-year-old woman who had no husband and no support."

Arloa sighed. "I read about your mother."

"What the fuck don't you know?" Jerry backed into the corner, her shoulders hitting the cement wall.

"I don't know what you're thinking right now."

Raising her gaze to the ceiling, Jerry shook her head. "My mother gave everything for me, including her dignity."

"She was a good mother, someone who loved her daughter." Arloa's voice was gentle, soft, imploring. Jerry wanted to reach out to her, wrap arms around her shoulders and break down in the way she hadn't allowed herself to do since she'd been rescued—again. "She's someone to look up to."

"She made stupid choices. She got involved with Miriam and couldn't get out."

Arloa's breathing increased, her breasts pushing against her corset as she took one simple step closer. "Jer, you aren't your mother."

But she was. In so many ways she was. She'd never managed to get out from under Miriam's hand. No matter how many times she'd tried, she'd always come running back when she needed help. She always depended on other women to get things done. She wasn't worthy of being called captain, and she certainly wasn't brilliant enough to figure out what started the pandemic they found themselves in.

"I'm no one."

"I don't believe that for a second."

"Then you're lying to yourself." Jerry clenched her hands into fists, struggling with the weight of emotion she'd just landed in the room, the explosion of feelings still threatening to erupt from her. "I am no one in this world. I'm an ex-con, now I'm an escaped ex-con. I can't use my name. I can't live. I can't be captain of my ships. I can't do anything!"

"You can do this. You can be here and be present. You're Jeraldine Adelric, and when I met you, you had the world at your fingertips."

"I had nothing but my ship, and now I don't even have that."

Arloa had somehow managed to get to her, standing right in front of her. Jerry bent her neck, looking into those eyes like she could have all the answers in the world, but Arloa had nothing for her. Nothing but hope—and Jerry didn't want that. She couldn't have any of that in her life because it wouldn't last. It never did.

Arloa reached up, curving her fingers around Jerry's cheek, her fingertips cold against her skin. "You are a survivor, and you're not stupid, Jer. You know what the world has to offer you, which isn't much, unfortunately. You deserve all of Penum. You are what makes this world a better place."

"Don't lie to yourself."

Sighing, Arloa dropped her hand. "I'm not going to put up with listening to your self-deprecation. If you would like to join me in finding answers, then feel free, but I'm tired of hearing this nasty talk."

She went back to the small cot, sitting on the edge of it and pulled up the papers to set them on her lap. One last look in Jerry's direction—a pointed look that meant business—and she was back to work. Just like that the argument Jerry had been searching for was gone—vanished. How had she managed to do that?

It took Jerry longer to move away from the wall and sit on the cot. She grabbed the file she had abandoned and opened it, staring at the words and trying to understand what was even in it. Thus far, she hadn't seen anything that was shocking or that she didn't already suspect. Raegina was struggling to survive. It had been for decades, even before Jerry had been born, but it had gotten significantly worse right before the virus took hold of them.

"I don't even know why I'm looking at these. I don't understand half of what I'm reading." Jerry's voice was poignant in the quiet room.

Arloa shifted her gaze in Jerry's direction, that icy look saying so much that Jerry couldn't read. Her lips thinned even more, as if Jerry were about to be chastised.

"I'm not smart enough to read these," Jerry said quietly, a resigned frustration in each word. "I'm uneducated, and while I understand the main process and big picture things, these words on this piece of paper are meaningless."

Arloa drew in a slow breath, letting it out through her nose. She took the paper from Jerry's fingers and skimmed it. She set it to the side. "There's nothing there."

"But what's the point of picking up another one—" Jerry grabbed the next one on her pile, waving it back and forth in the air "—and reading it if I can't understand it? There's no point because I won't know what it's saying."

Arloa snagged it and set it on Jerry's lap. "You're far more intelligent than you think, but perhaps the most important quality you have is your intuition."

Arloa flicked her gaze up to Jerry's face and then back down to the paper in her lap, as if the conversation was over. Jerry pouted and closed her eyes, trying to gain a hold on herself. She was out of drugs. That was exactly what this entire conversation was. Her body was depleted.

"Do you want to tell me what this is really about?"

Jerry pressed her lips together hard, immediately falling silent. What was she supposed to say to that? "I'm tired."

"So get some rest."

"Not that kind of tired. I don't know if I can sleep again, honestly."

That caught Arloa's attention. She put the papers down next to her, making eye contact. "What's going on?"

"I'm tired. Nothing is going to change. We're searching for answers, but what difference is it going to make? Nothing is going to happen."

"You don't know that."

"I do know it. I know it better than you. I've lived it my entire life. You have options. I don't." Jerry pressed a hand to her chest. "You have the world in front of you. Hell, you're a senator. And what am I? Nothing, because I can't even be who I was."

"Oh, Jer." Arloa wrapped her fingers around Jerry's hand. "You deserve the world."

"I deserve nothing." Jerry leaned in, making her point. "And I don't know why you think I do. I don't. I'm no one."

"You are someone. To me you are, and I know that sounds awful to say, but I wouldn't be here if you weren't. To Yafe and Azar and the others, you're someone. You matter. You always have—ever since I met you."

"You don't need to lie."

"I'm not lying." Offense filled Arloa's gaze.

Jerry bit her tongue, holding everything back. She'd been an emotional mess since her return—well, if she were honest, since the virus started.

"Look." Arloa took Jerry's hand. "I've gone after you so many times I've lost count. Doesn't that say something?"

"Says you're an idiot."

Arloa snorted. "Or obsessed?"

Jerry lifted her gaze. She'd thought that once before too, that she was obsessed with this woman. For some reason she couldn't ever stop thinking about her, and any time Arloa asked for something, she gave in.

"You're intelligent, Jer. It was one of the first things I noticed about you." Arloa's lips curled upward, her cheeks tinging pink with a blush. "You're independent, you understand this world in a visceral way that most of us don't. And you don't give up. The number of times you could have..." Arloa trailed off, her voice thick with emotion.

Overcome with emotion, Jerry brushed her fingers across Arloa's forearm, the most tender touch she had likely ever given her.

"But you didn't," Arloa finished. "And I found you again, and here we are."

"Reading fucking paperwork." Jerry smiled, genuinely. Her lips curled upward, her cheeks tightening as they pulled up, her muscles in her shoulders relaxing.

"Yeah," Arloa agreed. "It's a bit of a disaster, isn't it?"

"Every day is." Jerry rolled her shoulders, but she didn't want to move her hand from Arloa's arm. Instead, she leaned in, pressing their lips together. It was a brief brush of mouths— simple, easy, comforting. That was it exactly. Jerry was safe with her. No matter what happened, Arloa would find her, take care of her, be there for her. Grinning against Arloa's mouth, Jerry deepened the embrace for one more moment. "Let's figure out the disaster, okay?"

Arloa beamed. "Yes."

Arloa grabbed the paper she had set aside and put it back in her lap. Jerry mimicked her move and stared down at the small words neatly printed on the paper. She got halfway through it before blinking and reading again. Her stomach twisted hard, and her heart raced.

"Arloa."

"Hmm?" Arloa didn't lift her gaze.

Jerry set the paper in Arloa's line of sight. "What's this?"

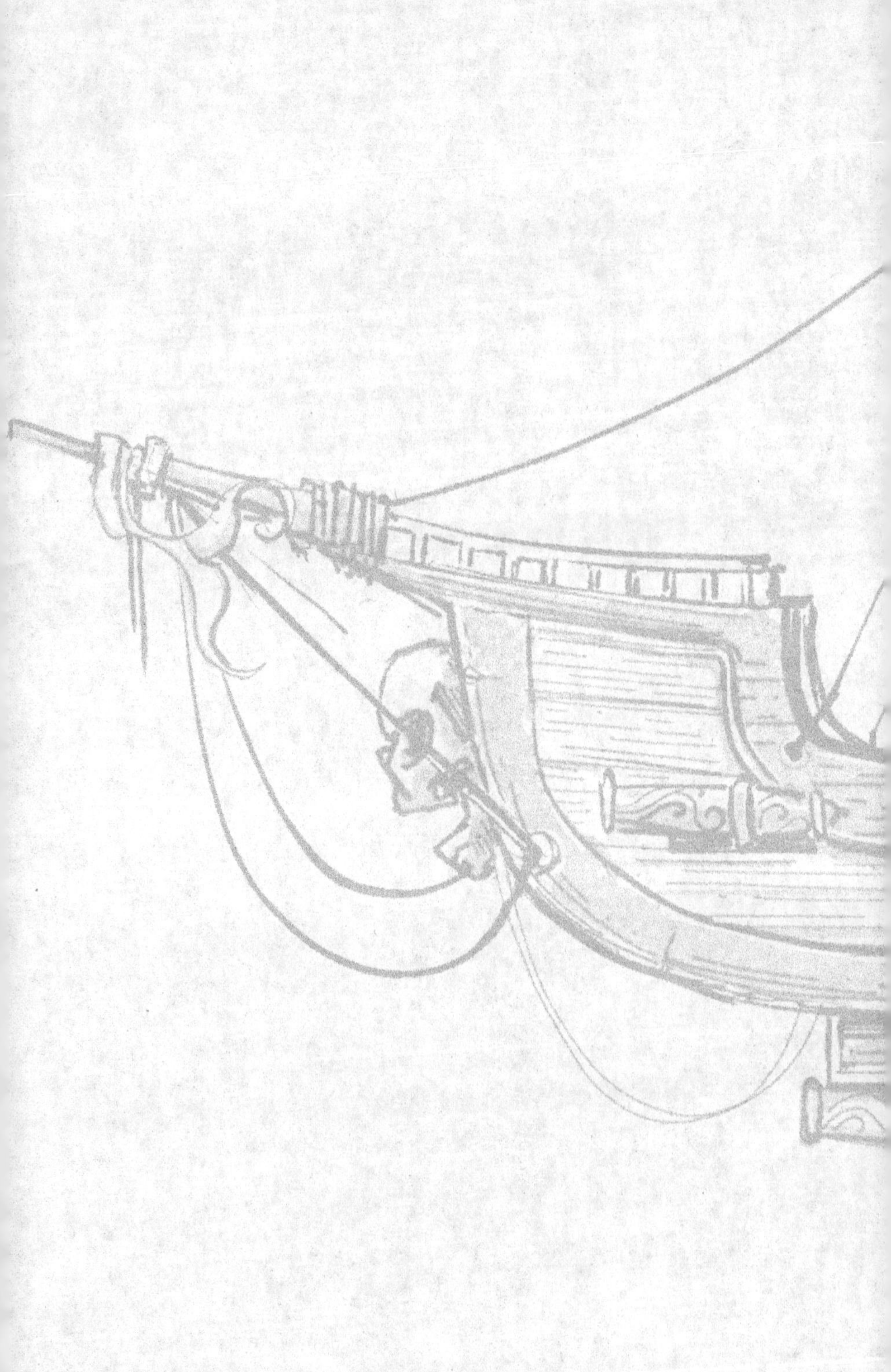

CHAPTER 12

Arloa slid the paper from Jerry's fingers, as if she was scared to see what was on it. Jerry held her breath, still trying to read the details but not fully understanding what it meant. The math on the page was over Jerry's head. She eyed the details. Arloa put her finger on it, sliding down to the bottom of the page and then flipping it over.

"It's not all here."

"What's not?" Jerry asked, hovering over her shoulder.

"This is only one piece. It's missing the beginning and the end." Arloa shoved the paper into Jerry's lap and grabbed another stack. "Where did you pull this from?"

"Um…" Jerry narrowed her gaze as she tried to remember. She picked up a stack of papers next to her that could very well be where she got it from, if she was lucky. Diving through, she looked for something similar to what she had found and hoped it would be the right piece of paper that Arloa wanted.

Tension rose back in her chest, but this time it was because of the tension in the room, the stress and excitement rolling off Arloa in waves. Jerry flicked through the papers, looking for anything similar to what she'd just discovered. That stack resulted in nothing, so she grabbed another one, trying to remember desperately where she had pulled the paper from.

Jerry got through the second stack and found nothing. Arloa made it all the way through hers and cried out in frustration, dropping the papers onto the concrete floor before standing and pacing the small room. She put her hands on her hips, her chin tilted toward the ground, and her breathing coming in rapidly as she walked back and forth. Jerry remained on the cot, watching this amazingly strong woman unfold in front of her.

"It's not here," Arloa finally said, raising her chin. "That piece of paper was an accident."

Jerry instinctively reached for the paper that had gotten the adrenaline going. She stared down at it again, still trying to parse out what it said and what it meant and getting absolutely nowhere.

"I can't believe he fucked this up." Arloa's voice went from quiet with excitement to loud.

"What is it?" Jerry asked, still staring down at the paper.

Arloa swung around, her skirts rustling as she sat next to Jerry and pointed at the middle of the page where a formula was handwritten into a printed box. "This is a formula."

"No shit." Jerry clenched her jaw, still wondering what all the damn excitement was for.

Arloa ignored her and forged ahead. "If I had this formula, I would have been able to manufacture something similar to vestigen. This is what we were missing the entire time."

Cold washed through Jerry, the numbers and lines and symbols in the center of the page not something she ever expected to see. Her heart raced with the possibilities. "Can you still do that?"

"Yes, not right away since the team has significantly dwindled over the past year, but yes, with this we can make a drug that will at the very least sustain you."

Jerry nodded slowly, then pointed down at the paper. "What is the formula?"

"It's for a vaccine." Arloa shifted her finger up and to the top of the page. "You can see it here, at least the end of it and the formula solution they came to."

"But does it work?"

"No idea." Arloa fisted her hand, putting it down next to her. "Without the rest of the papers, I have no idea if this is the middle of the process, the beginning or the end."

"Then how is it helpful in making vestigen."

"It's a better place to start than what I had, which wasn't much."

Jerry dragged in a deep breath, still holding that damn piece of paper in her fingertips. "So what do we do with it?"

"We have to tell someone."

"But how? You stole this. We can't exactly share what we have without someone else tracing it back to you and your thievery."

The muscles in Arloa's jaw tightened, and Jerry hated that she was the one who had done it, but it had to be said.

"You aren't going to throw your career away because of this."

"It'll be worth it."

"No, it won't." Jerry's voice raised.

They had a standoff, each looking at each other as if they were going to get their way, but this was one time Jerry wasn't going to back down. Arloa had power, and with that power came influence Jerry could never dream of having. She wasn't going to let Arloa throw that to the wind simply because Arloa thought it was the easiest way out of this.

"I can talk to Vivian," Jerry suggested, not hinting that she was already in communication with her.

Arloa frowned.

"She's good with tech, and I'm sure she can find some way to leak this."

"We need more than this to leak."

Jerry had known that from the start, but that didn't mean she wasn't ready to start ripping open all the damned secrets. "We need to start with doubt."

"Sowing seeds of doubt amongst your class isn't difficult. You all are suspicious of us anyway."

"With good reason," Jerry muttered.

"Agreed." Arloa clasped Jerry's hand, the tug and pull between them easing. "We're on the same side in this conversation, I promise."

Jerry had to trust that, but everything she had seen from Arloa so far proved that was true. "We start with rumors. But where?"

"In the government house?" Arloa closed her eyes, concentrating.

"Will that get to everyone else?"

"I don't know. We're experts at keeping secrets."

"We need pressure from within and without." Jerry rolled her shoulders, flopping back onto the cot, her hand still captured in Arloa's grasp.

"We do."

Arloa moved, leaning against Jerry's side, the first time they had been this close, pressed together, since she'd returned from Joab. The peace that overcame Jerry was indescribable, so she stayed where she was, turning slightly into Arloa's petite form.

"I can start the rumors in the government house. I know who is likely to spread the gossip like wildfire."

"And how will you protect yourself when he comes after you?"

Arloa's mouth thinned. "I can take care of myself."

"I know you can, but that doesn't mean he won't do something drastic." Jerry held her breath, not quite sure how to convey everything she was thinking beyond that moment. She trusted Arloa to hold her own, but she didn't trust Bert Riley. Not after what she had heard and witnessed. "What's to prevent him from coming after you?"

"Nothing." Arloa looked her directly in the eye. "He can come after me if he wants, but he can't touch my position. I'm an elected official."

"He can censure you."

"He won't get the votes. I'm liked well enough."

Jerry sighed. "For now, but when you drop something like this on the Senate Leader? No one is going to like you much."

"I don't care if people like me or not."

"It matters if you remain a senator. They can veto the votes. They can put you out."

"They've haven't done that in decades," Arloa argued.

"Fuck that shit. Yes, they have, and you know it. Quit thinking you're invincible." Jerry held her gaze, waiting desperately for Arloa to agree with her. She couldn't stand to see her throw it away. Someone like Arloa, who gave a flying fuck, in a position of power, was her only hope that the government might change.

"I don't matter so long as all of Penum knows what he did."

"What we suspect he did," Jerry corrected. "We don't have proof that this is what we think it is. We don't, and until we get that, we need someone who has the connections when we do get that proof. You need to keep your position for this to happen."

Arloa's lips parted.

"No, don't talk yet." Jerry put her fingers to Arloa's lips. "You need to hear me. Until we have definitive proof that Riley started this whole thing, that he is the cause behind our people dying, then you need to stay right where you are."

"I know," Arloa whispered. "But some days, I don't want to be there."

Tears brimmed in her eyes, and Jerry's heart shuddered at the pain she witnessed.

"It's so hard to be the stalwart one. I know why I'm there, I know exactly how I got there, and it wasn't by accident. I know what I need to do, but some days, I just don't want to do it. I want to be with you instead. I want to run away on *Yarrow* and escape this hellhole."

"You don't have to do it on your own." Jerry's voice was soft, gentle. "But I don't have *Yarrow* anymore. I'm as stranded in this society as you are."

Arloa traced a finger down Jerry's cheek, her hand falling off her chin. "We're both a ship awash on the sea, aren't we?"

Jerry wrinkled her nose. "We're here to do a job."

"I'll start the rumors in the government house."

"And what will happen when he comes after you?" Jerry wasn't going to let this one go.

"I don't know how to slip in the rumor without telling someone about it."

"We need a direct trace back to Riley, and we need to drop it inconspicuously so the discovery can't be traced to you."

"I understand what you want, but I don't see how it's possible."

"Let me talk to Vivian. Let me see first what more information she can find out for us, and second, if there's a way to spread the information widely enough. She can send out a news blast or something that will get everyone's attention in the government house."

"That's not an awful idea, but I don't know about bringing someone else in on this. That increases the risk of tracing it back to us, and with you in hiding..."

Arloa trailed off, but Jerry understood the message. They didn't have many people they could trust, and every time that circle widened, the risk increased. But Vivian already knew Jerry had escaped.

"We can trust Vivian."

"Are you sure? Miriam I understand, but I don't know Vivian."

Jerry snagged Arloa's hand with her own, holding it firmly. "We can trust her."

"Then yes. But no one else."

"I understand." Jerry breathed a sigh of relief. If Vivian could do what they were asking, it would take some of the heat off of

Arloa. Which would make her safer, and ultimately, it would keep Jerry safe from the authorities.

"So that's how we get the information into the government house. Then what?"

"We can't stop there," Jerry murmured. "We need to make sure the suspicion is deep."

"Then we need more information."

"We know it exists, so let's find it." Energy burst from Arloa. "It's not here. I'll need to—"

"No more stealing his papers for a while. He'll start to suspect you."

Arloa paused. "He will. I'll need to find a different way."

"A better way," Jerry affirmed.

"Yes, a better way." Arloa shifted so she was pressed more firmly against Jerry's side. The warmth from her body and skin seeped through Jerry's clothes, easing more of the tension that had built up over the last few months she'd been in Joab and in the prison of her hideout.

"Why would he do this?" Arloa asked the one question they had both avoided. "Why would anyone do it?"

"All we have proof of is an attempted vaccine."

"This was created before the virus hit. There's no way he didn't know it was coming."

"Perhaps it was for something else."

Arloa shook her head. "No, it was for this."

Jerry turned on her side, facing Arloa, the papers crinkling underneath her weight. "This isn't anything new. For centuries they've been killing off the lower class. When we become too many, it scares them, and a virus, a fire, some sort of law comes into place that forces us to live below our means and forces us into a death spiral. This is the worst that I've seen happen, and certainly the worst that I've read about, but it's nothing new."

"I know," Arloa whispered. "But *this* is genocide."

"It is." Jerry brushed her fingers over the tops of Arloa's

breasts, reveling in the softness of her perfect skin. She hadn't been sure she would ever be able to stand to be this close to another person again, let alone in this way. "But I expect genocide."

"You shouldn't have to."

"But it's how I grew up. No one gives a shit about us. You're an exception to that rule. Other governments are the same."

"Should we tell them? If he started this virus, then it spread throughout Penum. They are just as affected by it as we are, and they ought to know who is to blame."

Jerry hadn't considered that. Potelia was the country that was best off, but the rest of them were struggling as much as Raegina was. Jerry mulled over the idea, closing her eyes and breathing in Arloa's scent. Finally, she nodded her agreement. "Do you think they'll listen more?"

"I hope so. Maybe they can exert some pressure that we can't from the inside."

"Maybe. I think I want to add one thing to our plan."

"What's that?" Arloa's eyes were so blue, so perfect, that Jerry felt she could fall into them for days.

Jerry took Arloa's hand, threading their fingers together because she knew this was going to be an argument in and of itself. Especially after what she'd just held firm with Arloa about her role in everything. "I'm a ghost."

"I suppose."

"I'm a ghost. I don't exist in Raegina any longer, and as soon as Miriam gets my new cards in, then I can go anywhere and do anything that I want."

"I'm not going to like this suggestion, am I?"

"Probably not, but I want to confront him. I want to call him out to his face and create a bit more drama to the rumors, and I want to do it before the mass release goes wide. I want to be the faceless accuser."

"Why? What would it accomplish?"

That was the question, wasn't it? But Jerry had found her purpose. If she could use her anonymity to do this, then she would. "It would put a person behind the accusations. I don't have to be named. I don't even have to exist after that moment, but to give a person the power, someone who isn't from your class—"

"It would make them have to listen," Arloa interrupted, finishing the line of thought.

"Exactly."

"You're right. I don't like it." Arloa squeezed her hand. "But I understand it."

Jerry leaned in, pressing their mouths together. She closed her eyes, focusing everything she had on the touch. She needed it, the connection, the comfort. Parting her lips, Jerry deepened the embrace and slid her tongue across Arloa's thin lips. Their breath mingled, and her heart settled. Arloa was exactly who she had needed all along. Jerry was willing to take every risk there was out there in order to survive. Arloa was right about that. She wasn't a quitter.

Reaching behind Arloa's head, Jerry tangled her fingers in the mass of curly locks. She held Arloa to her, taking the strength that Arloa always seemed to possess and stealing it for herself. She needed it more than Arloa did in that moment. Breathing heavily, Jerry sucked Arloa's lower lip, the soft flesh wet. Arloa hummed her pleasure, and Jerry smiled against her. This was something she didn't want to give up—ever.

They had found each other in the most unusual of ways, a place where neither one of them should have been. And here they were, again, in that same moment, stashed away from the world spinning around them. Jerry kept still, not ready for any more, but enjoying what they shared. As she eased away from the embrace, she took her time. She pressed their foreheads together and closed her eyes.

"I don't know what I would do without you," Jerry whispered.

Arloa kissed her. "I feel the same. I never thought I would find someone like you. I was afraid you didn't exist."

"There are times I don't want to." Jerry opened her eyes and leaned back to get a full view of Arloa. "But somehow you always bring me back to Penum."

Arloa smiled brilliantly, her lips curling upward and her eyes widening. "Did you just tell me you love me?"

"Not quite." Jerry leaned in and kissed her hard. "But we do need to clean up this disaster."

Arloa laughed lightly. "We do. I need to put all these back in the morning."

"Except the one?"

"Except the one. It's not supposed to be there to begin with, so I doubt it'll be missed."

"And how will we trace it back to Riley?" Jerry sat up, putting the stacks of papers back together.

Arloa's eyes lit up. "Oh, leave that to me when it's time. I've got a plan in the works for that one."

"Do you?"

"Absolutely."

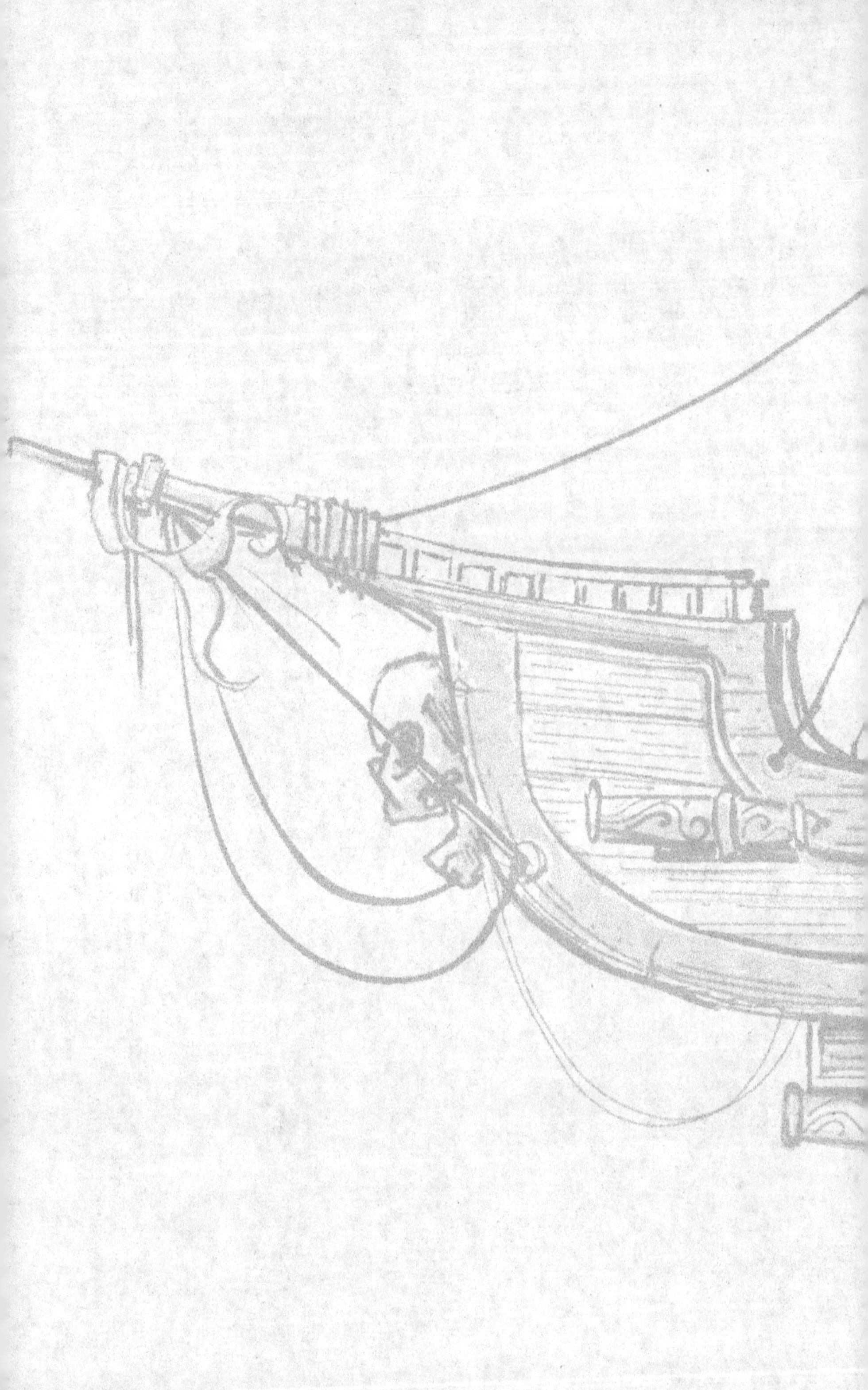

Jerry dressed like a man. The tunic was loose against her chest, the jacket wide across her shoulders. With her hair short and clipped in a stylish way against her scalp, she smiled down at Arloa. "Are we ready for this?"

"For the first step toward restitution? Yes."

"There's no restitution," Jerry replied, her lips still curved upward. "But at least there might be some semblance of justice."

Arloa buckled the jacket, her fingers swift against the metal. She threaded the buttons up Jerry's neck, hiding the fact she didn't look like a man but also matching the rich style that it would take to be part of the upper class. Jerry rolled her shoulders when Arloa was done, feeling for the first time ready to face Raegina.

Her steps had been lighter since the decision had been made and the plan put into place. Instead of hiding away, Jerry was going to do something, and she was going to be free. At least as free as she could be when the entirety of the authorities were after her.

"Do you have your cards?" Arloa asked, pressing earrings to her ears.

Jerry reached into her pocket and pulled out the cards, checking them over. Miriam had done a wonderful job with them. She shoved them back into the silk-lined pocket and cracked her knuckles. She was beyond ready to do something. Arloa came back over, pressing her palms against Jerry's shoulders.

"This has to work."

"It'll work."

Arloa drew in a steadying breath, as though she was attempting to convince herself more than Jerry. "It has to. We don't have a backup plan."

"It'll work."

"Don't panic when they take you. Please." Worry etched lines across her face.

Jerry leaned in, pressing their mouths together in a comforting kiss. She couldn't decide if it was more for Arloa or her in that moment, but it didn't really matter. They were there for each other, no matter what. Arloa hummed, her eyelids closing as she stayed still.

"I promise not to panic, but don't make me be with them for long."

"I won't." Arloa squeezed her hand. "See you soon."

Arloa turned and left the small hideout in a twirl of her skirts. Jerry had to smile as she left, her mass of curly hair halfway up and hanging down her back nearly to her ass. The curls swayed with her movement, and Jerry would never be able to get that image out of her mind.

"This'll work." Jerry clenched her jaw tightly and picked up her personal device. She sent a message directly to Vivian to make sure everything was in place on her side. It took an hour to receive confirmation, but once she did, Jerry's nervous energy took over.

She had until the midday toll of the bells until she could leave, but sitting and waiting in silence was doing nothing for her. She needed to move. She wasn't used to this kind of planned action like Arloa was, but they had thought it best to catch Riley on his way in from the midday break. That way there would be more people in the vicinity and they would be guaranteed to catch him in the public part of the government house.

Another tedious hour of waiting and the midday bells tolled. Jerry gathered up her courage and snagged the copied piece of paper she was bringing to light and headed out of her hideout. This time, when the sun's rays shone on her face through the smog, warmth and hope filled her. Things were finally happening.

Jaunting through the streets, Jerry clenched her jaw as she drew closer to the government house. The walk eased her nerves and spent some of the extra time since she couldn't afford to arrive early. Stepping through the double front doors of the building, Jerry straightened her shoulders. She had to assume the role of an aristocratic man, someone who had power and authority—which was something she'd never had in her entire life.

She stood in the middle of the wide-open entryway. No one was there. *Damn it.* She was too early. Jerry clenched her jaw, keeping her shoulders rigid as she waited. One quick glance at the sky out the large looming window told her it wouldn't be much longer until everyone returned. Sure enough, she turned around as the double doors to the front of the building opened again. This time, men in all varieties of expensive dress strolled into, their chins raised and their eyes set on their destinations.

Jerry held her breath as she waited for the one man she was there to see. Her lips pulled tight as soon as she caught sight of his top hat over the rest of them, his added height lending the ability to see him. Tightening her grasp around the paper in her hand, Jerry waited for him to be fully inside the building before she stalked forward.

Her entire body was set on him, and she would find him. Men disappeared behind her, going into the offices and to head back to work. Occasionally a woman passed her. Jerry stopped right in front of Bert Riley, and he had to halt all forward motion or risk running into her which would be an offense of touching without permission.

His eyes widened, and he cocked his head at her. "Can I help you?"

"This is an atrocity!" Jerry dropped her voice into a lower register and raised her chin defiantly.

Riley jerked back, clearly confused by what she was saying, which wasn't surprising. Her voice echoed through the marble hall, the words ricocheting off the walls. Everyone froze on the spot, turning to stare at her and Riley.

"Excuse me?" Riley said, quietly.

"You're a murderer." Jerry scrunched her nose, keeping her tone low to mask who she really was. She worked the muscles in her mouth, pinpointing her accent so they wouldn't be able to tell exactly where she was from. "This proves it."

She held her hand up in the air, the paper rounded from the force she held it with. She swallowed, staring directly into Riley's eyes, seeing that fleeting moment of fear race across his gaze until he masked it. *Oh, he's so damn good at that, but he wasn't expecting this.*

Jerry resisted the urge to grin, keeping the anger she'd brought with her front and center. That would make her able to complete this task. Riley tentatively took the paper from her hand, but Jerry jerked her wrist back and shook her head at him.

"*You* started this virus." She gathered spit in her mouth, waiting for the moment when he would try his next attempt to stop her. His jaw dropped, his eyes widening. Jerry kept her gaze locked on him as she hocked a loogie directly onto his cheek. "You *killed* everyone. It's your fault!"

"I don't know what you're talking about, sir. If you wouldn't mind…" He hovered his hand over her elbow, as if he was going to usher her away but didn't dare touch her. His other hand was out in front of him.

"What's all this about, Riley?" Lukatt stepped forward,

breaking through the crowd. He didn't seem overly concerned with Jerry, instead his focus was on Riley.

"I have no idea," Riley answered, bewildered.

Jerry scrunched her face up, shaking the paper in her hand again. "I have proof you knew this would happen."

"You have no such thing." Riley's voice rose, and Jerry swore she detected a hint of worry in the notes. "No proof exists."

"Sure about that?" Jerry lowered her chin, glaring directly at him. "Because this paper says otherwise."

"This paper that you have yet to show anyone. What kind of show is this?"

"Not a show. It's a declaration of truth." Jerry tossed the paper at him, knowing that Vivian was at that exact moment releasing the trace back to Riley along with a copy of the full paper to all the news outlets in Raegina and across Penum. Soon enough everyone would hear Riley's name in association with this virus and twenty years from now it would be impossible to separate the two.

Riley's gaze dropped to the paper, which he immediately crumbled into a ball. His cheeks reddened. Lukatt, thank all things holy, snagged the paper from him and unfolded it. His eyes widened before they furrowed in confusion. "What is this?"

"A vaccine for the virus," Jerry affirmed. She held her ground, not taking her gaze off Riley. She wasn't going to let him get away with any of this.

"There's no proof that this came from Bert." Lukatt folded the paper and shoved it into his pocket.

"Not on it, no. But there is proof." Jerry kept her eyes locked on Bert's face, looking for any sign of how this news affected him. Her breaths came in quick. "*He* is a murderer."

"And who are you that you should call me a murderer?" Riley stepped in closer, only inches from Jerry.

She held her position. "I'm no one. I hold no position here. You stole it all for your own gain."

Riley snorted and shook his head. "This is a fantasy you've made up to target me."

"Hardly." Jerry softened her tone, showing she had control in the moment. "Why would I risk my life to come here and accuse you of something you say you didn't do?"

"You already said you had nothing left to lose."

"Except my life." Jerry sneered, dropping her gaze down his form. "Just admit it, Riley. You don't care about Raegina. The only thing you care about is you. You didn't even care about your son."

"I don't have a son." Riley's face morphed into one of glee at her slip up.

Jerry shook her head slowly, whispering loud enough that those immediately nearby could hear. "Matthew Laurier."

All the color washed from Riley's cheeks. Jerry held onto the tense moment, letting the quiet that had fallen over them linger.

"Exactly."

The authorities rushed toward her, and the Senators backed up. Jerry's hands and wrists were immediately confined by the authorities, strapped behind her back as she held still and let them restrain her. The only thing they could get her on was spitting at Riley, and in this case, she doubted they would charge her, not with her new cards in her pocket.

They held her still, firmly. Riley stayed three steps away. Lukatt turned to him, mumbling something and handing over a cloth for Riley's face, which he finally cleaned up. Jerry refused to look away from him. Authorities surrounded him, too, but they didn't touch him. That was exactly what he thought he was, untouchable, but Jerry had proven him wrong that day and would continue to do so.

Her heart raced, her wrists aching from being tied behind her back so tightly it hurt. She remembered this from when she was dragged to Joab the first time, but this time would be different. She had to trust that. She had to hold on to the hope that Arloa would rescue her again if that was where this did start to go.

They mumbled with Riley, no doubt asking if he knew who she was and where she had come from. Hopefully they were also asking if there was any truth to what she was claiming, though she doubted they did. The authorities worked for the government, and to question the laws and those with power would stick them right where they didn't want to be. With the unmentionable creatures of Penum. Right, where Jerry had just escaped from.

"Jeremy Laurier," the authority next to her muttered.

She faced him, recognizing him in an instant as the man who had tried to accuse her of harming Matty when she'd first met him nearly two years ago. He looked so much older now, the age lines in his face not doing him any favors. He didn't seem to recognize her at all, but as soon as he'd said her last name, Riley's chin jerked up.

Jerry grinned at Riley and waited to see what was going to happen next. They pulled her away from the center of the main room, allowing those who were returning from the midday meal to go back to work, but she and Riley and Lukatt were left. Everything became hushed whispers, and Jerry didn't answer anything beyond what she absolutely had to. She gave no reason for her causing disorder and chaos, not wanting to give any more reason for guilt.

Eventually they dragged her outside and shoved her into a horseless carriage, one that had bars attached to the windows. Two new authorities took her away from the government house and to the edge of the center of town, right by the inner gates. The authorities' offices were located right on the other side, not worthy of being in the richest part of the town. She'd always found that amusing, but they too were considered well below everyone else who had power.

Jerry held her silence as they took her inside. She took deep breaths, easing the anxiety that reared its ugly head as soon as she stepped into the building. She was put into a long line, tied to a chair that would keep her there until they were ready for her. She'd done this so many times in her youth that she'd lost count. The last time she'd been to Joab there had been no question as to her guilt. They had skipped all this and taken her straight there.

This time, however, she wasn't the same person she was before. Jerry waited, keeping her shoulders squared as if she owned the building they had marched her into. She had a role to play, and she wasn't going to let Arloa down. She reminded herself repeatedly why she was there, that this entire situation was planned and on purpose. She and Arloa had talked it through endlessly, how she would get out, how she would use her position—as no one with cards that said she was someone—to do something good for the rest of Raegina. Jerry really had nothing to lose.

"Cards." The older authority barked at her, not even looking up into her eyes.

Jerry eyed him down, raising up one eyebrow at him. "In the front pocket of my jacket."

The authority dug around in her jacket and pulled out the thin pieces of paper. "I'll be back."

She snorted lightly as soon as he was out of sight. Nothing had been this simple before, but she supposed that was also on par with the difference between being male and female in their world. Right now she was everything the upper class male would be, down to the clothes Arloa had purchased for her, the short hair they'd managed to make look decent between the two of them, the way she held herself. The ability to have immediate power and privilege just because she was now considered one of them was amazing, but it also sickened her. This had been what she'd missed out on her entire life, what the laws told her she should have but could never quite grasp fully. It was intoxicating.

He came back over and shoved her cards back into her pocket, which was something that had never happened when she'd been there before. Apparently this time, he thought she deserved them back, or her crime wasn't that heinous. Jerry held her ground, the panic that swelled in her chest easily tamped down by how different this experience was to previous ones.

She was taken to a small room with a table and two chairs and seated, without being chained, in one of the wooden chairs. Jerry held her tongue, still only answering questions that required direction and not about what had happened at the government house.

The third midday bell rang. No one had come in to talk to her yet. The fourth midday bell echoed, then the fifth. When the first evening bell tolled, the door to the room opened. Arloa was led in by an authority. Their gazes locked, but they didn't say anything, and Jerry had to work hard to keep her face passive.

"Is this him?" the author asked.

"It is," Arloa answered, simply, disappointment in her tone. "May I bring him home now?"

"Do whatever you want. Riley isn't pressing charges."

Arloa nodded at the authority and then locked their gazes together again. "Let's go."

Jerry slowly rose, her muscles protesting the move since she'd been sitting still for so long. Jerry walked two steps behind her with her chin tilted toward the ground as if embarrassed. Instead, she was elated. Everything was working exactly as they had planned it. Arloa stopped in between the interior doors and the exterior doors. She gave Jerry a firm look. Jerry nodded at her before walking out of the building and down the cobblestone road toward the small hideout she'd been staying in, which was in the interior part of the city.

She was free. She could hardly believe it, but elation built in her chest, and she struggled to keep it tamped down. It was the only time since she was thirteen that she'd been brought there and released on the same day. Her heart hammered as she took confident steps. She kept her eyes wide open in case anyone tried anything, never trusting Riley and his reach. Someone would no doubt be after her, and in some ways, she'd been safer with the authorities surrounding her than she was alone on the street.

Then again, he wouldn't dare try something so soon after her accusation of him. Jerry got to the building and disappeared into the alley. She stepped down the basement steps and shut the door behind her, locking it. She was free, and their plan was in full motion.

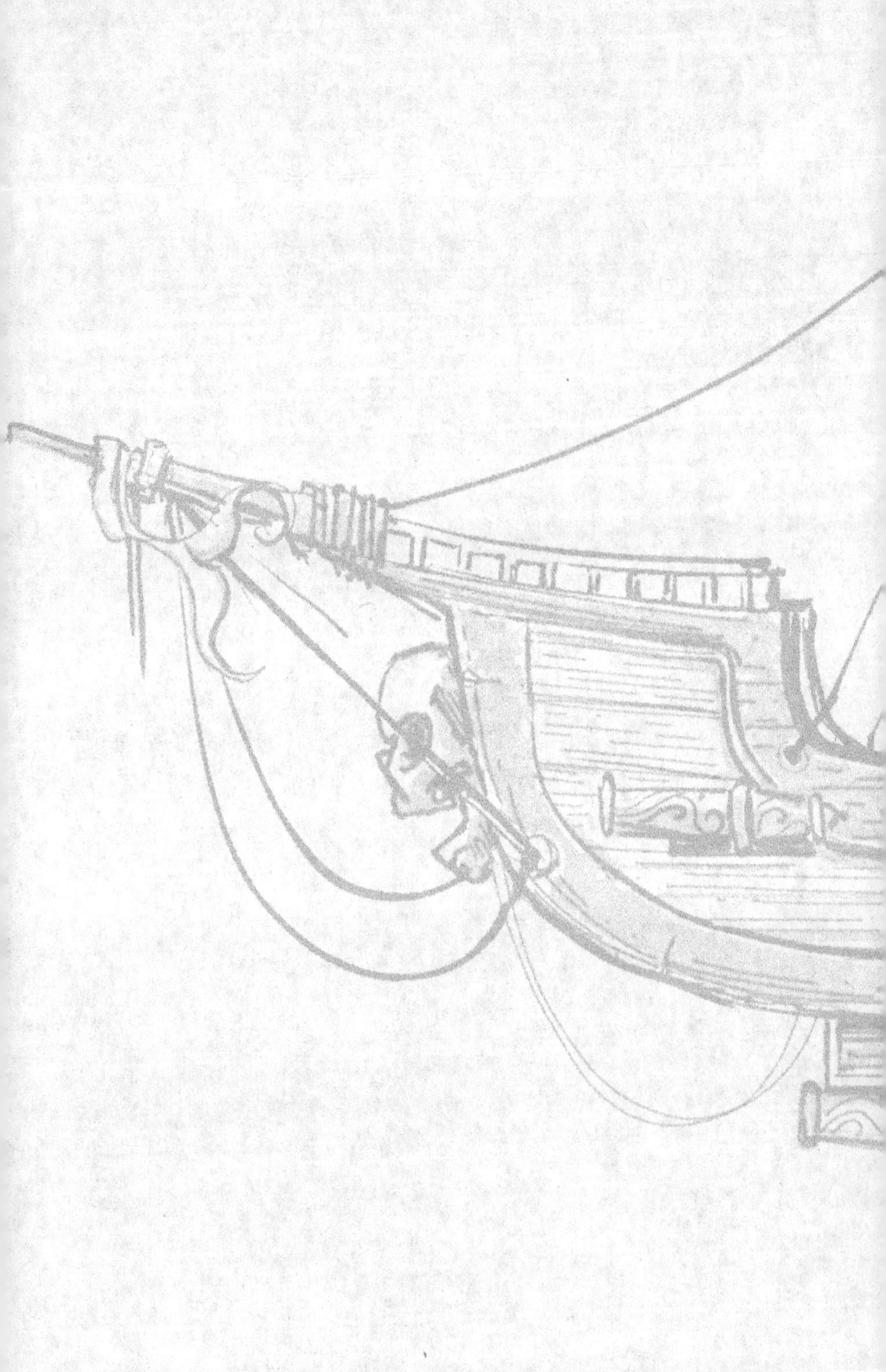

CHAPTER 14

Staying in the small room with energy bubbling around her was harder than Jerry had ever anticipated. She paced back and forth, nerves running through her entire body from the top of her head to the tips of her toes. She stripped off her clothes, freeing herself from their confines, and stood in nothing other than a tight pair of britches and her tunic.

Jerry leaned against the desk and turned on the radio. She needed to know what they were saying about the information Vivian had dropped, if it had made any dent in the monotonous monologue that was typical for the news outlets. She bounced on her bare toes, the cold from the floor seeping into her skin and reminding her that she was alive.

She had spent hours with the authorities, and she had survived. They hadn't once figured out who she was or where she had escaped from. She had done the impossible. She had recreated herself as someone new, someone who didn't have a checkered history.

The radio beeped, catching her attention. "The death toll rises from this virus, the new variant raging through the Omar Region and the Kilgorii Region."

Jerry's heart sank. Even if they did out Bert Riley as the cause of everything, the devastation was already done. The amount of people who had died because they were killed out of fear of the virus or because they couldn't find drugs to keep themselves sane—they'd literally torn themselves apart. Jerry had witnessed it so many times—too many times.

The door snicked open, and she was surprised she hadn't heard Arloa coming down the long hallway. Straightening her back, Jerry put her hands on her hips as Arloa stared at her with wide eyes. "They didn't talk about it on the news outlets."

"Not at all?" Jerry frowned.

Arloa shook her head. "I kept it on all day, waiting."

"Just in Raegina or everywhere?"

"Everywhere."

Disappointment filled her. Jerry sat on the edge of the table and closed her eyes, dropping her chin to her chest. "What do we do now?"

"We wait. Maybe they'll pick it up in the morning."

"They won't. Don't put hope where there is none."

Arloa pulled off her gloves and dropped them onto the table. Immediately she pulled off her overcoat, undoing the buckles and tossing it over the back of the chair. Jerry had to struggle to rip her gaze from the edge of the corset, where Arloa's creamy skin pushed against the tight confines of the material, to Arloa's steel-blue gaze.

"We start a secondary plan then."

"How?" Jerry asked, her voice getting caught in her throat.

Arloa put her hand on her hip. "We need to increase the pressure on Riley, and we need to find more information about him and what he's done. I already have some people on it."

"You can't keep putting yourself at risk." Jerry reached forward, snagging a loose curl and wrapping it around her fingertip. She gave a swift tug. "I need you here."

Arloa's gaze softened. "I am here."

"I was starting to panic this evening, waiting for the bells to toll."

"I know," Arloa murmured, stepping in closer. She put her

hands on Jerry's sides, wrapping them around her back to pull her into a sweet embrace. "But I'm here."

"You are." Jerry closed her eyes and drew in a deep breath, Arloa's scent surrounding her. That scent had brought her back from the brink so many times. If there was one person she could trust outside of those on her ship, it was Arloa. She had risked herself so many times in order to bring Jerry home, in order to save her and take care of her.

Jerry did the impossible. She pushed through the self-doubt and fear, the intangible emotions she refused to name. With a finger under Arloa's chin, she raised Arloa's mouth to meet hers. The kiss went from tender and exploring to fiery in an instant.

She threaded her fingers into Arloa's curls, tugging as she tried to deepen the kiss and tame her ferocity. But she couldn't. This had been such a long time coming. Jerry spun them around, pushing Arloa against the table. The entire thing shifted into the wall from the force of the move. Jerry nipped at Arloa's lower lip, sucking it hard.

Arloa moaned, the sound vibrating through Jerry and moving straight between her legs. For the first time since before she'd been taken back to Joab, Jerry wanted nothing more than to sink her face between Arloa's legs and taste her. Every block she'd had before now tumbled down in a second. Jerry moved away from Arloa's mouth, pressing kisses and nips along her jawline and down her neck.

Arloa's breath was ragged, her breasts pushing against the corset when Jerry dropped her mouth to the supple flesh she had been entranced with only moments before. Arloa tugged her short hair before pushing Jerry's face into her.

"Are...are you sure, Jer?"

Jerry didn't want to answer. She didn't want to break whatever spell she was under, whatever curse she had broken.

"Are you ready?" Arloa asked again, but she didn't move Jerry away or make her stop.

Using her tongue, Jerry traced a line right at the edge of the material before going back over the path with a light scrape of her teeth. Arloa whimpered, her nails digging into Jerry's scalp lightly.

"I need to know," Arloa murmured. "Because I've wanted this for so long."

Jerry said nothing as she knelt down onto the cold ground. She pushed up Arloa's skirts, and thankfully Arloa held onto them. Jerry placed ginger kisses along Arloa's bare legs, her fingers working at the ties on her boots and dragging them off. She wanted to tell Arloa everything, to spill the words from her lips, to tell her that she too had been waiting months for this, but she couldn't bring herself to say anything.

She tugged off Arloa's boots and then kissed her way back up. The skin was so soft on the inside of Arloa's thighs, so warm and smooth. Jerry tugged down the undergarments, and Arloa stepped out of them. She kept the skirts in place, not wanting to bother with them yet. Blowing a breath across the short curling hair between Arloa's legs, Jerry bolstered herself. She did want this. She had wanted to find normal for so long and it was finally within her grasp.

Pressing a sweet kiss against the top of Arloa's mound, Jerry worked to find the same strength she'd had only minutes before when she'd started this, when she'd been the one to initiate more. Arloa had been so damn patient with her, but this wasn't Jerry paying her back for that. This was so much more.

"Jer," Arloa tried again, her quiet tones filling the room and Jerry's ears.

Jerry closed her eyes, pressing her cheek against Arloa's thigh as she drew in deep breaths, the scent of Arloa's arousal spurning her on even more, but she needed to calm her racing heart. She needed to find her footing again, the equilibrium she'd managed to acquire throughout the day.

"Yes, I'm ready." The husky quality to her words was unexpected, but Jerry felt every scratch against her throat like it was new.

She didn't hesitate again. Pushing at Arloa's hips, Jerry shoved her back and up onto the edge of the table. Her mouth was on Arloa's clit in an instant as Arloa lifted her legs and circled them around Jerry's back and pushed her heel into the top of her shoulders. Jerry sucked hard, closing her eyes and enjoying the slick flesh, the heat that filled her, the taste she had longed for.

Arloa keened, her hips rocking, and her fingers diving back into Jerry's short hair. Jerry didn't let up. She wasn't going to stop until Arloa shuddered under her touch, until she was somewhat satisfied, but that connection between them that had been missing was rebuilt. Jerry continued to press her face between Arloa's legs, focusing everything she had in that one moment on making Arloa feel everything they had both been missing, everything they needed. Tears brimmed in her eyes as she pushed through the shame and guilt, the fear that had taken root inside her. She didn't want it anymore, and she had no reason to keep it around.

Releasing the demons that had kept her company since she'd tried to end it all on by jumping off the side of her ship, Jerry gave all her hurt to Arloa. She trusted that Arloa would vanish it, that she would smother it until it no longer existed. Arloa cried out, scraping her nails along Jerry's scalp as she leaned back in an attempt to hold herself up on the table.

Jerry dipped lower, dragging her tongue through Arloa's folds and gathering her juices on her tongue. She swallowed, slowing her breathing and savoring every moment they had together. She hadn't known that she would see Arloa or ever get to feel Arloa's skin against her own again. She kissed down Arloa's thigh to her knee, dashing her tongue against the sensitive skin at the back of her knee.

Arloa shuddered as Jerry stood up and pulled her off the table. Her skirts dropped to the ground, and they came together. This kiss was so different than any other kiss they had shared. Jerry gave herself over to it completely. Arloa tenderly traced her fingers along Jerry's curves, along her spine, her cheeks, her hips. Jerry held on to Arloa, her lifeline, and Jerry wasn't going to give that up anytime soon.

When she pulled away, Jerry closed her eyes and pressed her forehead into Arloa's shoulder. She tried to catch her breath, but she was so overwhelmed with a sense of ease and comfort, something she hadn't experienced since she was a little girl. Again those tears brimmed in her eyes, but she refused to let them fall. She refused to let herself show any kind of weakness.

"Help me take this off." Arloa's voice was rough from crying out her orgasm. But she turned around and pulled her hair, giving Jerry full access to the ties of her corset.

As if no time had passed, Jerry pulled at the leather and stuck her fingers in the pulls to loosen everything. Arloa held it up against her chest when she turned back around. "Are you sure you're ready?"

"Yes," Jerry answered simply, not wanting to drag it out any longer.

Arloa moved her hands, dropping her dress to the ground. She reached up and pulled Jerry's tunic over her head and let it follow the same path as her clothes. She twirled a finger around Jerry's small breast, her nipple already hard from the chill in the air.

"I love you," Arloa murmured reverently. "I'll do anything for you."

Jerry warmed, her entire body relaxing. She pulled Arloa into her, their mouths cascading against each other. The air in the room heated, and Jerry dragged Arloa toward the small cot in the corner of the room, pushing her onto it as she stood over her. Reaching for the ties on her pants, Jerry undressed completely.

Arloa scooted farther onto the cot, her legs spread and her fingers playing between them. Jerry shook her head, a smile playing at her lips. She climbed over Arloa on her hands and her knees. Kissing Arloa senseless, Jerry pressed her thigh between

Arloa's legs and rocked hard. Arloa gasped, her fingers digging into the backs of Jerry's arms as she held on.

"Weren't expecting that, were you?"

Arloa giggled lightly. "I never know what to expect with you."

"Good." Jerry bent down, sucking hard on the soft spot right where Arloa's neck met her shoulder. She scraped her teeth, she rocked harder, and she did everything she could think of to bring Arloa up higher than she had before. The heat at her thigh was a bright spot in the midst of everything. Arloa wanted her, even after everything she had done and been through, Arloa wanted her like this.

"I missed you," Arloa whispered, moving along with Jerry.

Jerry had missed herself too, but something in the last few days from connecting with Vivian again to finally taking her life back into her own hands had shifted the balance of who she was to who she was becoming. She liked it, and she wasn't about to give it up. Jerry bit her way down Arloa's chest, her pert breasts, her shoulder, back to her mouth and her plump lower lip.

Arloa crested through her second orgasm, clenching to Jerry like a lifeline. Jerry softened her kisses and touches to ease Arloa down. Sweat formed along her skin, and Jerry licked it up with her tongue, savoring the salty flavor. With a shudder, Jerry fell to her side and trailed one finger over Arloa's body as she caught her breath. She was soothed by being in Arloa's presence, no matter how many ways she looked at it, that was the only conclusion she could come to.

Jerry propped her head up with her hand and waited for Arloa's steel-blue eyes to turn to her expectantly. She wasn't disappointed. Arloa's lips curled upward, and she shook her head with a laugh. "You've been holding out on me."

"On both of us, I think." Jerry flicked Arloa's nipple, pleased when it tightened and hardened even more.

"I'm glad you're not anymore."

"Mmhmm." Jerry kissed Arloa's cheek. She breathed out as she closed her eyes. "What's next?"

"Whatever you want, Jer. This is all for you and about you."

Jerry paused in the moment, the love radiating from Arloa more than she could comprehend. She'd never felt this with anyone else before. She reveled in it, the willingness of Arloa to give to her, the tenderness she found in just lying in her arms.

They stayed there for minutes before Jerry finally spoke. "Get on your knees."

Arloa complied, turning to face Jerry with a curious look on her face. Jerry shifted to the center of the cot and crooked her finger at Arloa, beckoning her to come closer. Grinning, Arloa walked on her knees so she was positioned right over Jerry's mouth. Jerry tested her, her tongue running through her, circling her clit, and moving back down to slide into her. Arloa gave a heavenly sigh. Jerry immediately teased her, not wanting to hold back. They had never held back from each other sexually. Everywhere else in their life they had, but this was one thing they had managed to find together where they both thrived.

Arloa pressed her hand against the wall, holding herself up as she leaned back, her free hand snaking between Jerry's parted legs and teasing her. Jerry hummed her pleasure, closing her eyes and focusing on everything she was doing and all she was receiving. She hadn't realized how much she needed this.

Jerry gasped when everything in her body pulled straight between her legs. It took her entire concentration to keep moving her tongue against Arloa's clit, teasing her and dragging Arloa right along with her. Jerry couldn't hold on any longer, and she clamped down on Arloa's fingers. She paused her own tease and drew in sharp deep breaths, her face scrunched as she let the pleasure seep through her entirety.

This was perfect. She should have given in sooner, but she hadn't been ready before. Moaning, Jerry pressed her face into Arloa's thigh, breathing steadily as Arloa gently continued to play her body like a fine-tuned instrument. Once she caught her breath, Jerry started again, bringing Arloa through her third orgasm in a matter of minutes. She flipped Arloa onto the bed, soothing her with fingers across her chest, her stomach, her cheeks.

They stayed there for hours, not moving. Their conversation eventually turned from sex to talks of their backup plan to out Riley to the torture Jerry had experienced in Joab. Their bodies cooled, and when Arloa shivered, Jerry dragged her into her chest and pressed kisses to the top of her head. She closed her eyes, never wanting these hours to end.

For the first time in her life, she was relaxed. The tension in her shoulders was gone, the conversation wasn't hard, and she wasn't worried about what Arloa was looking to take from her. They fell asleep to the sounds of the radio playing the news cycle, their bodies entwined, and the thin blanket covering them waist down.

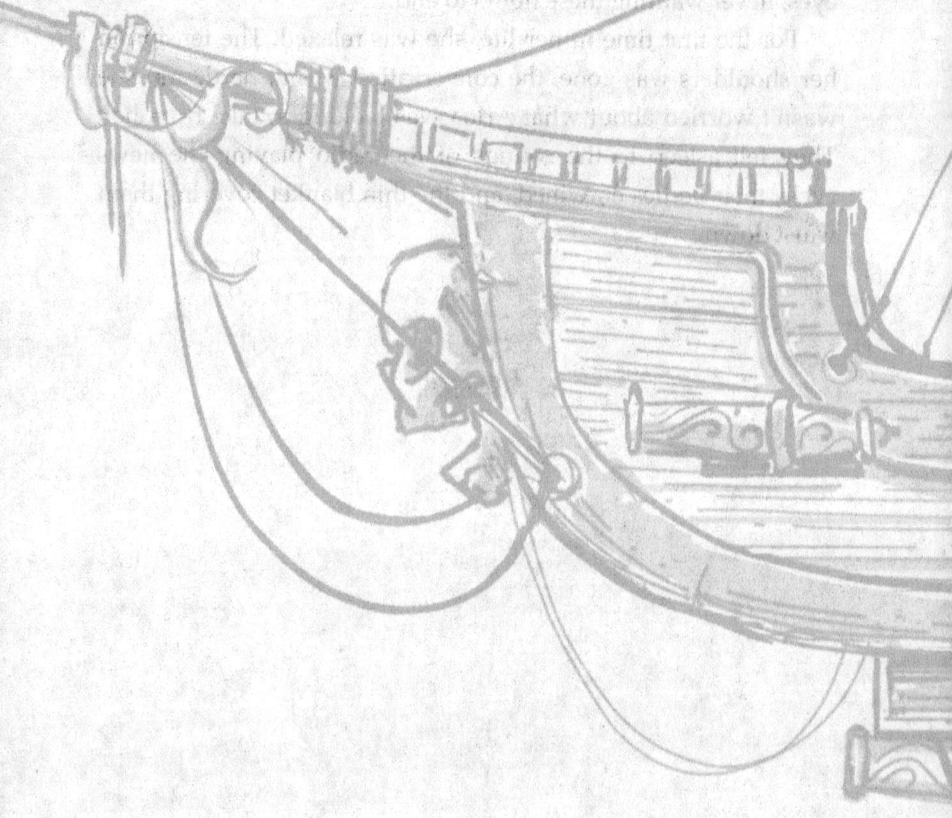

CHAPTER 15

erry pried her eyes open when the dawn bell tolled. Arloa was wrapped in her arms, her scent surrounding them, and she didn't want to let go or move. Jerry closed her eyes again, reveling in the comfort she'd found. She might not know who she was in the world any longer, but to Arloa she hadn't changed. Despite all she had been through, Arloa was still there waiting.

She didn't want to move. No matter what happened with Riley and outing him, she at least had this, and that was more important than Jerry had ever thought possible. Arloa was someone she could rely on, had been able to rely on several times over the past few years. Jerry touched her lips to the middle of Arloa's forehead. This was perfection.

"What time is it?" Arloa murmured, her voice filled with sleep, and her eyes still closed.

"The dawn bell just tolled."

Arloa hummed, snuggling deeper into Jerry's embrace. "I'm not ready to get up yet."

Jerry's lips curled slightly. She understood the sentiment, not wanting to leave the oasis she had discovered. All it had taken was for her to find her feet again, not a direction or a path, but to know that there was something out there for her that was beyond *Yarrow*.

"You don't have to get up," Jerry answered, tangling her fingers in those long locks. "Truthfully, I don't want you to get up."

Arloa chuckled, her face still pressed into Jerry's shoulder. "We will eventually have to leave."

"But not yet," Jerry whispered. She would take as much of this peace she could, the hope that she had discovered. Tracing her tongue along the shell of Arloa's ear, Jerry held on to what they had still. She stayed right where she wanted to be, not giving in to leaving. Not yet anyway.

Arloa wiggled against her, and Jerry turned, pinning Arloa to the bed. She pulled her arms above her head, holding them firmly while she lifted up. Jerry eyed Arloa's body, the way her breasts lay against her, the curves, the perfection of her skin that remained unmarred. Arloa's nipples hardened, and just as Jerry was about to dip her head down, she froze.

The radio they'd left on the night before sounded. Three loud beeps, meaning there was something important that everyone needed to pay attention to. Jerry cocked her head to the side, waiting to hear what was about to be said, but she didn't move from Arloa. If it wasn't that important, then she wanted to take exactly what was being offered.

"We have received unsubstantiated allegations that Senate Leader Bert Riley is connected with the virus currently raging through our planet."

The wind knocked out of her lungs. Jerry flopped onto her side, her eyes glued to the radio.

"We want to repeat that these allegations have no hard proof backing them, but we felt it prudent to share the accusations."

"Holy shit," Jerry muttered. "I didn't think they'd do it."

"Pressure from other countries, no doubt." Arloa pulled herself up to sit, holding the blanket across her chest. "I need to get dressed."

Jerry sat stunned into silence as the radio continued on about the papers that had been sent to multiple news outlets and countries, about how there was no way to verify where they came from or if they were directly from Bert Riley himself. Her heart thrummed with anxiety.

It was all out there now. There was no going back on this plan. Her hands trembled, so she grabbed her legs as she bent them and leaned against them. Arloa pulled her skirts on, tightening the ties behind her with confidence. Jerry couldn't even bring herself to look at her like she normally would.

"Bert Riley is alleged to be connected with the resurgence of this virus through the creation of vaccines against an ordinary ailment."

"Which every rich person on this planet would get while us unsightly creatures wouldn't." Jerry scrunched her nose, remembering after the fact who she was in the room with.

"Very true," Arloa answered as she pulled her corset on. "Do you mind? It'll be faster if you help."

"Sure." Jerry stood up, her bare feet on the floor cold. She stood naked behind Arloa and pulled the leather ties tight. Arloa adjusted her breasts while Jerry worked. She tied off the ends and tucked them into the top of the skirt to hide them.

"There are rumors that Riley has access to a vaccine that would halt the virus's advances."

Jerry raised her eyebrow at that. "We never sent that."

"Maybe someone else jumped on the wagon to look into him and what he's been up to." Arloa grabbed a clean dress and pulled it over her front. "Tie me please."

Jerry obliged, though she'd much rather be untying the clothes instead of dressing Arloa to go to work during a catastrophic news cycle. She had no idea when she'd even see her again. When Arloa was dressed, Jerry grabbed her by the waist, spun her around, and kissed her hard. She tangled her fingers in Arloa's long locks, tugging and pulling when she could.

Arloa moaned, leaning against the small table as she pushed into Jerry and trailed cold fingers across Jerry's naked skin. Jerry nipped at Arloa's lower lip when she pulled back. "I guess I'll see you whenever."

"Soon, I hope, but likely a day at the very least."

Jerry nodded. "I can wait."

Arloa kissed her lightly before stepping through the door and out into the hallway. Jerry shut it behind her, locking it. She put her head against the wood and closed her eyes.

"If these allegations are true, and there is evidence to support these efforts, then it is likely Senate Leader Riley will be removed from his position. That means Senator Lukatt will step into that role until another election cycle can be arranged."

"Lukatt…" Jerry shook her head. He wasn't much better than Riley, but at least he didn't have the brains to plan a viral genocide.

She took her time getting dressed, listening to the rest of the speculation on the radio. They dropped in a few other items in the news cycles but always went back to the chaos Jerry, Arloa, and Vivian had dropped on them in the last day.

Jerry managed to keep herself occupied until the early morning bell, but she had to get out of the hideout. She needed to feel the sun on her face, to stop listening to the speculation, and to finally make her stance. She squared her shoulders and left her hideout. Finding her way to the city gates, Jerry slipped through them with no issues. She walked down the road, the cobblestones catching on the shoes that were two sizes too big.

She stopped short when she reached a large house right before she would leave the gates. She'd been to that house once before to find a girl, Whitney. She'd be eighteen or nineteen now. Jerry couldn't quite remember. Jerry raised her chin up to the window she'd first seen Whitney sitting in.

"Do you have any work I could do for credits?"

Startled, Jerry looked down at the young woman in front of her. Her hands were red and dry from the weather. Jerry pressed her lips together tightly before reaching forward and waving a finger indicating she wanted the woman to lift her gaze. Her stomach dropped at the sight.

"I don't have any credits to spare. What is a young woman like you doing out here?"

She shrugged and tried to walk off. Jerry almost gripped her wrist but held off, clenching her fist.

"Answer me," she stated firmly, using her lower tone to her advantage in that case.

The woman stumbled, and when she spun around, Jerry saw the fear in her gaze. "I'm doing nothing, sir."

"I'm not going to contact the authorities because you're begging."

Relief flooded her eyes.

"Answer me."

"I have nowhere else to go."

Jerry held the tense moment, her mind swirling. She cringed as she tipped her hat up, wondering if Whitney would recognize her. When nothing crossed her gaze, Jerry dropped her chin again. "I can give you shelter."

"I don't want shelter."

"What do you want credits for, then?"

"A water vial."

"Fuck," Jerry muttered. "Come with me."

Jerry took her time walking through the gates and down toward the harbor. Whitney followed her, two steps behind as was proper for a woman of her status compared to the one Jerry had in that moment. When they reached the harbor, Whitney hesitated.

"Come on, girl."

"I...I've only been on a ship once."

"I have friends who will give you shelter and food, and if they don't, I will provide it." Jerry clenched her jaw, just wishing Whitney would listen. She had to believe that she still had some pull with Yafe and Azar even though *Yarrow* wasn't her ship any longer. They would no doubt expect her to take over.

Whitney shook her head.

"Would you rather stay on the streets? Perhaps the underground can use your body."

Whitney's eyes widened, which answered Jerry's unasked question. She hadn't resorted to that yet.

Jerry held her hand out in front of her. "You trusted me once before, trust me now."

Whitney's brow furrowed in confusion, and she finally lifted her chin the entire way to look into Jerry's eyes, but again, there was no recognition there. Jerry gave it another minute before Whitney took a step toward her and onto the pier. They walked side-by-side now until they reached *Yarrow*.

Jerry reverently touched the wood hull, closed her eyes, and breathed relief. She had missed *Yarrow* desperately, but she wasn't sure they would ever be together again, at least not like they once had been. Jerry clenched her jaw and put her hand against the sensor on the side of the dock. To her surprise instead of alerting the crew to her presence, the exterior door lowered down and connected.

"Vivian." Jerry rolled her eyes. She must have gone in and put Jerry's codes back in just in case she wanted to return. "Yafe will skin you for that one."

They walked across the door. Jerry commanded it to close behind them before hitting the interior door to unlock. Her stomach was in knots, and she was unprepared to see Yafe standing on the other side of the door with Jerry's gun in her fingers pointed directly at her stomach. Jerry jerked her hands upward.

"Hey there."

Yafe's beautiful face morphed from anger to joy. "Cap? Holy shit! Azar!"

Yafe launched herself forward, wrapping her arms around Jerry's shoulders and pulling her in tight for a hug. Yafe didn't let go, her entire weight in Jerry's arms. Jerry held on tightly, closing her eyes and letting the moment of happiness sink in.

When Yafe stepped back, Azar peered his head around the corner, his eyes widened, and he proceeded to wrap Jerry up in another tight hug. "Where have you been, Cap?"

Jerry snorted. "That's a long story."

Azar clapped her on the shoulder. "Sacha and Vivian will be excited."

"For sure." Jerry nodded. "I brought a guest."

Yafe's gaze flicked over Jerry's shoulder. "To stay?"

"If you have room."

"Are you staying?"

Jerry grimaced. "We can talk about that in a bit."

"Doesn't sound good."

Jerry shrugged. "Galley?"

They all climbed up the ladder to the floor above. Yafe took out a couple packets of water and food, giving them to Whitney as she sat down. Yafe looked back at Jerry. "She looks awful."

"Living on the street."

"What about the underground?"

Azar shook his head. "Miriam is retiring. At least that's the rumor."

"Is it?" Jerry raised an eyebrow in curiosity. "How long has that rumor been floating around?"

"Month or so now I suppose."

Jerry said nothing. Soon enough Sacha and Vivian joined them, both greeting her with the same wild hug. "Did you find new work yet?"

Yafe shook her head. "Not since we fired Mortimer."

"Good for you." Jerry hadn't liked working with him much for various reasons, but she'd never had the guts to pull out of that deal.

Azar leaned back on the small stool. "We still have *Astilbe*."

"I've seen her in the harbor." Jerry had watched every chance she could risk it and had seen them coming and going.

"How long have you been out?" Yafe asked. Whitney struggled to open the food packet, so Yafe took it and ripped the top open.

Jerry clenched her jaw. "Not too long now. Enough time to heal for the most part."

Vivian had remained suspiciously quiet, and Jerry was thankful for that. It was clear that she hadn't told Yafe and Azar about the work they were doing behind the scenes. Jerry made eye contact with her. "How did you get out, Cap?"

Jerry paled, cold washing through her. "That's a long story, but they didn't let me go. I'm no longer Jeraldine Adelric."

"Then who are you?" Sacha asked, her sweet voice positing the one question none of them dared to say out loud.

"I'll keep that to myself, I think. In case I need to keep you lot safe from what I'm up to."

"And what's that?" Azar crossed his arms over his chest after grabbing a second food packet and ripping it open to hand to Whitney. "Because I don't see why you can't come back to the ship."

"I can't captain, not on record. I don't exist. I'm an escaped convict, a ghost."

Hushed silence filled the room. They all stared at her as if she should have the answers to everything, but she didn't. It was bittersweet to be there. She loved being amongst her family again, but she knew she couldn't go back to the way it was. She couldn't bring herself to put them in that kind of danger—not again.

"Since we can't talk about that. Let's talk about what you all have been doing."

Azar snorted. "Pirating. What else?"

Yafe elbowed him lightly. "Since we gave up the legal side of things, it's been easier to pirate."

"Are you still rescuing strays?" Jerry nodded toward Whitney, who's eyes finally seemed clear of the glassy look they'd had since they ran into each other again.

Yafe slid over another water packet. "Not since you left. It was too hard to hide them and us for a while there. We changed the name of the ship, claimed *Yarrow* went down, and got new papers. Vivian was helpful for that."

"I have no doubt of that." Jerry winked at Vivian before focusing back on Yafe. "You're doing really well from what I've seen."

"As well as can be expected without our proper captain."

Jerry sighed. "I won't be returning as captain. I've accepted that, and you need to as well."

Yafe didn't look as though she wanted to, but Jerry wasn't going to let her off that easily. She held her ground. Eventually the conversation turned toward updates on Azar's crew and what they had managed to pirate, sharing stories from their time together on *Yarrow* and stories from when Jerry had left them. She also got the full story of what happened after she was arrested by the authorities.

Night had fallen, and the midnight bell tolled before Jerry slipped from *Yarrow* and back onto the pier. She left Whitney there, glad to have at least helped her out as much as she could. She made her way back toward the center of the city, knowing she wouldn't see Arloa that night. She would catch the last of the news outlets' reports before she fell asleep.

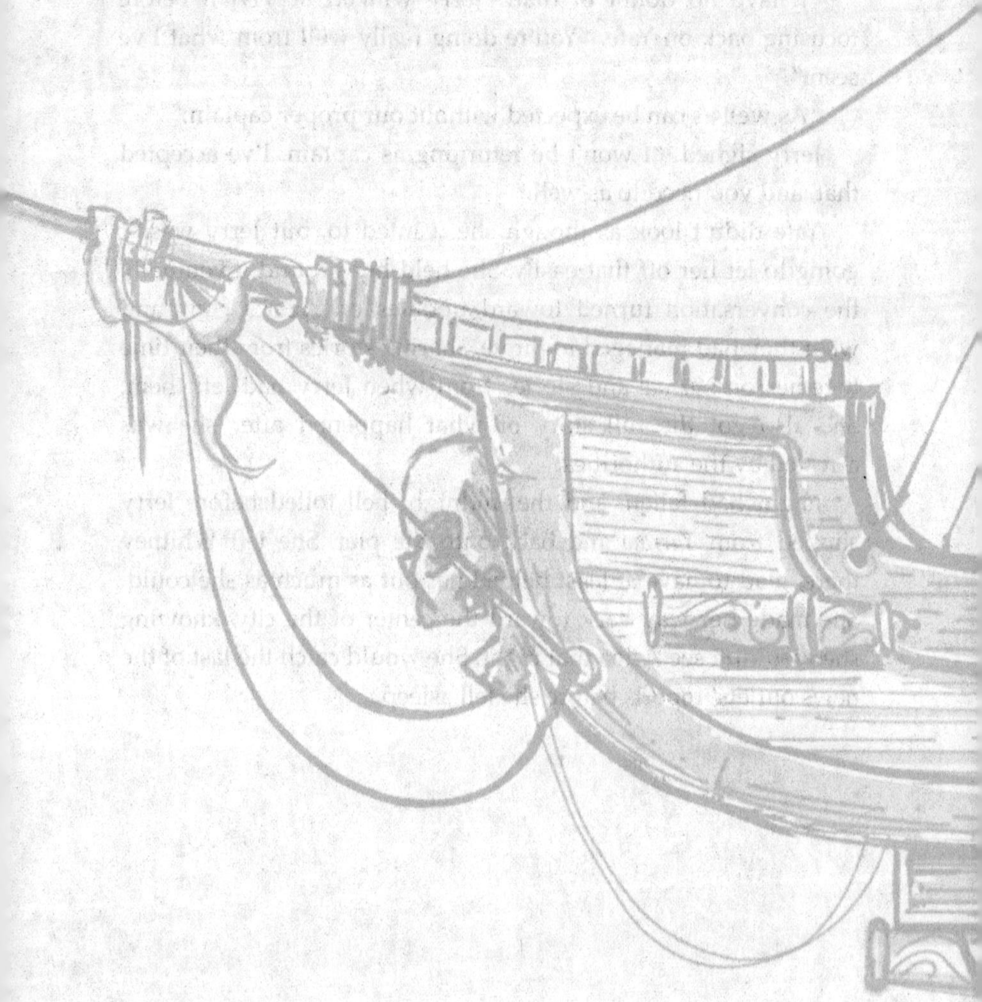

CHAPTER 16

erry flicked the radio on first thing in the morning, listening for the conversation on Bert Riley and the accusations she and the others had thrown in his direction. Instead, she was greeted with another missing person report, although this time it wasn't a senator. Jerry pursed her lips, her hands folded in her lap as she closed her eyes and concentrated on everything the radio said.

"The entire Melora family was killed in a brutal slaughter late last night and were discovered by an employee early this morning."

Jerry shuddered. She'd never met the Melora family, but Jenkins was one of the richest men in all of Penum. He wasn't involved in government directly, but he had considerable influence on policy and owned a good portion of the land surrounding Raegina. Jerry tensed her shoulders and immediately tried to relax them.

"Jenkins Melora was killed in his study, his head severed and not recovered. His wife, Caila, was murdered in their bedroom. His mistress, a Ms. Laney, was found in her bedroom."

Shaking her head, Jerry scrunched her nose. He certainly was living the life with wife and mistress in the same home. She wondered how that worked for a moment before her attention was dragged back to the news outlet.

"The oldest Melora son was found murdered in the sitting room along with his pregnant wife."

"Fuck," Jerry muttered. It was a damn massacre, and unfortunately for them, what it was doing was covering up the biggest news report that she needed out there.

"There are rumors of a connection between Jenkins Melora and Bert Riley."

Jerry's ears perked up at that. This was entirely new information to her, and she would have to ask Arloa what she had missed while she'd spent time on *Yarrow*. Warmth spread through her at the thought of her ship and her family. She missed them, but there was no way to be with them for now and not risk their lives. Not yet, not until she got through the drama with Bert Riley and truly left her mark on Raegina in her new personhood.

"Melora and Riley attended school together, graduating two years apart."

Jerry's attention was drawn back to the radio.

"They weren't known to run in the same circles during their school years, but evidence discovered by the authorities during the investigation leads us to believe that Riley and Melora had formed a business relationship."

"What?" Jerry's eyes widened. She itched to grab her personal device and contact Arloa, but with this news, there was no way that she would have time to answer any of Jerry's hundreds of questions. She scratched the back of her head, her short hair rustling with the move.

"Twenty years ago, Riley and Melora formed a business called Teawicks. It's still unknown what exactly this business does, and our investigators are continuing to look into it. As expected, when there is such a brutal murder of upstanding citizens—"

Jerry snorted.

"—it is expected Senate Leader Riley and Grand Master Paradise will make an official statement this afternoon. We will have reports on that later."

They moved on to hashing out the rumors on Riley next, but there was no new information in it. Jerry clenched her jaw, staring at the small table across from her where the radio sat. Even if she couldn't get hold of Arloa to ask questions, this was information she had needed, another connection that she hadn't found before.

Jerry grabbed her personal device and sent a message to Vivian with expectations of research into that connection. When she received the "already on it" in response, Jerry was elated. She dove into her own research, though Vivian's would likely be far more thorough with her hacking abilities than Jerry's run-of-the-mill ability to read what was widely available.

Her device beeped with an incoming communication. Jerry hit *Accept* without waiting. "What is it?"

Vivian's beautiful face filled the hologram, the purple hues adding to the lines of her face. "We need to talk. Now."

"Where?"

"Come to *Yarrow*. We're still in port."

"I'm not sure that's wise. People might connect—"

"You don't have a choice. There's nowhere else to meet where we can all fit."

"All?" Jerry furrowed her brow. "What did you find?"

"Now." Vivian ended the communication.

Jerry growled as she dropped the device next to her and got off the cot. She dressed quickly and grabbed her top hat at the last minute. Ducking out of her hideout, Jerry jaunted down to the harbor. The urgency in Vivian's tone was what had gotten her. She needed to know what was about to go down.

She was nearly out of breath by the time she entered her codes into *Yarrow*, the door extending down until she could step onto it and walk across. Jerry managed to look out to make sure no one had followed her before she pressed her palm to the door and closed it. Once she was safely locked inside, the internal door opened.

Vivian met her, her hazel eyes and the dress Jerry had bought her gracing her fine-boned body. "Took you long enough."

"I came as soon as I could." Jerry scrunched her nose. "What's the emergency?"

"This way." Vivian's skirts swished around her as she spun around down the corridor and to the ladder. They climbed up and found themselves in the galley, the place they always gathered it seemed. Vivian leaned against the small counter, taking a deep breath, as the radio continued to sound behind her, the tones muted. Azar sat at the table along with Yafe and Sacha. It seemed the necessary people were here.

"Anyone going to let me in on the secret?" Jerry raised an eyebrow at them. "I don't appreciate being left in the dark."

"Nothing worse than what you've done to us these past few months," Sacha muttered.

Jerry swallowed the guilt that gurgled up. She deserved that one—she could admit to it. She nodded at Vivian, waiting for the explanation.

"I found a direct connection between Jenkins Melora, Bert Riley, and Arloa Kauket."

Jerry's stomach clenched tightly, bile swimming in with that guilt. Fear shocked through her. *Arloa in cahoots with them?* It had to be a misunderstanding, something simple. Jerry tightened her jaw and flatted her tongue to the roof of her mouth. She would say nothing until Vivian finished her explanation.

"They were all in school together." Vivian crossed her arms, her voice the only sound that mattered. "Not only were they all in school together, Arloa was presumed to be in a relationship with both of them."

Jerry wasn't sure she believed that. Arloa had never shown any inclination of being interested in men, though she was younger back then, so perhaps she hadn't figured out where her proclivities were. Jerry had to work hard to keep her breathing even, but sounds rushed to her ears, making it difficult for her to focus.

"She's the one who could have introduced them."

"Is that it?" Yafe asked. "The only connection between her and them?"

Jerry knew Yafe was asking for her sake, and as much as she was thankful for it, she wasn't sure she wanted the answer.

"No." Vivian swept her gaze to Jerry.

They all stared at her, as if she was going to break any second. Jerry nodded. "Don't stop now."

"After school, Arloa went to work for her father, but a few years later, she went out on her own in business. Seems she has a good head for chemistry."

Jerry already knew that. Arloa had never explicitly told her, but she had guessed as much based on their conversations together.

"She joined forces with Melora and Riley to go into pharmaceuticals."

Which would explain why Arloa had the facility to reverse engineer vestigen. It explained why she had a line on cirax. Jerry's stomach plummeted, bile rising upward. *Has she played me the entire time?* She wasn't sure she could breathe. Arloa had come off as such a mercenary through everything, plying Jerry with vestigen when she ran out, healing her, giving her tips about where to find more drugs. But it was all for her benefit, wasn't it?

"Something happened ten years ago that ended their working relationship."

"What happened?" Jerry ground out, but she couldn't bring herself to look in Vivian's eyes.

"I don't know. But the business crashed, and aside from professional conversations with Riley, she hasn't spoken to either of them from what I can find."

"So the connection to what we're accusing Riley off—"

"Is slim," Vivian finished for Jerry. "It is, but when we throw our next volley, Arloa might end up in the middle of it."

"She can handle herself." Jerry squared her shoulders, the room falling silent around her. Everything in her life relied on Arloa, and it was scary to think what might happen if she didn't fall in line with what Arloa might want.

"Cap." The pity in Yafe's voice was too much.

"What else did you find?" Jerry interjected, wanting to get it all out on the table.

"Nothing about Arloa."

"What *else* did you find?"

Vivian sighed and took her time answering. "Melora benefited financially from this virus."

"What rich person didn't?" Sacha spat, crossing her arms and pouting in her chair.

Jerry agreed with the sentiment, but if Vivian was bringing it up, then there was more to it than that. Vivian glanced at Jerry. "He was the manufacturer behind a recent vaccine."

Jerry knew instantly what Vivian was talking about, and very likely that was what had landed Melora dead. Her stomach churned. Since they had released that information into the world, anyone could have connected the dots. They had put a target on the wrong man's back. She couldn't stay in that room anymore.

Panicking, Jerry stood sharply and escaped. She climbed the ladder to the wheelhouse, stepping out onto the deck. The cold air wasn't fresh, but it felt wonderful against her cheeks. She closed her eyes, tilting her chin up toward the smog-covered sunlight. She hadn't expected this. She'd gone from being completely independent to relying on someone she knew nothing about, someone who had an entire life before her. She was such a fucking idiot.

"Cap."

Jerry couldn't do it. She couldn't talk to Vivian and find out any more. Not yet anyway. She needed a few more minutes to center herself, to regain the calm that she'd finally found in the last few weeks.

"Cap, there's more."

Jerry sighed. "What more could there be?"

"Riley signed off on the newest vaccine that was distributed right before the virus started."

Vivian gripped Jerry's hand. "I'm so sorry."

"For what?"

"Being the messenger."

"There's no proof she did anything."

"There's no proof she didn't."

Jerry knew that, even if she didn't want to admit it. Everything they discussed left Arloa in a very precarious spot. But again, Jerry was starkly reminded that Arloa could handle herself. Jerry was the one who had needed rescuing time and time again. Her heart raced.

"What are you going to do, Cap?"

"Don't know," Jerry mumbled. "But I can't come back here, before you ask."

"Do you even want to?"

Jerry's eyes filled to the brim. "Always. *Yarrow* is my home. You're all my home. But I'm on the run and illegal. If they catch you with me? It'll be the end of us all."

"I think we're all willing to risk it."

Jerry grimaced. "I won't let you. As my last act as your captain—I won't let you."

Vivian frowned. "I wish you would."

"Me too."

They stood in silence for a bit longer, Jerry finding her balance again as Vivian stood with her. Eventually Yafe joined them, wrapping her arms across her chest as she eyed Jerry up and down. "You good, Cap?"

"For now."

"Then let's figure out what we're going to do about this."

Jerry followed Yafe and Vivian back down to the galley. Once they were all seated, Jerry crossed her arms, ready for whatever they had to throw at her next. Silence filled the room, each of them looking to her. No matter how damn hard she tried not to be their leader, they seemed to always thrust her back into that role. She didn't want the damn responsibility though.

"Riley is giving a report tonight," Jerry started. "If I'm going to make a move, I think it should be then."

"I don't think you should do it alone." Yafe eyed her, that dark gaze never wavering.

Confused, Jerry shook her head. "Do what?"

"Confront him."

Damn Yafe for already knowing what she had planned. It would be Jerry's second time sticking her neck out in order to bring out the truth, and to do it again might land her in far more trouble than it had the last time. However, it was a risk she was willing to take. She was no one. She was dead. It was a risk she could take when others didn't stand a chance.

"No," Jerry stated firmly, again not wanting to drag them into any of her drama. It seemed to be all she did anyway.

"Yes." Vivian stepped forward, squaring her shoulders as if this was going to be the battle she chose to fight. "Every one of us deserves to know if he did this."

"If?" Jerry raised an eyebrow. She held the silence as she stood slowly and moved into Vivian's space. "If he did this?"

"We know he did, Cap," Vivian whispered. "Let's prove it."

"This isn't proving anything."

"It will if he folds."

"Riley isn't an idiot. He's not going to bow just because we put pressure on him."

"Then we'll push on him in as many directions as possible."

Jerry pressed her lips together hard. "I don't want you to do it."

"To be fair, Jerry…" Sacha's use of her name instead of her title sent shivers down Jerry's spine. As much she wanted it, she didn't like it. "…you're not our captain anymore."

Turning slowly, Jerry locked her gaze on Sacha before flicking it to Azar and Yafe. They were the ones in charge, the two leaders who now legally owned the ships. Jerry held her breath, hoping they would listen to her one last time.

"I say we do it." Azar's voice was firm, his gaze direct at Jerry when he finally spoke.

"I agree," Yafe said.

Fuck. Jerry closed her eyes and collapsed in on herself. She wasn't going to win this one as much as she wanted to. "Fine. Then we plan it and all possible outcomes."

"Are you going to help us with the plan? Or not."

She didn't want to. Jerry wanted absolutely nothing to do with putting them in danger again.

"It'll be easier with you, Cap. You're brilliant."

She knew she should. If they were in it together then they would be more likely to succeed. But it didn't mean she wanted to. She had always wanted to protect them. No matter what. Yes, they always agreed to her crazy ideas, but they were her first priority—save them and she could maybe save herself.

"I don't like this."

"You don't have to like it, Cap." Azar seemed to finally find his voice. "You just have to go along with it. We're your family, remember?"

"Oh, I remember." Jerry tightened her grasp on her elbows, not wanting to give in to their desires. "And I remember I've nearly gotten you killed several times."

"It's what we signed up for. All of us," Yafe added.

Jerry looked at each of them. They nodded their agreement to the terms. Jerry wasn't going to win this one, no matter how much she might want to. Closing her eyes, she drew in on herself. If Arloa truly was a part of this nefarious plan, which she still doubted, then she truly had no one else to rely on.

"Fine. What are we doing?"

Yafe and Vivian grinned. Azar's lips twitched upward in as

much of a smile as he would ever give. Sacha clapped her hands and bounced in her boots. Jerry rolled her eyes.

"At the report. We'll do it then." Yafe fisted her hand on the top of the table, as if she was ready to go into battle. "We'll drop enough information to investigators to allow them to turn the conversation from Melora's murder to his connection to the vaccine."

"We don't have enough proof to even bring up the vaccine again," Jerry argued. "We need more proof."

"I'll work on that." Vivian shifted and grabbed her personal device, as if she was going to start her research now instead of when they were done with the conversation.

"And if you don't find anything?" Jerry eyed her. "We need some sort of plan even if we don't."

"Does it matter if we have proof or not? Or does it matter if we create enough doubt?"

Jerry couldn't fault Azar for that logic. Perhaps the focus of the attack shouldn't be proof, but rather to create more doubt for when proof was found later, whether they discovered it or someone else did. Jerry mulled through that one, debating. Eventually, she nodded.

"All right. The goal is to cast doubt."

"Perfect," Vivian agreed. "That is something I think we can accomplish."

Jerry sat at the table, her hands folded on top of it. "Then let's make a plan."

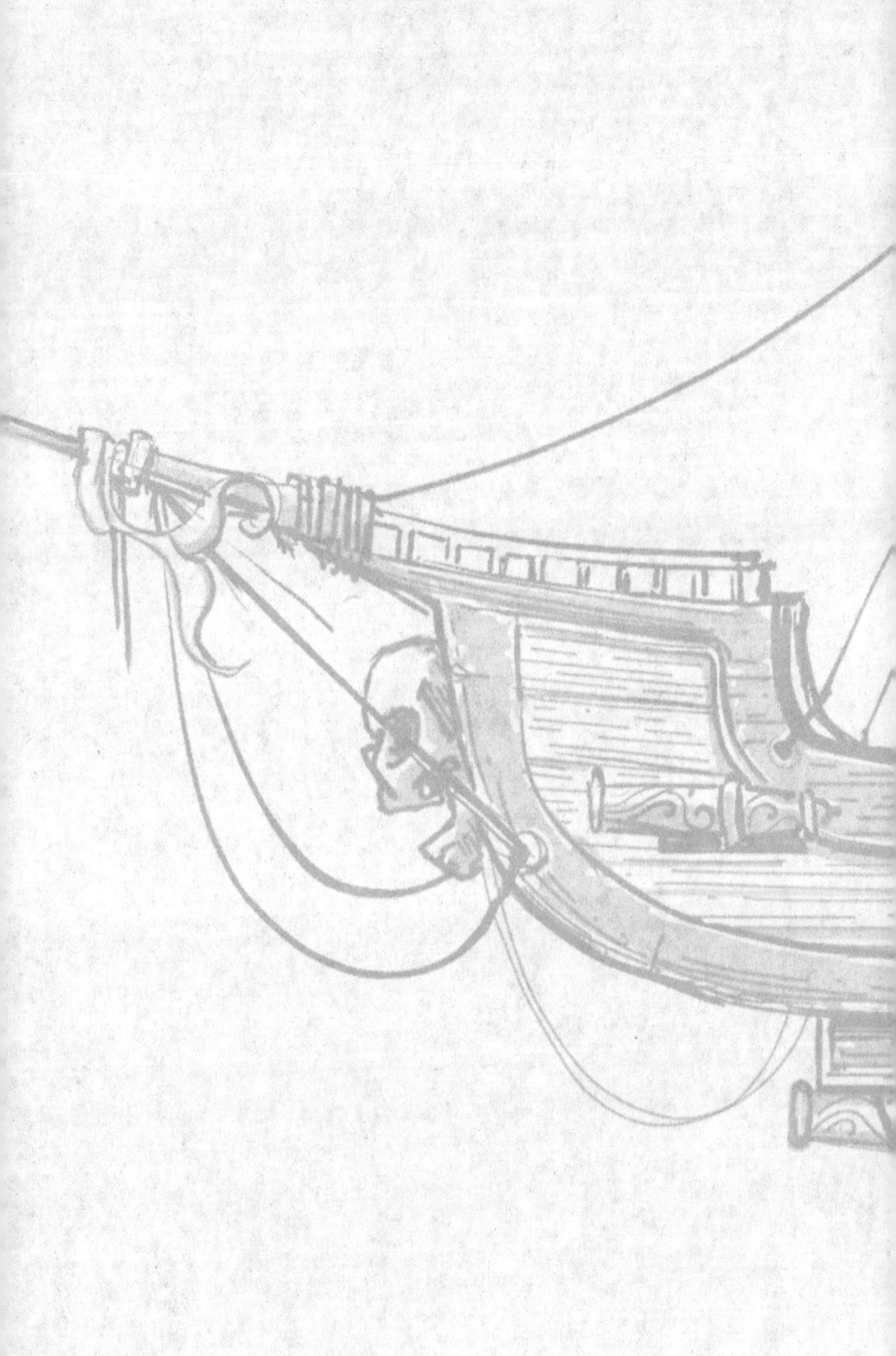

CHAPTER 17

Jerry leaned against a wall in the center of town. The news outlets had moved in, setting up their equipment in rows.

Jerry lifted one boot to press it against the wall of the building she stood against, tilting her top hat down to hide part of her face. With her arms crossed over her chest, she waited for the announcement to begin.

As Senate Leader, Bert Riley was charged with explaining the brutal and senseless murder. On the one hand, Jerry didn't envy him that job, but on the other, she was curious what he would say and if he would talk about the connection between him and Melora. She doubted that he would.

With forty minutes to go until the release, people filled the square, standing close together. In the midst of a virus raging with multiple variants, Jerry was surprised they were even doing this. Then again, how else would they? They needed to hear it straight from the horse's mouth.

Jerry kept her position, making sure she could see the majority of the square and who was there. Oddly enough, she found authorities stationed at each of the entrances into the square. They stood on either side, their shoulders squared as they kept their eyes wide for whatever they were looking for. She wished she'd had a moment to speak with Arloa and find out what the drama was all about. She'd never attended a news release before, but this surely wasn't normal.

Was it?

Several other senators arrived, standing just behind the main podium where the majority of the amplifiers had been placed. Jerry raised her chin, going down the list to see who was among the chosen. Not surprisingly, Arloa wasn't part of that crew of men. Wrinkling her nose, Jerry stayed as still as possible. She didn't want anyone to catch wind that she was there or that she had another plan to accomplish.

Riley strode in, flanked by two more authorities. Was it his safety they were concerned about? Especially with the attack on Melora? Jerry pressed her lips together hard, watching as he took the podium and put out his hands to quiet everyone down. He straightened his shoulders as he prepared to speak.

"Good people of Raegina…" he started.

Jerry gagged. He didn't give a flying fuck about anyone but himself and his own enterprises, and the majority of Raegina knew that. Unfortunately those weren't the people who would show up at a release like this.

"I was saddened to hear the reports about the Melora family and their brutal killing."

Jerry tried hard not to roll her eyes. Moving her focus from him to control her reactions, she looked around for the people she knew would be there, the ones who were supposed to help her. The square filled up even more now that Riley was speaking, people showing up from the outskirts to stand and listen.

"The Melora family were my friends. Jenkins and I went to school together, and I stood up at his wedding to Caila." Riley paused like he gave a shit. Jerry very much doubted that.

Out of the corner of her eye, she caught sight of Azar standing with his arms crossed directly across the square from her. If he was in place, then Yafe would be as well. That left Vivian, and Jerry knew she was stashed away hidden while all the focus was on the square. They'd left Sacha behind to take care of Whitney. Jerry moved from the wall, slowly lowering her boot to the cobblestone below.

"What are you doing here?" Arloa's quiet hissing startled her.

Jerry slowly moved to look into Arloa's steel-blue eyes, her hair perfectly done up for a release and one of her best dresses on, the embroidery of two women in the throes of passion along the top edge far bolder than it had originally been.

"Listening to the release," Jerry answered, her tone terse and her shoulders squared.

"Bullshit." Arloa reached out to grab Jerry's arm, but Jerry jerked it back and out of Arloa's reach. Confused, Arloa lifted her chin. "You can't be here. They'll see you."

"I'm a new person, and I can walk in broad daylight."

Arloa locked their gazes together, put off by Jerry's earlier refusal to let her touch. Jerry could see it in her gaze, the distrust that was building. Well good—now Arloa felt the same way Jerry did.

"You're risking everything we've fought for."

Jerry's forehead creased. "*We* fought for?"

"You need to stay hidden."

"I can't stay in that little room for life. I deserve to live if I'm here. I've done enough surviving, and I'm tired of it."

Arloa's chest heaved as she breathed heavily. Jerry wasn't going to back down from this one, however. She needed Arloa to understand that she wasn't someone to be locked away. It would be only slightly better than Joab in the long run if she was.

"What are you doing here, Jer?"

"Nothing that concerns you."

"If it concerns Riley, then it concerns me."

Jerry shook her head slowly, bending down so her lips were inches away from Arloa's ear. "No, it doesn't."

With a flair, Jerry spun on her toes and stalked away. She knew it was cruel, that Arloa had no idea what was going through her mind at that point—or her heart—but Jerry couldn't stop to take the time to explain. She could blame it on lack of brain later, even though she knew she'd eaten some just before arriving at the square.

"Jenkins was found to be murdered last, and we suspect he was forced to witness the killing of his wife and children. We suspect this is the work of a serial murderer who has been attacking political influencers for the last year."

Jerry stuttered at that, her steps faltering. She kept her gaze to the ground and absorbed everything Riley said from the podium.

"We have no suspects in these killings, but I promise you that the authorities are working on the situation, and we won't stop until we find this ruthless killer. He has no place to hide."

She had been waiting for this. Riley paused and Azar called from the edge of the crowd. "Liar!"

Riley hesitated before he continued. "We will find who did this, and they will face the repercussions of their actions."

"You did this!" Yafe shouted before vanishing.

Jerry's lips quirked at the onslaught Riley was about to face. Arloa twisted her arm, pulling her around and making eye contact. Her steel-blue eyes wide with fear, and she shook her head, mouthing, "Not like this."

Jerry gave her a hard stare back. Arloa had kept her out of the loop, so Jerry had decided this was the best course of action right now. Arloa didn't need to know everything about what she did, and it only made the situation worse. They had to keep secrets, especially if Jerry had any hope of living instead of dying. Being with her crew again had rekindled that. They were her family, and she wasn't willing to give them up.

"You started the virus!" Azar shouted from a different location, having disappeared and reappeared for a quick moment.

Everything worked perfectly. Jerry's turn was almost up, but she couldn't tear her gaze from Arloa.

"You made us sick!" Yafe shouted, this time from behind Riley.

Finally their voices were heard over the din of people, through the amplifiers that were used to bring Riley's voice to so many people. Jerry lifted her hands, cupping them around her lips. Breaking eye contact, Jerry shouted, "You killed us!"

When she went to look back at Arloa, she was gone—vanished, nowhere to be seen. Jerry flitted her gaze around the square, hoping to catch sight of blonde curls and the deep sapphire dress she'd worn that day but there was nothing for her to find.

Azar and Yafe continued their verbal assault, getting so loud and attracting so much attention that the two authorities who had come in with Riley stepped up to flank him. Jerry smirked as she took a step and started phase two of their plan. She could only hope Vivian had managed to get what she needed already because there wasn't much time left.

Jerry disappeared into an alleyway. Yafe and Azar would do what they were there to do and Jerry would take over as soon as she could. Riley's voice echoed throughout the square and into the rest of the center of Raegina. She stalked carefully to the glasswares shop, glad to see that it was locked and the owner out.

It took her no time at all to pick the lock and find her way inside. Jerry breathed in a sigh of relief as she walked through the shelves of items, still surprised that any shop like this was able to make it through the virus. Keeping her head down, Jerry walked confidently to the small tunnel that connected this building to the government building next door.

It wasn't long before she slipped into Riley's private office and sat in his chair, putting her feet up on his desk and leaning back. Azar and Yafe would be doing exactly what they needed, which Jerry knew put them at risk. She had to trust everything was going to plan because there would be no way she would find out otherwise.

It took longer than she'd anticipated, but when Riley entered the building, Jerry received an alert on her personal device.

Shoving it into her pocket, Jerry stood up, smoothed down her jacket, and stepped out of Riley's personal office, into his main office, and into the hall. She made sure to lock the doors behind her as she went.

She waited.

It only took three minutes for heavy footfalls at the end of the hallway. Her lips twitched into a smile that she schooled in an instant. He had no authorities with him. They must have stayed closer to the entrance, assuming the government building was safe because no one had been seen coming in during the release. Jerry stayed in the shadows, wondering just when Riley would see her.

He stopped a few paces from her, his lips parted. Jerry raised her chin, her hands shoved into her pockets. She eyed him gleefully, as though she was about to out him to the entire world. And she wished she was, but today would have to be a conversation between just the two of them. Jerry had Riley alone. Bracing her feet shoulder-width apart, Jerry waited as he came closer and tried to walk past her. He didn't see her.

Jerry cleared her throat and straightened her spine, giving herself another inch of height. She glowered at him. Riley stepped right next to her, and Jerry spun on her toes quickly to catch his attention.

"It's all true, isn't it?" She kept her voice low. She dropped her gaze down his body, resting on his face. He looked unsettled, his lips parted, his eyes wide, and his cheeks pulled tight as if he were clenching his jaw. Whether it was from her or from what happened at the release, she had no idea.

"Excuse me?" Riley sounded affronted, putting his hands on his hips as if to scold her.

Jerry shook her head slowly. "What they said out there?"

Riley raised a bushy eyebrow at her. "What who said?"

"At the release." Jerry kept as still as possible. She wanted him unnerved, but she didn't want him to run away from her—not just yet at least.

"Were you there?" Riley seemed almost in disbelief.

The hall was still empty, which meant he likely came back before anyone else did. Jerry kept her gaze on him, listening for footsteps and voices just in case someone was coming up from behind her.

"I was there. Quite the accusations."

"Rumors." Riley didn't even seem disturbed by them.

Jerry held her ground. "Are you sure about that?"

"There's no proof."

"Not even another denial." Jerry shook her head, letting out a soft chuckle. "You know, to me that spells guilt."

"I'm sorry. Who are you?"

"Jeremy Laurier." Jerry raised an eyebrow. "Don't you remember?"

"Ah, yes, the little man who thinks he knows everything."

Jerry cocked her head to the side. "I do know a considerable amount."

"Except no one knows who you are."

"Not quite true." Jerry rolled up on her toes, holding the tension. "But about these *rumors*. How much truth do you suppose is in them?"

"One thing you'll learn about politics, Mr. Laurier, is that truth doesn't matter. If you'll excuse me." Riley turned toward his office and walked inside without another word.

More convinced than ever that he had something to hide, Jerry stayed put for another minute. If he came back out, she wanted to catch him by surprise, but she knew that she couldn't linger for long. Her personal device buzzed in her pocket. Jerry snagged it and read the message from Vivian. They had more files and information to go through. Smiling, Jerry turned on her toes and sauntered happily toward the front door.

She grinned. Everything had gone to plan—mostly. She had managed to get an unofficial confirmation that Riley was hiding something. Now all they had to do was find the proof he thought didn't exist and expose him. She was just at the door when Arloa burst through it. Her gaze morphed from annoyed to angry.

Jerry swallowed hard, her fingers tingling. She shouldn't have been so harsh with her, especially because Arloa had no idea why she was pushing back so much. Still, Jerry had to protect herself from everything, even if that included Senator Arloa Kauket, the one woman she had managed to fall in love with.

Arloa's lips parted, but she said nothing. Their gazes locked, tension filling the empty space between them. She knew Arloa had questions, that they needed to talk about what had happened, but now was not the time or the place. They needed privacy for that.

"Tonight," Arloa muttered under her breath. "The ninth bell."

Jerry nodded sharply in confirmation. She stepped around Arloa and through the main doors to the government house. She didn't glance over her shoulder despite how much she wanted to. She couldn't let Arloa see how much this affected her. She needed to keep herself sane.

Instead of meeting her crew back at *Yarrow*, Jerry took an alternative route and stopped by her hideout. She packed everything she had in that room into her two small rucksacks and shoved them over her shoulders. She locked the door on her way out, only glancing back twice at the door. She would be back tonight, since that was where Arloa would no doubt expect to meet up. But Jerry couldn't stay there any longer. She needed her family, and she needed her ship.

Walking out of the city center filled her with relief. She wasn't made to be one of them, and despite how many times she had played at being richer than she was, it wasn't her. She was Jerry Adelric, captain of *Yarrow*, daughter of a whore, and heir to the underground.

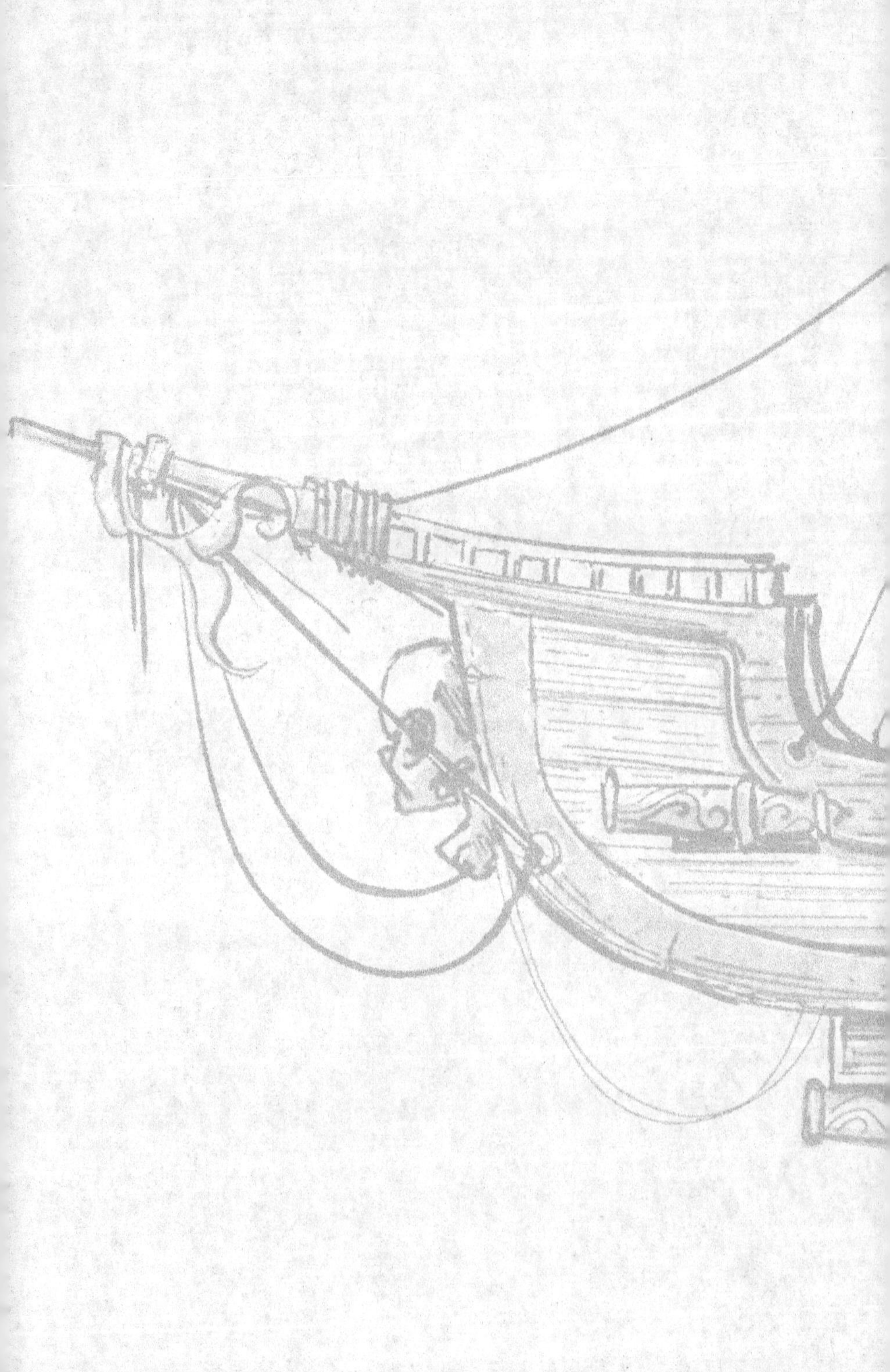

CHAPTER 18

Arloa stormed down the small hallway to the room at the end. Her boots clacked loudly as she stomped. Jerry straightened her shoulders, the relief she'd found as soon as she got herself on *Yarrow* gone in an instant. Arloa was in for another shock as soon as she stepped inside.

Jerry stood in the center of the small room, her hands shoved into the pockets in her pants and her body as relaxed as she could make it. This was going to be a battle for control, and she had to win. She couldn't live like this anymore, and she needed to know exactly what Arloa's history was with Melora and Riley.

The door slammed open, Arloa's petite frame filling it as she stopped short. Her steel-blue eyes roved the room before landing on Jerry, her lips pursed, her jaw clenched, and her gaze narrowed. "What's all this?"

Jerry swallowed. "I can't stay here anymore."

Arloa didn't speak right away. She took another sweep of the room before stepping inside and shutting the door behind her, locking it. Jerry's heart raced, knowing the battle for control had finally begun. There was no more waiting.

"I'm not a pet to keep locked up."

"I never said you were." Arloa's voice came out hushed, a harsh whisper into the still air between them.

"That's exactly what you've done."

"I've done no such thing." Arloa's voice rose, and she cut her hand across the air. "I rescued you from Joab. *I* brought you back to life. *I* saved you."

Jerry clenched her fists in her pockets. "Is that all I am to you? Someone who needs saving?"

"No." Arloa loosed the air in her lungs before dragging in a slow breath. She tried to control herself—Jerry had seen her do it before though never in an argument between them.

Arloa started a step toward Jerry but stopped short. She blinked as she raised her gaze to Jerry's. "May I come closer?"

"Why?" Jerry's back was up. The door to leave was behind Arloa and it was locked, but to go back to the conversation of asking before touching, asking before being in each other's space, meant there was far more distance between them than Jerry had originally anticipated.

"Please."

"No." Jerry raised an eyebrow, daring Arloa to break the confidence of her word. But she didn't. True to the moment, Arloa stayed put right where she was.

Arloa sighed heavily, brushing her fingers through her hair and closing her eyes. "What am I to you?"

Jerry ground her molars. She wasn't going to answer that question if she could avoid it. It didn't matter what they were to each other—what mattered was that they couldn't ever be in the same world. They were too different. Jerry didn't belong here and Arloa didn't belong on the open seas. They weren't compatible from the beginning.

"This started as a fun fling."

"And what is it now?" Arloa fired back, not missing a beat. "Because I think both of us knew it was beyond a fling the first time we were together."

Jerry's heart raced, thumping in her chest. Her shoulders were tense again, and she took great pains to relax them and lower them. "You're an aristocrat."

"But what else?" Desperation lit the edges of Arloa's voice.

Jerry held the moment, keeping the tension from sliding away. "You can't be anyone to me."

"Why not?" Arloa held her ground, though her body shook and she listed forward.

Their gazes locked again, tears brimming in Arloa's. Jerry wanted to go to her, wanted to hold her and kiss her, touch her in the ways they just had. "What's your relationship with Jenkins Melora and Bert Riley?"

"That's irrelevant." Arloa spun on her toes, moving to the small table and leaning against it.

Jerry shook her head. "I promise you, it's not."

Sighing, Arloa covered her eyes with her hand, her fingers trembling. "I went to school with both of them. Bert was a year ahead of me and Jenkins a year behind, though he and I were the same age. We did go together when we were in school, but nothing ever happened. We were young, and I was trying to impress my family—my parents—but nothing I ever did impressed them. They wanted a demure, silent daughter, and they'd been graced with a loud-mouthed, opinionated girl."

Jerry held her ground. She wasn't going to interrupt this rant because she knew most of this already. Vivian had managed to find records of it.

"I never went with Bert. I never really liked him, and when Jenkins and Bert became closer, I cut off my relationship with both."

"And what about the pharmaceutical company?"

Arloa jerked her chin upward, shaking her head slowly. "It was a failure. We couldn't work together. The two of them have no head for business or taking risks when it comes to profit."

"Is that what you were using to reverse engineer vestigen?" Jerry stayed perfectly still. In her gut, she knew the answer but to have Arloa say it would bring everything home.

"Yes. I reopened the plant with a few select chemists and healers."

"Maisie?"

"Yes, Maisie." Arloa frowned. "She was killed in this war."

"What war?"

Arloa blew out a breath. "The war for power. This virus isn't about killing people, Jer. I know that's what you see it as, but it's so much more than that. They want complete control of Penum and are willing to go to extremes in order to accomplish that."

"Who is *they*?" Jerry still kept the space between them, needing it to keep herself steady. She'd known Arloa was hiding far more than Jerry knew about. She always had secrets upon secrets, and Jerry felt she was finally at the first surface of them.

"Bert. Jenkins was part of that. Fudala had his hand in it. My father and brother. There's more, but I haven't been able to figure out who everyone involved is. I can't stop them all. I don't have the power or the following to do it."

"What would do it?"

"I don't know," Arloa murmured. "The upset at the press release today was minimal. Without proof, no one is going to change their opinion of their beloved Senate Leader. But they don't know what he was like. Bert has managed to put this image of himself out there, one that is infallible. This city gave him power, and he never should have had it."

"And what's your role in all this?"

"I'm nothing but a lowly senator trying to expose the truth."

Jerry raised her chin. She knew there was more. Arloa wasn't telling her anything, but this was deeper into the vat of secrets than they had ever managed to go. Jerry pulled her hands from her pockets, clenching and unclenching her fists. Arloa looked so small and defeated, her shoulders drawn, her face tilted down. She'd never seen her look like this before.

"I love you," Jerry whispered. "I'm obsessed with you, and I love you."

Arloa chuckled lightly and shook her head slowly back and forth. When she finally raised her gaze, tears were in her eyes, big droplets streaming down her cheeks and falling off her chin into the fabric of her dress. "I never thought you would say that."

"It doesn't change anything."

"Of course it does."

"Stop it." Jerry pulled what little anger she could find and held it in the center of her chest. "We're too different for this to work. We'll never find a moment to be together without everything else going on."

"We can. We have managed that." Arloa shifted, standing again. "I have to believe that we can."

"Why?"

"Because I need one good thing in this life to survive it."

Jerry held her ground, not taking a step closer as much as she wanted to. She had to keep her distance because she knew what would happen if Arloa got too close. "I'm infected. I'm a pirate. I'm an escaped convict. I can never be seen in the world again, but I can finally be me."

"So what will you do?"

"I have a plan. Don't worry."

Arloa stumbled forward. Jerry resisted the urge to put her hands out to steady her. "I need you."

"You've never needed me," Jerry whispered. "Just like I never needed you."

"You're right." Arloa reached out, ghosting her hand along Jerry's arm and pushing the boundaries Jerry had set up at the beginning of the argument. "But I want you—desperately."

"We can't have each other."

"I'll find a way."

"I'm not worth it, Arloa."

Arloa dragged in a deep breath, her breasts pushing against her corset and her hand dropping to her side. "It is worth it."

"I can't cure this virus and neither can you."

"No. I can't. There is no cure." Arloa looked her directly in the eye. "But I can and will find a means for you to live with it, successfully. The war going on in the government shouldn't affect you in this way. It's unfair."

Jerry snorted and rolled her eyes. "Nothing is fair about being an unsightly creature."

"You're not unsightly to me." Arloa stepped in closer, their bodies only inches apart. Jerry knew exactly what Arloa was doing, that she was trying to use her physical influence to sway Jerry's opinion. "I love you."

"It doesn't change anything."

"It does and it doesn't," Arloa agreed. "I plan to get rid of Bert Riley, strip him of his power and control in the government, make him the unsightly creature he abhors."

"And how do you plan on doing that?" Jerry's fingers itched to reach up and curl around Arloa's cheek, feel the soft skin against her fingertips, the warmth from her body.

"I need to expose him, but I need proof first. I haven't been able to find any."

"I have." Jerry wasn't sure if she would regret that confession or not. Arloa was her greatest ally in this fight, but that didn't mean that she could be trusted.

Arloa's eyes lit up. "You found proof?"

"Some."

"What did you find?"

Jerry shook her head slowly. "I need your connections to get it out there."

"Yes, anything. He's dangerous, so we need to be careful, protect you."

Swallowing hard, Jerry gave in and cupped Arloa's cheek. She brought their mouths together in a soft kiss. This was coming home more than returning to *Yarrow* was. Arloa moved under her, gripping the fabric at Jerry's sides and holding firm. She didn't push for more than Jerry gave but took everything. Breaking the kiss, Jerry closed her eyes and rested her forehead on Arloa's shoulder.

"We found the chemist who was working on the virus."

"Who was it?"

"Malek Rahl."

"Maisie's father?"

Jerry nodded as she lifted her head. "He's a healer and chemist."

"And dead."

"Suspected dead."

"No, he's dead." Arloa straightened her shoulders, so confident in that answer that it unnerved Jerry. "How do we connect him to Bert?"

"They worked together. After you left, Bert and Jenkins hired him along with Maisie. They worked together for years." Jerry knew whatever moment had been between them was done now. She straightened her back and took a step away from Arloa. "Malek was reported missing by Maisie six months ago and hasn't been seen since. There was no trace of him."

"He's dead." Arloa nodded firmly. "Trust me, there were traces, and he's dead."

Jerry canted her head in Arloa's direction. "What traces? We haven't managed to find any."

"You wouldn't, please just trust me. Malek Rahl is dead. He's not coming back."

"All right." Jerry shoved her hands back into her pockets. "So now what?"

"We expose them. All of them, and we let the masses do their work on them." Arloa vibrated with excitement. Jerry was glad to see it instead of the tears she'd had moments before, but she also knew that this would be the end of whatever relationship they had. Jerry needed to get back to her ships, and she needed to talk to Miriam about her plans for the future.

Jerry stayed still, not knowing what to say. They did need to make a detailed plan, but she couldn't bring herself to break the spell of Arloa's sudden happiness. This was exactly why they had to stop seeing each other after all this drama was done. Jerry couldn't be trusted to keep her head on straight when Arloa was around, and with what the future had in store for her, she knew she would need to.

"What proof do you have?" Arloa was back to business as usual.

Jerry sighed, pulling her mind back to the conversation. "We were able to prove that he worked with Malek for years, and that Malek is the one who created the virus. He left his mark all over it, considering there is a base form of magic involved, which is why you were never able to find a cure."

"So there is a cure?"

"No. There's no reversing it."

"But if we can persuade the government to manufacture vestigen again, then we can at least stop people from dying." Arloa, always and ever hopeful, never gave up. Jerry hated to shatter that.

"We're born to die, Arloa. Until you understand that my people are expendable, you'll never understand the world. No one cares about us."

"I do."

"And I still don't understand why, but you still don't understand us. We're here to die. You're here to live in a marble house on the hill."

"That's not fair."

"It's the reality of the situation."

Arloa stepped close, brushing her fingers down Jerry's arm until they twined their hands together. Lifting her chin, Arloa looked Jerry directly in the eye. "It's not a reality I want to bring into the future."

"Good luck changing that."

"Jer, you have to trust me."

"I can't trust you." The words were out of her mouth before she could stop them. Backtracking, Jerry tried again. "I trust that you'll help us expose Riley because it's to your benefit and what you've been working for. Beyond that? I can't allow myself to trust you. Every time I have, it's put me in danger."

"But I saved you from that."

"You saved me from the situation you sent me into, multiple times." And there was the reality that Arloa didn't want to admit.

"I didn't tell you to go back and get *Yarrow*. I told you to forget her."

Jerry scratched the back of her head, anger flashing through her. She tried to pull her hand from Arloa's, but her grasp was tight.

"We need to work together on this."

"Yes, we do. But anything else? We don't work together on that."

"Jer..." Arloa's lips parted. "I want to work together with you from here on out. I love you."

"That changes nothing."

"It's everything. I won't give you up."

"Now who's the one obsessed?" Jerry tried again to break their grasp, but Arloa held firm. "Let go of me."

"Not yet. I don't understand where this is coming from. You can live here or on your ship, you can live with Miriam. I don't understand why we can't be together."

"We can't!" Jerry's voice echoed through the small room. Anyone else would have shrunk back, but Arloa held her ground. "There's no way we'll have a normal relationship."

"I don't want *normal*. What I want is what we have."

"You always want more than I can give."

"No, I don't." Arloa paused, steadying herself. "Look, let's put this conversation to the side for a moment. Let's deal with Bert, get him out of power, and then come back to this."

"There's no point." Jerry towered over her. "We'll release the information to the news outlets, and we'll push it to the other countries. What are you going to do?"

"I'll file a request that he step down while an investigation is in process."

"Good." Jerry straightened her shoulders. "I'll see you

around, Arloa."

"No. We're not leaving it like this."

"We are."

Arloa tugged Jerry hard, moving them around and shoving her against the small table. Jerry knocked back into it, and Arloa was against her, their mouths pressed together. Arloa was hot on her, their lips pushing into each other. Arloa nipped at her lip, her fingers slid down Jerry's front and over her breasts.

"I'm not willing to give you up," Arloa murmured before she went back in.

Jerry relaxed, using the physical touch to ground herself. This she could handle—the physical—but Arloa had always seemed to want more. What had started as fling nearly two years ago had gotten way out of control. She understood Arloa though. Jerry didn't want to give her up either, but it was inevitable.

"I need to go," Jerry whispered, bringing Arloa's mouth back to hers.

"Where are you going?"

"*Yarrow.*"

"Right." Arloa nodded and stepped away. "When are we doing this?"

"We'll release the information tomorrow, which gives you time to get some things into place."

"I understand."

Jerry stepped toward the door and clicked the lock. She pulled it open, looking over her shoulder at Arloa's soft, unhindered gaze.

"I'll come find you when it's done, when he's been suspended," Arloa stated firmly.

"Isn't that when the real work for you begins?"

"Yes." Arloa raised her chin. "But I love you, Jer, and I'm not going to give you up for nothing."

Jerry kept quiet. She hardened her gaze and walked away. She knew it wasn't the last time they were going to see each other, but it was the start of the inevitable end.

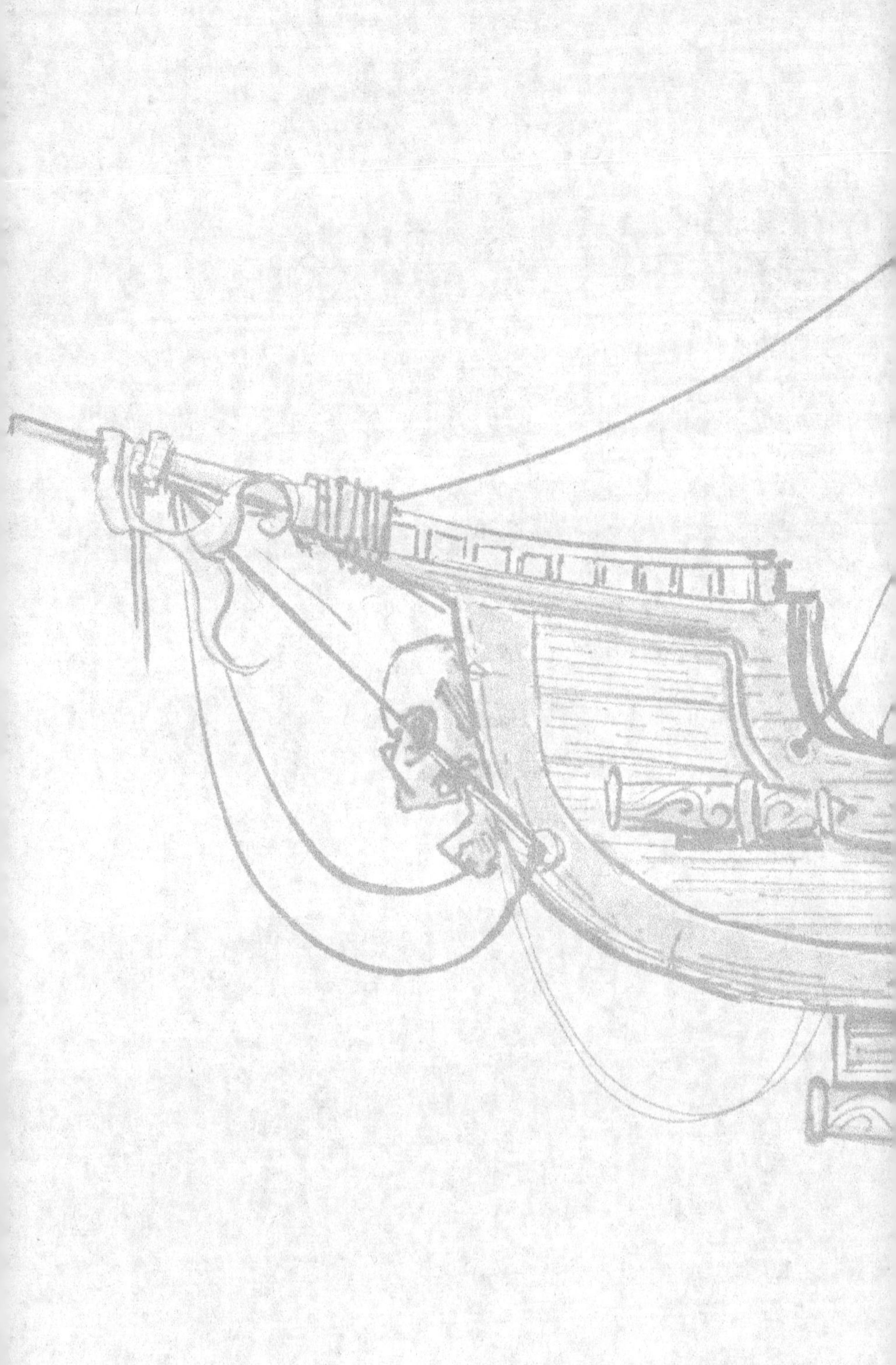

CHAPTER 19

t took nearly all day for the news to make the reports. Arloa sent a message right before they hit to let Jerry know. Jerry brooded on *Yarrow's* topside, glad to finally be home. She sipped some moonshine that Yafe had managed to make in one of the storerooms.

"What's going on, Cap?" Yafe slid next to her.

Jerry scrunched her nose as she took another sip. "Take this before I'm too drunk to confront Miriam."

Yafe's brow furrowed in surprise, but she took the glass jar and put the lid back on it. "What does any of this have to do with Miriam?"

"She made me an offer, and I'm not going to refuse it."

Yafe opened the moonshine and sucked down a few gulps. "All right, I'm ready now. What did she want?"

"The rumor Azar heard is true. She's retiring, and she wants me to take over."

"The underground?" Yafe's eyes widened in shock.

Jerry said nothing but continued to stare at the edge of Raegina, the harbor only a few steps away from the slip. She was always on the outskirts of life, wasn't she? Never quite accepted into the full city and never quite a complete outcast. But that was who she was, and it was about damn time she accepted her fate. Jerry glanced down at *Yarrow's* deck.

"I couldn't bring myself to stay in the city. I didn't think I could live without being on the open seas."

"So what will you do?"

"What can I do? I can't work legally. Me being on *Yarrow* is a risk, and I'm putting you all at risk by being here."

"I don't think we care about that." Yafe's voice was so gentle. "We're all pirates."

Jerry dragged in a deep breath and closed her eyes. "Would you come with me?"

"Anywhere." Yafe settled her head against Jerry's shoulder.

Sitting in this moment was exactly what Jerry had needed but hadn't had since returning from Joab. She hadn't been able to find this peace stuck in the city, but here on *Yarrow* with her family surrounding her, she knew she could at least have some semblance of it.

"I want to run the underground from *Yarrow*, and I don't want to be stuck in harbor."

"Where will we go?" Yafe whispered.

"We'll do what we do best in the meantime. We'll pirate."

Yafe turned her head up to look into Jerry's eyes. Her full lips parted, but Jerry saw the recognition of the opportunity in them. This would give them both freedom from everything that tied them to Raegina and kept them running in fear. If they could go where they wanted and have the backing and support to do it then why would they take any other option?

"Miriam really wants you to be her successor?"

"I think she's been planning this since I was a child and just didn't tell me."

"What do you mean?"

Jerry furrowed her brow and rolled her shoulders. "When I was a kid, she took special interest in me. I always assumed it was because of my mom and to get me out of the way when she was working, but I'm not entirely sure of that now."

"Cap, you're not making sense."

"I know." Jerry rubbed her hands together. "Miriam used to take me into her office and have me help with different projects, like finances and connections and running things from place to place. She gave me quite a bit of freedom for a kid."

"And your mother?"

"She encouraged it." Jerry raised her eyebrows. "Kept telling me that someday I would be smart enough to take over the world if I wanted. She was an idiot of course. Who would want a zombie like me to run anything."

"But the underground?"

"It would be the perfect solution to keep hidden and still be able to do something."

"You could retire."

Jerry snorted and then laughed loudly. "Me retire? Do nothing? Live off what spoils?"

Yafe shrugged. "We could still give you a commission from the ships since you bought them."

"No. You know I can't do that."

"It was worth the suggestion."

Jerry rubbed her hands against her thighs. "I'm going to speak with Miriam. Do you know what you're doing?"

"It's all planned out, Cap."

"Good." Jerry stood up and rolled out the kinks in her shoulders. "I'm off then."

"Cap?"

"What?" Jerry raised her chin, looking into Yafe's easy eyes.

"Are you back here permanently?"

"I think so."

Yafe grinned broadly. She jumped up and wrapped her arms around Jerry's shoulders with a tight hug. "I've missed you, Cap."

Jerry was struck speechless. She had no idea what to say or how to respond. Wrapping her arms around Yafe's back, she embraced her, closing her eyes and reveling in the comfort she found there. It was so easy with Yafe, everything was. Clenching her eyes tight, Jerry drew in her scent before stepping back.

"I'll see you tonight."

Miriam's office was quiet, and she sat at the table with her head buried in papers while Jerry stood awkwardly at the door and waited. She had no idea how to begin the conversation that she'd abhorred so much earlier.

"Good work on Riley," Miriam murmured but didn't raise her gaze.

Jerry cocked her head to the side, her hands wrapped together in front of her. "What do you think I've done concerning him?"

"You're not taking no for an answer, and you're figuring out where you can throw your weight around." Miriam raised her head up, her gaze beaming with pride. "You're growing up, Jeraldine. Your mother would have been proud of you."

Confused, Jerry stayed still and said nothing. "She'd be something, that's for sure."

"She died far too young." Miriam put down the papers she was studying and stood up, coming around the table to lean against the side closer to Jerry. "But I don't think she's what brings you here today."

In some ways, she was. Her mother had introduced her to this life, and Jerry had never been able to escape it. Now it was time to embrace it. "Does the offer still stand?"

"Which offer?"

"You know which one."

Miriam's eyes lit with joy. "To take over?"

Jerry nodded sharply.

"You were born for this," Miriam said, elated. "You've grown up in this world, and it'll be to your advantage that you have."

"Isn't there someone else?"

Miriam cocked her head to the side, lifting one leg up onto the edge of the table and resting her chin on it while wrapping her arm around her shin. She studied Jerry in silence. Anxiety and fear spread through Jerry like wildfire. Now was where the judgment began.

"Miriam."

Miriam shook her head slowly. "There's never been anyone else. It's always been you. I thought you knew that."

"I didn't want to know that," Jerry admitted. "But I can see it now."

Humming, Miriam stood up. "I'll give you everything you need to make this yours."

"I won't do whores."

"I know you won't." Miriam moved to the side wall. She snagged the edge of a cloth and pulled it back, revealing a worn piece of wood in the wall. She pried it open with her fingers and pulled out a small leather-bound book from the recesses before closing everything up again. She walked quietly toward Jerry and handed the book over. "Start here."

"What's this?"

"An accounting of several major projects I've worked on throughout the years. All you had to do was ask."

"It wasn't ever relevant before to know what you were doing."

"It is now."

Jerry didn't answer, knowing she was right. It was time for her to learn everything she could about Miriam's influence before she officially stepped into her new role. As much as she'd spurned the offer before, it sat right on her shoulders now. "What did you mean *make this mine*?"

"You think I'm not without influence in Penum? Silly girl, I run this city."

Jerry kept her gaze glued to the book in her hands, her lips pressed together hard. She wasn't sure if Miriam was exaggerating or being honest about what she truly had power to control. If she was telling the truth, then Jerry could potentially make even more changes than she'd anticipated. Instead of just running a business, she could change the way her people were perceived.

"Ah, before you get any grand ideas..." Miriam trailed off, her voice low as she sat back down in her chair "...some things can't be changed, others can, and even more things are in place for a reason."

"What reason?"

"Balance is important. For one to be rich, someone else must be poor. Don't let your ideals be your folly."

Clenching her jaw, Jerry opened the book and skimmed the first few entries. It was divided into sections based on the different businesses that were run. It was far more than whores, drugs, and jewels. Jerry, instinctively, always knew that, but to have the proof at her fingertips was something she never expected to happen.

Jerry stood while Miriam went back to work. She flipped page after page until the name Kauket caught her attention. Cold washed through her, fear ratcheting up, her heart thudding loudly. Swallowing the lump in her throat, Jerry focused on the name and read the next line. *Election.*

The date matched.

Her ears rang loudly, and her stomach dropped. She couldn't faint. She couldn't do anything but stand there and stare at the words written in Miriam's perfect penmanship. Jerry raised her chin and pinned Miriam with a look.

"What's your involvement with the Kaukets?"

"They keep to themselves. The family has more influence and power than I do in some arenas."

"And have you done business with them?"

"Several times." Miriam didn't even look up from her table.

Jerry ground her molars together and resisted the shudder. She should have finished that jar of moonshine. She needed it in order to make it through this. "What for?"

"Most recently, I helped Senator Kauket break you out of Joab."

"You what?" Tingles raced through Jerry's spine.

"She didn't tell you?"

"No."

"Hmm." Miriam raised her chin, making eye contact. "She needed a ship to get you across the waters along with names of guards who could be bought. The rest was her doing."

"What else?" Jerry needed to know everything.

"You should speak with her on that, but she is one of my strongest connections to the government at the moment."

"Because of this?" Jerry slapped the book onto the table.

Miriam slowly took it and moved it around so she could see what Jerry had been looking at. She pressed her lips tighter tightly before making eye contact with Jerry. "Not because of that, no."

"Did you buy her the election?" Miriam said nothing. Jerry squared her shoulders and shook her head slowly as she stepped away. "I need to check on some things."

Without another word, Jerry raced from the small office and down the flights of stairs. As soon as she was out in the alley, she struggled to breathe. She couldn't get a grasp on anything. Her nerves raced with fear, and her stomach twisted with betrayal. She stood in the alley for as long as she dared before she pulled her hat down and lowered her chin to the ground. She stepped into the street and stopped immediately.

People filled it. They burst through the city gates and pushed toward the center of town. Jerry moved along with the throng, her anger moving her to follow instead of lead for just one damn time. She didn't want to be the one who had to be reasonable any longer.

They went past Arloa's apartment building, all the doors still shut and locked. The mass of people moved beyond the government building, where guards were stationed out front. Jerry moved closer to it, but she couldn't see inside any of the windows with their tinted glass. Scrunching her nose, she ducked her chin and moved with the people. She hadn't seen this amount of people in one place since well before the virus took over.

On the north side of town, where the hill rolled into Raegina and stopped short, the crowd burst into rage. Jerry moved to the side as they filled the space in front of a large looming house. Jerry watched in amazement as citizens gripped the bars on the gate and shook it as hard as they could, but the metal didn't budge.

Slouching into a corner and away from the chaos, Jerry held her ground as curses and screams were tossed in the direction of the house. Glass shattered against the bars, liquid pouring down the gate. Finally one was lit on fire and thrown over the top of it, reaching the front door on the other side.

"As soon as the report hit, the mob started." Azar's voice was loud enough that she could hear what he said, but quiet enough no one else around them would pay any attention.

Jerry turned over her right shoulder and raised her chin up to look him in the eye. "Have any of ours joined in yet?"

"No. They're obeying the command to stay back and only incite."

Humming, Jerry nodded. "Good. If anyone breaks that, I want to know who."

"You got it, Cap."

Crossing her arms, Jerry watched the onslaught. Vivian and Sacha had done a beautiful job getting everyone together to focus on one thing—Bert Riley. Authorities were stuck on the edge of the mob, trying to make their way in to get everything under control, but they had managed to get the road there ahead of them.

"What did you find with Miriam?" Azar asked.

"Nothing." Jerry tensed. She couldn't very well tell him that Arloa's entire election was fake, that the only reason she was in office was because she had stolen the vote to win. She wasn't even sure what she could do with that information yet. If she was willing to out Bert Riley for genocide was she willing to out Arloa for faking the election? Because she needed Arloa. They still had plans they needed to complete to get Riley out of office and ditch his career in the sea.

The sound penetrated her thoughts, bringing her back to the reality of the moment. They had caused all of this. Careful planning, people in the right places, information in the right hands—everything had been prepared to get to this one moment. What happened next was out of her control, and Jerry had to hope that the government did the right thing for once. But she had her doubts, especially if it was filled with people like Arloa.

Turning to Azar, Jerry looked at the building behind them as she raised her voice so he could hear her. "Get our people out of here. I don't want any of them arrested."

"Understood, Cap."

Jerry walked away, sliding through an alley and climbing a ladder to the roof of the nearest business building. The others would have to sneak away too, but they'd all planned and practiced for it. It was easier to avoid authorities in Raegina than it was on the seas.

She walked across the rooftops, dropping down just outside the main city gates. The cobblestones under her boots were worn, like she had been in the past few months. She should have asked Miriam sooner—hell, she should have asked Arloa. For loving the woman, Jerry had no idea exactly what Arloa had her fingers in.

Jerry would confront her about it. Not then. First, Arloa needed to do her job, and then Jerry could take up their issues.

They needed to finish this, and Riley needed to be ousted from the government before he could do any more harm. The walk back to *Yarrow* was quick, but Jerry stopped just on the edge of the harbor. Turning on her toes, she went back to the underground. If she was going to go into an argument with Arloa, exposing everything she did, then Jerry wanted to have as much information at her fingertips as possible, and since Miriam insisted on keeping those records handwritten and away from technology, Jerry had no other choice but to head back to her lair.

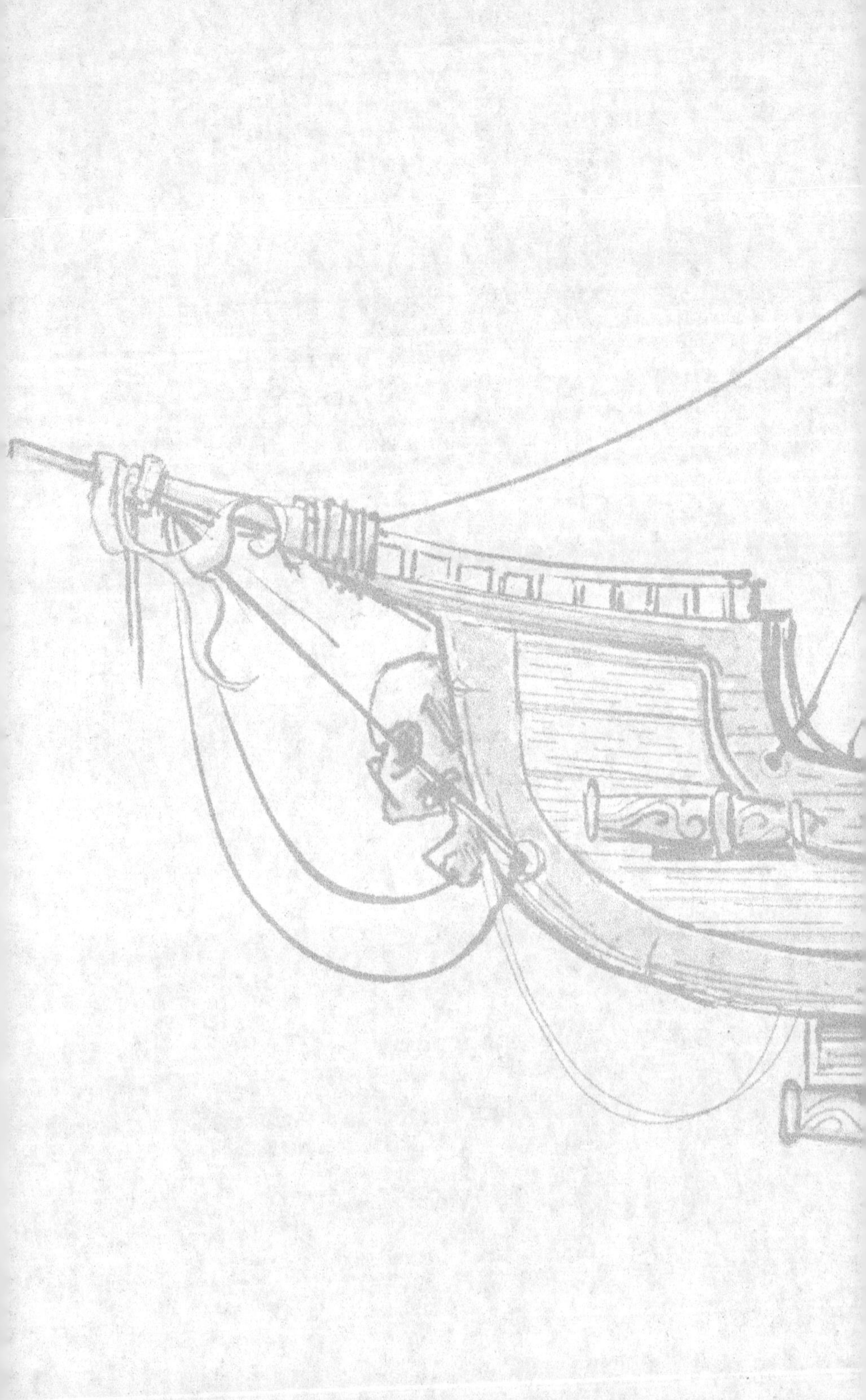

CHAPTER 20

Arloa slammed her door shut but stopped short two steps inside. Jerry eyed her from the small sofa, her arm stretched along the back, her ankle crossed over her knee, and her leather clad fingers tapping against the wood. She had waited hours already, the alcohol she had stolen from Miriam's stash already burning through her system so she was way more sober than she wanted to be.

"How did you get in here?" Arloa took deep breaths, her breasts pushing against her corset and her cheeks flushed.

"I know a few tricks still," Jerry answered. "Seems you do, too."

"I'm not in the mood for an argument today, Jer." Arloa cut her hand across the air as she dropped her work bag onto the small table.

Jerry stayed put, not willing to move until they had this out. She wasn't going to let Arloa get away with it anymore. She needed to know everything—she deserved that at least.

"The Senate denied my motion to have Riley removed or at least put on suspension during an investigation." Anger seethed through Arloa's words as she walked into the galley. She came back with a dark-colored bottle with a thin neck, and immediately Jerry recognized it as her preferred drink. "They said they'll investigate internally, but I have my doubts how forth-coming they'll be."

Jerry snorted loudly. Arloa expecting the institution she was in to be honest and truthful was hypocritical. Coming from a woman who had bought her way into office, it had to be a joke. Surely she could see the idiocy of the comparison. No one in government was without dirty hands, and the one person Jerry had thought she'd found who was mostly clean wasn't in the least. She was one of the dirtiest.

"I can try again when they find something, but until then, I'm at a standstill." Arloa poured herself a glass, drank it in three swift gulps, and poured herself another. "Want any?"

Jerry looked Arloa over, not answering. Her voice was so calm, and Jerry knew she wasn't prepared for the argument they were about to have. Nothing would prepare them for it. Anger simmered in her chest, and she was ready to let it loose. She was ready to have it out, to figure out for the first time who the real Arloa was.

"When we met..." Jerry started with a calm tone, noting Arloa's confusion at the lack of answer and the change of topic "...at the bar on the harbor, what were you doing there?"

"Having a drink." Arloa's face pinched. It was such a small change that no one else would have noticed it, but Jerry had spent the last year and a half figuring out who this woman was and what she meant when she didn't speak.

"What else?"

Arloa's lips parted, her eyes widening. "What is this about, Jer?"

"You got a message while we were talking and you had to leave rather abruptly. What was the message?"

"You're not making any sense."

"I'm making perfect sense!" Jerry's voice boomed through the room.

Arloa raised her chin, stepping closer after ditching the bottle and cup on the small table off to the side of the sofa. "I received a message from a contact that I was meeting that night. The issue was time-sensitive so I had to leave immediately."

"You were waiting for directions." Jerry knew exactly what the message had been. She'd seen the records of it because Miriam was fastidious. "You were meeting with Miriam."

Arloa released a breath, standing in front of Jerry with her hands at her sides. "Yes, I met with Miriam."

"To buy your election."

"Yes." The simple word fell off Arloa's lips in a whisper. She didn't offer any excuse or explanation, which irked Jerry. The least she should do is defend her decision to cheat and lie her way into power.

Nodding, Jerry straightened her shoulders and took her time standing up. "What were you thinking?"

"It was the only way." Arloa raised her chin to look into Jerry's eyes. "I might be a Kauket, but I'm a woman with no experience in politics. My family has stayed out of the government as much as possible—at least the overt side of government. I wanted to make a difference, and this was the only way."

"You could have won fairly."

Arloa shook her head, curls bouncing against her shoulders. "I never would have won. I still won't. I need Miriam in order to win re-election next year."

Jerry clenched her jaw tight. Arloa didn't know. No one knew. But next year, Miriam wouldn't be here, and everything would be Jerry's decision. "How much would you have given her?"

"As much as necessary."

"You wanted power that bad?"

"I wanted access." The distinction wasn't clear, but Arloa seemed determined to make it.

Jerry paused, standing toe-to-toe with the one woman on this damned planet who could shatter her. "Access to what?"

"The world."

"And did you get it?" Jerry raised an eyebrow, taking slow breaths to keep herself from doing anything stupid.

"No," Arloa whispered. "But I got you out of it."

"What do you mean?"

"If I hadn't been there that night, we never would have met. You can't deny that would be a loss for both of us."

Jerry tightened her hands into fists. "What else aren't you sharing with me?"

"There's so much." Arloa's voice broke, and she stepped in closer, her skirts brushing against Jerry's boots. "But I can't go through it all with you tonight. You have to trust that I would do anything for you and that I will tell you in due time."

"How deep are you in with Miriam?" Jerry wanted to reach up and touch her, run fingers through her hair and soothe the obvious upset she had caused on top of what Arloa had come home with. But she held her ground, needing this one last question answered.

"How deep are you?" Arloa riposted, her voice raspy. "We've both made our decisions in life, Jer. Look at where we've gotten ourselves, how far we are from where we started. We both made those choices with eyes wide open and knowing there would be consequences. I don't want whatever is between us to be one of those."

Words left her. Jerry stared down into that steel-blue gaze and had no idea what to say. She hadn't gone into her relationship with Miriam with eyes wide open. She'd been born into it, and perhaps that was the stark difference between her and Arloa. Jerry understood every single facet of how the underground worked, including that no one was safe and everyone died there. She preferred to think of only the immediate things she could gain from it, the credits from jewels and the things she stole, but there was so much more than that.

Miriam had been right. It was an infrastructure that took over all of Penum. Raegina's portion was only a very small part of that, and Miriam was only in charge of one part of how the underground made Penum function as a planet. If anything, Arloa should have gone into those politics. Jerry had ignored the meetings, the people she had met through Miriam for too long, and she needed to rely on what she knew worked, not on the wild card in front of her.

"Jer, I love you."

"I know," Jerry answered, finally reaching up to touch Arloa's cheek. Arloa closed her eyes, tilting into the caress. "I don't know how this is going to work, especially with what's coming, but I do know you're right about one thing. The only thing that will come between us is us."

Jerry crashed her mouth against Arloa's, taking her by surprise. Arloa's squeak set Jerry's body on fire. Arloa pushed into her, running her fingers over Jerry's chest and down to her waistband as she groaned, her eyes still shut. Jerry watched serenely as relaxation covered Arloa's features. It was one of the few times she ever seemed to let the world vanish around her, and Jerry envied that. She brought everything with her no matter what she did.

"Jer," Arloa hummed as she broke the embrace. "Jer, touch me."

Whipping Arloa around, Jerry pulled sharply at the ties on her corset. She wanted Arloa completely naked against her this time, to see her muscles ripple as she came, the softness of her skin, the flush as it rose all over her chest and into her cheeks. She shoved the cloth down Arloa's body to the floor and wrapped arms around her front, cupping her breasts. Jerry bit hard at the line of Arloa's neck and shoulder, sucking.

Arloa whimpered. "Take me. I need you."

Arloa was going to need Jerry more than she knew as soon as power was transferred to her. Miriam had already started the process before Jerry had returned the second time that day, and she knew she was going to be spending intense days learning at Miriam's side. It would happen swiftly and only key people would know.

"I need you in me." Arloa's voice was so soft. She rested her head against Jerry's shoulder, her eyes still shut in complete trust of what was happening. Her chest rose and fell, her breasts heaving as she touched herself in anticipation of Jerry taking over.

Jerry reached around Arloa's front and thrust two leather-clad fingers in, Arloa's breath hitching in an instant. She started a brutal pace, using the strength of her body to hold Arloa against her securely. "We're more entangled than you know."

Arloa's lips parted as if she was going to speak, but Jerry added her thumb into the mix and circled her clit. Arloa grunted in pleasure. Jerry bit and trailed her tongue all along Arloa's shoulder. "We're going to depend on each other."

"Yes," Arloa hissed, her nails biting into Jerry's forearm.

Jerry ripped her hand away and spun Arloa around again, pushing her onto the sofa. Her decision was made, whether she had anticipated that was what this night was about or not. She would work with Arloa, because she couldn't trust anyone else. Arloa bounced as she hit the cushion. Jerry got onto her knees and spread Arloa's knees wide as she scooted up between them. This time she didn't enter, using only her gloved fingers to swish back and forth in a hard, rapid succession. Arloa cried out, her hip bucking up while Jerry pushed her back down.

"I will do anything for you," Arloa said. "Just don't leave me."

Jerry leaned in, covering Arloa's breast and sucking hard on her nipple before swirling her tongue around it. Arloa always had pretty words and demands, but this time, Jerry knew they were true. Arloa wanted them to be together, never to be without each other, and yet, they were about to be in both opposition and cahoots with each other. There was no way to avoid their connection any longer.

"Jer." Arloa curled her fingers into Jerry's hair, pulling as she lifted her hips to get closer. Her body jerked, her hips moving rapidly, and her stomach rolling as her muscles worked. Jerry didn't give her a second to take a break.

Grabbing Arloa by the hips, she tugged and turned her around. Next, Jerry pulled her down onto the floor, her knees pressing into the hard wood. Jerry pushed a hand against the center of her back and rammed two fingers back in. Arloa groaned. Again and again, Jerry took her, pleasured her, pushed Arloa to the brink.

When Arloa came for a second time, Jerry stepped away. She stared down at her gloves, covered in Arloa's sweet juices, and swallowed hard. She hadn't come here for this, but she had at least gotten what she needed. A confession and a moment of truth between them went a long way. The fact that Arloa had barely denied Jerry's accusation before admitting it, that she hadn't given any excuses—she'd simply said why she'd made those decisions.

"What will you do when you're caught?" Jerry asked, raising her chin.

Arloa moved her head from the couch cushion, her cheeks flaming red, her eyes wide, and her hair so tousled there must be a million knots in it. She looked well and properly fucked, but her shoulders still held the poise of power she always had.

"I won't."

Jerry snorted. "You don't understand Miriam at all, do you?"

"I understand how she works." Arloa stood up, not bothering to fix her hair. She came closer to Jerry, stepping into her space. "I didn't go to her without doing research."

"But you didn't grow up with her either." Jerry bent down, raising an eyebrow. "She protects herself and no one else."

"And you," Arloa murmured. "She has always protected you."

"No, she hasn't."

Arloa started on the buttons on Jerry's pants, pulling them apart and pushing her hand between the fabric and Jerry's skin. "You're so wet."

Jerry grunted. "Hard not to be with someone like you. You should know that."

Arloa shuddered, goosebumps running all up her arms. "What are you planning, Jer?"

"Nothing you won't know about soon enough. Until then, you'll have to wait like the rest of the world." Jerry wrinkled her nose when Arloa gently played with her. The tension from earlier eased away. Jerry grabbed onto Arloa's shoulders, holding herself steady as she rocked back and forth with each tender swipe of Arloa's fingers.

"I love it when you let go like this," Arloa whispered. "For a time there, I was worried I would never see it again."

"I'm quite resilient."

"You would have to be, I should think. Jer, kiss me when you come."

They fell into silence, Arloa continuing the steady rhythm while Jerry stared down into her eyes. For the first time ever, there were no barriers between them, no boundaries. They knew where they stood, that they would take from their relationship what they could and hold it precious and firm between them. Jerry used her thumb to wipe a single tear that fell from Arloa's eye.

"When you do whatever it is you're doing, don't leave me," Arloa whispered her plea, the words wrapping Jerry tightly. She had no answer, so she bent down and took Arloa's lips as she crashed through her orgasm. Arloa wiped her hand on her thigh as Jerry redid the buttons on her pants. "When will I see you again?"

Jerry shook her head. "I don't know. I have business to take care of, and so do you."

"The Senate won't listen to me."

"Make them." Jerry raised an eyebrow. "Or you won't get what you need from Miriam. If you don't have sway, she has zero use for you in that capacity."

Arloa's lips parted in surprise, her eyes widening. "Are you doing her bidding now?"

Jerry squared her shoulders and shoved her hands into her jacket pockets. "No."

Leaving the small apartment, Jerry walked down the hall to the stairwell. She made it to the second floor and slipped out the window, jumping down to the cobblestones below. She knew Arloa would look for her out front, but she wouldn't give her that satisfaction. They had found what balance they could, and for now that was enough. Jerry slipped through the alleys until she reached *Yarrow*. Tomorrow she would start again.

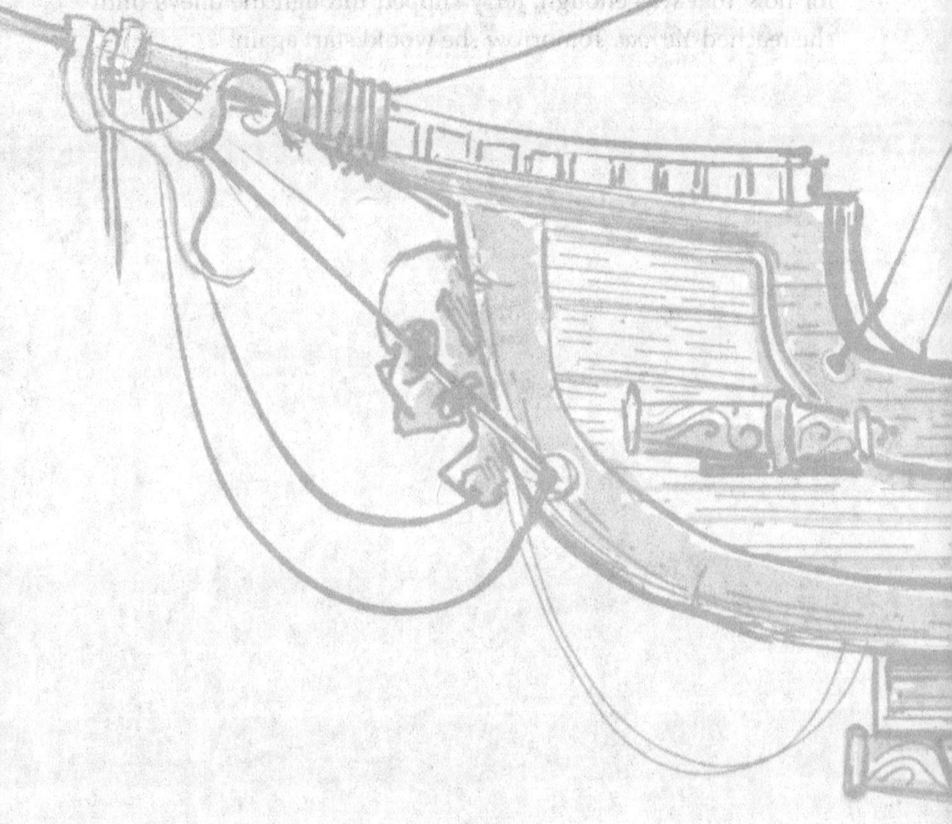

CHAPTER 21

Jerry slipped into Arloa's apartment undetected for the second time that week. Bert Riley's house remained under attack the entire week, requiring a band of authorities to protect it. On the one hand Jerry felt bad for his family, and on the other, the twerp got what he deserved. She'd spent days on end with Miriam, working through every business she had running, or at least the ones they had managed to cover in that short period of time.

In the meantime, Azar and Yafe prepared *Yarrow* to be out of the harbor for the long term and researched where to stash her off the main continent. It was a monumental task, but they were up for it. Jerry had yet to inform the crew, or even Yafe, of the change in plans, since she still wanted to keep herself hidden for as long as possible.

She stepped into Arloa's bedroom, the scent from her perfume hitting her hard even though Arloa no doubt hadn't been there in hours. Brushing her fingers along the edge of the vanity, Jerry looked at the different bottles and jars Arloa had set out there.

"How do you keep coming in here?"

Jerry's lips curled at the sound of Arloa's voice. She stayed with her back to the bedroom door, keeping her fingers running over Arloa's things. She wasn't sure how much longer she would be able to smell them, and the temptation to steal one so she would always have it with her was strong. Jerry picked one up and pulled the stopper out, bringing it to her nose to get a strong whiff. Surprise hit her belly when it didn't match Arloa's scent. She put it back down.

"That's for me to know."

Arloa sighed heavily and pulled off her light brown clothes, tossing them onto the vanity as she stood in Jerry's space. "Are you going to keep doing this?"

"As long as you allow it."

Arloa hummed, reaching out for Jerry's hand and lacing their fingers together. "I'll never deny you access to me."

Jerry cocked her head to the side, staring down into the depths of Arloa's eyes. She found only truth in the statement. "We need to clear the air."

Arloa frowned, the lines along her lips and eyes deep. Weariness crept over her face and her gaze flicked down. "Some other night."

"No. We're doing this now."

"I had a difficult day, Jer." Arloa sounded defeated. Jerry's shoulders squared as Arloa moved away from her and began stripping her clothes.

On instinct, Jerry moved behind her and pulled at the laces on her corset, loosening the material. She dropped kisses to the exposed skin and breathed in her scent. Depending on how their conversation went, she wasn't sure how much longer they were going to have moments like this, not once she left Raegina.

"What did you want to talk about?" Arloa moaned when Jerry dug her thumbs into her tense shoulders.

Jerry dropped another kiss to the base of her neck. "We need to be honest with each other."

"We're as honest as we can be."

"No, about everything. What happened that's got you so upset today?" Jerry scraped her teeth against Arloa's skin, leaving red welts in her wake which she soothed with her tongue.

Humming, Arloa stayed still, her fingers clasped around the metal of the footboard of her bed. Jerry had wanted to tie her to it at one point, and she would still be glad to do that and have her way with Arloa sometime. Perhaps that was what both of them needed. "I made the formal request for sanctions and an investigation into Riley on the Senate floor today."

"I take it you were denied."

"Not only denied, I was shut down. Told to shut up and look pretty." Tears welled in Arloa's eyes, and Jerry wanted to take that pain away from her.

"They're idiots." Jerry kissed up Arloa's neck, massaging her shoulders even more as she dropped the top of her dress to the floor beside them. She purposely didn't touch Arloa's breasts, the nipples already hard from the touches and cold air. "You're too brilliant for them."

"But I have no voice if they won't give me one."

"Since when have you ever let a man tell you what to do?"

Arloa grunted her agreement. It was one of the things Jerry loved about her, the audacity Arloa had along with her absolute brilliance. Jerry pressed a trail of kisses down Arloa's spine and back up. She was just about to ask a question when Arloa interrupted her.

"What are you doing here, Jer?"

"We need to talk," Jerry answered, not stopping her titillation. "I need to know what's going on, and so do you."

"Then what's going on?"

Jerry smiled. "You first."

They still had a long way to go when it came to trust, and Jerry wasn't quite sure she was willing to be the first one to share what she knew with Arloa, at least not all of it yet.

"Caprese, the Senator who denied my request today, has gone missing."

Jerry's heart thundered, and she faltered in her exploration of

Arloa's body. As soon as she had the full force of Miriam's power behind her, that would be one of the first items on her agenda. She needed to protect Arloa from anything that could potentially happen. Yet, Arloa didn't seem tense at all. In fact, she felt more relaxed than before, the muscles in her shoulders and chest were not as tight, her breathing more even. Jerry closed her eyes and used her hands to make sure that she wasn't missing something. "And you're not dealing with the fallout?"

"I can't. Not tonight. I'm too tired."

Reaching up, Jerry rubbed the edge of her thumb across Arloa's nipple and brought it even more to attention than it was before. Her mind whirred with the possibilities of what was going on. She needed to know and understand exactly what was going on in Arloa's world, but she instinctively knew that it was a harder answer to get than she ever thought possible.

"I'm not going to be in Raegina much longer."

Arloa blew out a breath, her eyes closed, and she leaned deeper into Jerry's arms. "I suspected the call of the seas would be too much for you."

Jerry bent down and rested her chin on Arloa's shoulder, her lips very close to her ear. "It's not just the seas. It's freedom."

"We're never free, Jer." Arloa tensed. "We're women, and we're of a different class and breed than the rest of the world. In order to survive we have to fight, and in order to fight, we need to be present."

"So you don't want me to go?" Jerry's brow creased in the center, confused by what Arloa was saying and not saying at the same time. "I can't stay here."

"I never thought you would."

"But you want me to stay with you."

Arloa sighed and shifted, turning slowly so she stood in front of Jerry, half-naked, but with eyes of steel. Arloa canted her head to the side, her chin tilted up so their gazes locked. "My place is here. Your place isn't. We can make it work if we want to. I'm not asking for a housewife."

Jerry smiled at that. Arloa would never settle for something as simple as that, and instinctively, Jerry knew that. "I'm worried for your safety."

"You shouldn't be." Arloa dropped her chin and started on the ties on the front of her skirts.

Jerry watched in curiosity, Arloa's deft fingers moving until they ran into a knot that she couldn't easily undo. Instead of helping, Jerry continued to observe. Arloa was flustered, and she couldn't figure out why. They had barely stepped into the conversation more than an inch. "Why shouldn't I worry for your safety?"

"I'm not in danger. Not like you are."

"I'm a ghost. No one is looking for me."

"*Everyone* is looking for you." Arloa's eyes bore into hers. "Just because you have a new identity doesn't mean they've stopped searching. You escaped Joab."

"With *your* help. You can't tell me that doesn't put you on someone's radar."

Arloa frowned, the lines creasing in her lips as she finally managed to pull the knot loose and drop her skirts to the floor. Immediately distracted, Jerry raked her gaze up Arloa's body and freshly exposed skin. Her heart thundered at the prospect of what they might get up to, but at the same time, she knew she needed to focus on the conversation at hand.

"I'll be fine," Arloa muttered and moved out of Jerry's immediate line of sight and pulled the ties on her boots to get them off, pushing them against the wall of the room. "I'm not in danger."

"You're not invincible."

Arloa said nothing as she reached for a gauzy shift, tugged it over her head, and started on her hair, pulling pins from it. Jerry gripped onto the bar of the footboard, holding herself up as she watched those golden curls tumble down Arloa's back. "I never said I was."

"You're acting like you are."

Arloa shot her a glare through the mirror as she plucked another pin from her hair. "I'm not the only one."

"Oh come off it."

"You leapt from your ship into the ocean, and you didn't think something would happen."

Jerry's heart skipped a beat, her chest tightening and her shoulders tensing. "How did you know that?"

"I read the reports when I was trying to find you. What did you think you would accomplish?" Arloa pulled another pin, the majority of her hair tumbling down her back. She spun around, her hands against her vanity as she leaned, her nipples still at attention, dark through the thin fabric.

Groaning, Jerry closed her eyes and dropped her chin. "That was the point of jumping."

"Escape?"

"Ultimate escape, yes."

Breath rushed through Arloa's parted lips, the hardness that had been present a moment before completely gone. "You wanted to die?"

"Anything to avoid going back there." Jerry wasn't going to hide from her anymore, not if she directly asked, and not if she could avoid it. This was the time for her to take a stand. "I tried more than once to kill myself while in Joab, and I never managed it. I was weak."

Arloa whimpered, and she stepped forward, snagging Jerry's hands in her own. "You are far from weak. I've never met a person as strong as you."

Jerry wanted to snort at the absurdity. She wasn't strong in any capacity. She survived, and most of the time, she wasn't even sure how she managed that. "What are we doing about Bert Riley?"

"Don't change the subject, not yet." Arloa lifted her hand and curled her finger around Jerry's cheek. "You've survived a great many things in your short life, and you should know that it's not by chance that you've managed that."

"Of course it is."

"It's not." Arloa's lips curled upward. "I never would have survived even half the things you've been handed. Our world isn't built to give women a hand up, and you have taken the cards you were dealt and you've run with them."

Jerry's stomach swirled. She wasn't used to the praise, and it unsettled her. She wanted to move away, but Arloa's grasp was firm on her hand and face, and she had to look into her eyes.

"I love you, Jer, and it's because of who you are and what you've done, not because of who I want you to be."

Warmth spread through Jerry's chest, her lips twitching into a small smile that she couldn't resist as much as she might want to. "Why aren't you afraid?"

"What is there to be afraid of?" Arloa murmured, stepping in close so their bodies brushed together.

Jerry hissed, resting their foreheads together as her eyes fluttered shut. "Why aren't you afraid that your position will get you killed?"

"It's a risk I was willing to take when I ran for senate. You can't tell me the same thoughts haven't floated through your mind when you turned to pirating."

Humming, Jerry smirked. "I didn't have a choice. You did."

"I want to make a difference, and this is how I'm choosing to do it."

"I admire you for it. I certainly couldn't." Jerry's stomach clenched. "I worry about you."

"I know." Arloa lifted her chin, pressing their lips together gently.

Jerry sighed into the kiss, losing herself in the humble touch. She was going to have to tell Arloa soon what the plan was, that she wouldn't just not be around as frequently, but that it would become more difficult for her to return. They needed to trust each other fully for this to work, and for the first time in years, she wanted it to.

"I'm taking over for Miriam."

Arloa jerked back, her eyes wide. She shook her head slowly. "What do you mean?"

"I'm going to be running the underground."

Tears formed along Arloa's eyes. "That puts us in quite a spot, doesn't it?"

"In some ways, but you already have dealings with Miriam, and you're not some squeaky-clean senator either."

Arloa's shoulders tensed, though Jerry couldn't figure out why. It was obvious Arloa had dealings with the underground, they had met in Miriam's lair more than once. "I've had my dealings with her, yes."

"You'll never escape her." Jerry knew that meant the two of them would always have dealings, whether their relationship continued or not. It was a thready road they walked. "When I'm in charge, it'll be the same."

"And when will that happen?"

"Soon." Jerry straightened her back. "What are you doing about Riley?"

"With Caprese missing, nothing for now."

"This isn't something that can wait any longer."

"Senators are going missing every week now, and it's causing stress on those of us who are left."

Jerry shook her head slowly and leaned down to make her point. "If you're not worried for your safety, then it shouldn't make a difference. If you want the power, I can ensure you have it."

Arloa pressed her lips together firmly. "I'm not in any danger."

"How can you think that?" Jerry's voice raised, thundering through the room. "You're in more danger than anyone else. You're opposing Riley!"

"Drop it, Jer."

"I won't just drop it. You're not invincible."

"And neither are you." Arloa's eyes widened.

"How is this ever going to work if you don't trust me?"

Arloa said nothing. She gave Jerry a hard stare, her glare deepening as Jerry held her ground. They weren't going to get anywhere tonight. Jerry knew it in her gut. Stepping away from Arloa, with her hands out at her sides, Jerry eyed her carefully.

"When you decide to trust me, then we can talk. Until then, Arloa, we have nothing more to discuss." Jerry left in silence, her heart shuddering from the weight of the ultimatum she had just given.

CHAPTER 22

Jerry had fire in her steps as she walked up the stairs to the government house. She wasn't going to take the end of their conversation the night before lightly. Arloa needed to do something about her safety, more than she already was.

Jerry pulled off her top hat as soon as she was inside, holding it under her arm as she stepped down the hall toward Arloa's offices. She stopped short when she ran face-to-face with a scruffy looking Bert Riley. She couldn't resist the smile that lit her lips at the sight of his harried expression.

"Excuse me, sir." Jerry bowed her head slightly, and he nearly walked by her but stopped short.

His dark gaze roved over her, his lips thinning to the point that Jerry couldn't even make them out anymore. Riley scrunched his nose in a sneer before he bent toward her. "The stench off you is disgusting."

"I take that as a compliment, sir." Jerry's eyes glittered with pleasure. He recognized her, but he didn't want to admit it, not when they were in public and others could see or hear. "I did want to talk to you and express my deepest condolences over what's been happening."

Riley narrowed his gaze at her. Jerry kept her tone low so as to distract him from truly recognizing who she was and just how many conversations they'd had. She kept her shoulders squared. "Do you have a comment on it?"

"Not at all, just my sympathy for what your family must be dealing with." She knew he had a wife and children, and that the attacks she had led on his house would affect them, but the fact that he didn't seem to be handling the situation well was a plus in her books. She had worked hard to cause chaos in order to disrupt his norm. "Are they well?"

"Yes," he hissed, his nose moving up into that sneer again.

Jerry had to hold back her chuckle. She bowed her head slightly. "What do you think the scoundrels want?"

"To blame someone other than themselves," he muttered, looking over Jerry's shoulder.

She wasn't sure what was behind her in the hallway, but there was no way she thought they were close to being alone. Any confession from him here would be hard won, so she wasn't even going to try. She was simply going to tease him while she could. "Tsk, poor fellows don't even know the difference between blame and cause, do they?"

Riley flicked his gaze across her face, his jaw clenching tightly. "What do you know of cause?"

"I know for every action there is a cause, and that cause is sometimes obvious and other times not." Jerry moved in closer to him, lowering her voice as she moved. She raised an eyebrow, keeping her persona as an upper-class male in the forefront of her mind. She needed to continue to fool him as long as possible. "I know that the cause of this virus isn't as hidden as some think it is, but we've all been distracted with the fallout from it, which has made it difficult to pinpoint the reason why it's here in the first place."

"And what do you think that is?"

"Power." The word smoothly fell from her lips, dripping with the very essence of what it was. She felt it as soon as it hit her chest, seeping into her pores and puffing out her chest. She had him exactly where she wanted him. "Everything on this planet is about power, don't you agree?"

"Yes," Riley whispered.

Jerry moved in closer, her breath brushing against him when she spoke again. "But the true question is who stands to gain it and who stands to lose it, and to what end?"

Riley slowly turned his chin toward her. "And who do you suspect that would be?"

Swallowing hard, Jerry dropped her voice even lower. "Now, Senator Riley, I think the people have spoken well enough on that one. But I'm glad your family is safe."

Spinning on the toes of her boots, Jerry made her way down the hall. She held back the grin from blooming on her lips until she heard the decisive clack of his boots against the marble floor. The grab to her arm wasn't unexpected, nor was the shove into a nearby room.

"What do you mean by that?"

Jerry raised an eyebrow at him, dropping her gaze from his face to his hand still on her arm. She could compel him to do so much with one simple accusation of a touch, though as a man like the world now saw her, the weight of the accusation wouldn't be as powerful as if she was still a woman.

Raising her chin, she eyed him over as soon as he let go of her. "The people seem to have chosen who to blame."

"They're wrong."

"Are they?" She held her gaze on him, wanting some sort of answer, needing him to just admit it already. "You have to admit, Senator, that the evidence against you is stacking up quickly."

Riley growled, the sound low in his throat. "Even if I did have something to do with this damn virus there would be no way to connect me to it."

"Are you sure about that?" Jerry was going to hold her ground no matter what. She didn't have what she needed to put a nail in his coffin, but she was going to do her damnedest to make sure he paid for the crimes he had committed. "Orchestrating genocide is no small feat. Sir."

Riley's lips curled upward. "False accusations are punishable by the law."

"They would have to be false first."

The tension between them skyrocketed. Riley bore down on her, moving into her space, his face so close to hers that she could butt her head against him in an instant. But Jerry remained still, keeping herself composed and holding firm in her stance.

"I'm untouchable," he growled, his voice barely above a whisper.

"No one is," Jerry answered. "You might not be the scourge of Penum, but consequences will resound as soon as questions are answered."

Riley's eye twitched. "You have no proof."

"I have more than you could ever imagine. The lab, the connections to Fudala, to Melora, to Caprese being in your pocket. I have everything."

Riley paled, his lips slightly parted, his eyes wide.

"You're bluffing."

"Am I?" Jerry wanted to push around him, to get the hell out of the small utility room and make her way to Arloa's office where she at least thought she might have some safety from whatever this asshole was going to try, but she couldn't do that just yet. "Prove me wrong."

He remained silent, fear sliding across his gaze.

Jerry chuckled. "You can't, can you?"

"So what if I did make the virus," he hissed, anger in each and every syllable. "I didn't distribute it."

"No, Fudala did when he approved the new vaccine at the beginning of the year." Jerry straightened her shoulders, glaring.

"I never gave that order."

"Sure, you did. Kent has the approval papers, and I've seen them. The world has seen them. They just don't know what they have." Jerry straightened herself, brushing invisible lint off her arm where he had touched her. "And Lukatt was in on it, too, when he issued the stay in place orders, causing those who were upper class and could afford to stay home to survive. Little did they know they were already immune."

"You have nothing."

"I have everything!" Jerry pushed forward into him. "And now I have your confession."

She shoved her arm against his shoulder and moved out of the small utility room. Without hesitating, Jerry marched down to Arloa's offices, stepping inside and locking the doors behind her. She nodded at Arloa's secretary and burst into Arloa's interior office, locking that door.

Arloa looked up at her, weariness in her gaze as her curls fell over her shoulder. "Jer—what—"

Jerry held her finger up to her lips and shook her head. She needed a breath. She needed to know first if Riley had followed her and if he was going to come after her. She needed to know that they would be safe for a few more hours before everything blew up in their faces.

When she was greeted with silence after another minute, she stepped toward Arloa's desk and then around it. She grabbed Arloa by the forearms and pulled her up, their lips connecting in a heated kiss. Jerry closed her eyes, their tongues tangling in a furious comfort. Jerry needed this—the one thing that she knew Arloa, and only Arloa, could provide her. She held her ground when she pulled away.

"He confessed."

"What are you talking about?"

"I ran into Riley on my way in here to talk to you about last night, and… I don't know what happened. I wasn't even trying, I threw bluff after bluff, and he confessed."

"To what?" Arloa's eyes widened.

"To everything." Jerry kissed her loudly. "He told me he made it, he told me exactly how it was distributed, everything we needed."

"And no recording." Arloa pressed her hands to her hips and scowled. "Of course he would tell you when it wasn't recorded."

"It doesn't matter. He did it, and we know he did, so we can use that to our advantage. We can make him pay for what he did."

"Jer..." Arloa shook her head slowly. "It's not that simple when it comes to men like this. He's powerful. He has contacts and safeties in place, I'm sure. He has someone who will take the fall for it."

"But he confessed."

"It doesn't matter." Arloa's voice raised, her hand moving upward until it dropped suddenly. "It doesn't matter. He has everything we don't have, and we have no proof of it."

"He said he didn't distribute it."

"And he may not have, but we have nothing to bring the authorities down on him for that."

Jerry clenched her fist. "I just got a confession out of him and you want to drown it in disappointment that it wasn't written and signed."

"Jer, that's not what I mean."

"It's exactly what you mean. I can't do anything that's good enough for you, can I?" Jerry's voice rang through the small office.

Arloa flicked her gaze from Jerry to the door and back again. "Watch your tone while we're in here."

Disappointment rang through Jerry's chest, the absolute failure on her part to get proof along with a confession, the inability to be able to do something that she had been working so hard for. What good was she if she couldn't even manage that.

"We just need more time and more proof."

"I'll never be good enough for you," Jerry whispered, the truth of her statement filling the space between them. She raised her gaze, knowing that Arloa couldn't refute it. She was a nobody. She was the scourge of the planet, born and bred to never exist in the eyes of the law. No one cared about her people

—no one but herself, that was. Arloa couldn't fake that, and her election was nothing more than a fucking lie.

"I didn't say that."

"But you did, didn't you?" Jerry nodded, confirming her understanding. "You did say it because I didn't get a recorded confession. I didn't get proof that he did it, and I can't do that without being who I was born, which I can't do without landing my ass back in Joab. Nothing I do will be for the good of us or Raegina. I am no one trying to be someone who doesn't exist."

"What are you talking about?"

Jerry swallowed hard, no lump in her throat this time as the truth of her decisions and the weight of her understanding came full force. "I came here to talk to you about last night, about your safety, but I can't protect you. You wouldn't want me to in any realm of this planet. I'm not good enough for that."

Arloa's face remained passive.

Jerry leaned in, whispering harshly. "I'm no one."

"Which means you're perfect for this." At Jerry's confused expression, Arloa grabbed her hands and pulled her in closer. "Listen to me carefully, Jer, because I'm only ever going to say this once. Miriam was no one. You are no one. You will be exactly who you need to be, a ghost, because you can slip through the cracks of life. You don't exist anymore, which means everything that you can accomplish and will accomplish won't be a struggle anymore. You won't need to prove yourself."

Jerry's breath was ragged as she sucked it in. "What are you talking about?"

"You need to run the underground. You need to take your place in it, and you need to figure out who you are in this world because you do have power. You have more than Riley could ever dream of having. You just haven't grabbed hold of the reins yet."

"I don't understand."

"You don't want to, but you do. You have skirted through life by walking the line, by positioning yourself right on the edge of following the law and breaking it, but Jer, that's not where you should be. You can help so many more people without being blocked in by the confines of rules that shouldn't exist."

"What are you saying?" Jerry knew in her heart what it was, but she wasn't ready to hear it out loud. Not yet. She'd just had the biggest breakthrough of the last few months, and Arloa wasn't even going to acknowledge it. "Arloa..."

"I love you," Arloa whispered. "I do, but please believe me when I say this is the destiny I want for you. I want you to have everything at your fingertips and more. You deserve to have as much privilege as I do, but you don't, and you should. This is your chance to have that. Take it."

"Take what?"

"Take over for Miriam, and don't look back. Don't question it. Trust that you are exactly who you're supposed to be."

Jerry's lips parted in surprise, unsure of what to say or do. Her entire body moved into Arloa, their lips touching in a tender kiss. It felt different this time. The comfort was still there, but Jerry felt confident in the embrace, as though she did actually have the answers she sought. Not just the ones about Bert Riley, but the ones about herself. She had been searching to be seen, and it was Arloa, the person who shouldn't see her, who finally shone the light in her direction.

"But what does that mean for us?" Jerry whispered.

"Trust me, I'm going to need you. Very shortly."

"What does that mean?"

"Nothing for right now." Arloa straightened her back and smoothed her hands down her skirts. "I wish we could talk longer today, Jer, but I have a meeting to get to about Caprese."

"He hasn't been found yet?" Jerry squinted when Arloa jerked her chin up in Jerry's direction.

"He hasn't, and he won't be."

A line creased in the center of her forehead, and Jerry bent her neck to stare into Arloa's eyes. She had no idea where to go with that statement, where to move to figure out exactly what Arloa meant—what she wasn't saying.

"What aren't you telling me?"

Arloa pressed her hand to Jerry's side, turning her. "We'll talk tonight, yes?"

"When?"

"After the new bell tolls."

Jerry frowned, her stomach swimming with unanswered questions. "That's the middle of the night."

Arloa nodded. "I know, but I'm going to be working late. I promise I'll explain everything tonight."

"Arloa," Jerry murmured. "Tell me now."

"Not here." Arloa leaned up on her toes and pressed a kiss to Jerry's cheek. "Tonight. I promise."

CHAPTER 23

Yarrow was quiet as they all sat around the galley. Jerry pursed her lips, the radio echoing in the corner of the room with the newest updates on what the news outlets were trying to discover about one Bert Riley. It still gave her a sense of satisfaction that she was the cause of that. Even if the rest of the government wouldn't listen and investigate, at least the people were for now. That would put more pressure on the government in the long run.

Yafe sat next to her, a small packet of food on the table as she nibbled at it. Vivian and Sacha were also there while Azar finished rewiring the communications devices to protect their communications even more than they already were. Since coming back, Jerry fit right in. She hadn't had to work to find her place here, knowing exactly where she could slip into the role she needed to play.

"I'm spending the afternoon with Miriam," Jerry mumbled. "If you can have everything set to go, I think we'll take her out soon and figure out where we'll be staying for the next while."

Yafe nodded. "I'll let Azar know."

"I want you in charge of *Astilbe*."

Yafe had been resistant to that idea since Jerry had floated it, but they needed two ships and two captains, even if Yafe worked under her. "Azar would be the better choice."

"Would you like him to be with you on the ship?" Jerry held Yafe's gaze, making sure that she caught all the nuances. "You can co-captain *Astilbe*, and Vivian can stay here instead of going with you."

"I'd like that, Cap," Vivian added in her opinion.

Yafe shrugged slightly but never dropped her gaze from Jerry's. "You really think this will work?"

"I won't do it any other way. I'm not staying in Raegina."

"Then let's do it that way. We can always switch it up later if it's not working."

"We can," Jerry agreed, falling silent as she slipped a vial of water between her lips. She relaxed slightly.

Sacha stood up and moved to the radio, turning the volume up when the reporter got more excited. Jerry stayed still at the small table and finished her ration of water for the day. Sacha stayed by the radio, and Jerry turned to look her over.

"Senate Leader Bert Riley is missing."

Jerry's stomach plummeted.

"There has been no sign of him since the lunch hour when he left the government house and didn't return to lead the current session. Senator Arloa Kauket reports that there is a grave concern for the lives of the current Senators, that they are being targeted and the authorities are failing to do their job in protecting them. She says they won't stop until Senate Leader Riley is found."

Yafe hissed. "What the hell is going on?"

Jerry's stomach was twisted in knots. Arloa was still alive if she was the one giving reports, but it only doubled the fact that they needed to find some sort of protection for her, that she needed to be more careful than she was, and that this was no longer an isolated incident. Arloa's life was in danger.

The news outlet continued, "We have been assured by the

authorities that they are launching a search for Senate Leader Riley and will not stop until he is found."

Bile swirled in Jerry's stomach as the news settled into her chest. She held back the need to puke, her fingers clutching the edge of the table. She wouldn't be able to see Arloa until that night when they had already arranged a time to meet, and she wouldn't be able to check if she was all right. She hated this.

Standing sharply, Jerry stalked to the wheelhouse to help Azar finish up. She needed to keep her hands busy if she was going to distract herself from what she couldn't do. As soon as she got into the wheelhouse, the tension in her chest ratcheted up another notch. Azar sat against the wall, listening to the same news report that Jerry had.

"What do you think happened to him?"

Jerry sneered. Fear over Arloa's well-being took over all of her senses. "Nothing he didn't deserve, I'm sure."

"And your Arloa?"

"Safe as far as I know."

Azar grunted. "I don't envy the trust you have to have with her."

Jerry stilled, her heart pounding a heavy rhythm. "What do you mean?"

"You're both independent women, Cap. In order for that to work, you each have to trust the other's ability."

Sitting heavily next to him, Jerry slid her way under the dash and stared up at the wires he had pulled. She clenched her jaw, working through how far he had gotten on redoing the systems. "I'm not independent."

Azar snorted. "You absolutely are."

He moved down next to her, showing her exactly where he had left off. Jerry said nothing as they continued to put the communications systems back together. Perhaps once those were back up she could at least manage to get Arloa a message to check in, but even then, maybe Azar was right. She couldn't crowd Arloa. But this was her safety that was the concern, and unfortunately, Arloa seemed to be so nonchalant about it, as if she was immune to the potential dangers of her position.

"You don't think…" Jerry trailed off, the thought that had been running around in her mind going silent. She shook her head. "Never mind."

"That your Arloa is involved?" Azar finished for her. "I wouldn't put it past a woman like her."

Had Jerry been so blinded by the attraction between them that she had missed something? Grinding her teeth, she finished putting the communications systems back together and slid out from under the dash. Azar moved out, staying on his back as he stared up at her.

"I need to speak with Miriam."

Azar raised an eyebrow at her. "For?"

"None of your damn business." Jerry shot up to her feet. She didn't take her time gathering what she needed before she made her way to Miriam's for the rest of the day. She didn't have anything new to discuss with her, though she understood that Bert Riley would come up in conversation. All of Raegina was no doubt talking about his abduction. Still, they had work to do if Jerry was going to take over the underground by the end of the month. Arloa would have to wait until that night and the meeting time they had already set.

Jerry gasped. Arloa was covered in blood. Her heart raced, and immediately she ran over to Arloa as she stepped through the door to her apartment and rested against it, a leather bag in her hand which she promptly dropped next to the door with a heavy thud. Jerry skimmed her gaze all over her, from her head to her toe.

"Are you okay?" Jerry ran her fingers down Arloa's arms and sides, looking for where the blood came from, where the dark stains were originating. "We need to get a healer."

Arloa cleared her throat and shook her head, closing her eyes as she pushed her head against the door. "No, I'm fine."

"You're covered in blood." Jerry pulled at the cloth, needing to see under it to make sure that Arloa was fine.

Waving her hand in the air, Arloa shifted out of Jerry's grasp and moved around her. "It's nothing."

"It's not nothing!" Jerry's voice raised. She needed answers immediately. With the conversations that had been running rampant in her brain all day, and then finally confirming Arloa was all right only to have her show up covered in blood was not nothing. "What happened?"

Arloa sighed as she walked swiftly to her bedroom, pulling at her clothes as she went. Jerry didn't help her this time as the material fell away. Arloa gathered the skirts and underthings, putting them into a pile next to the washroom. She glanced over her shoulder as she walked through the door completely naked. Jerry could readily see that she didn't have a damn scratch on her, only stains from the blood against her pale skin.

She waited in silence, sitting on the edge of Arloa's bed as Arloa bathed and washed off the blood she'd come home with. The questions outweighed the answers, but Jerry wasn't even sure where to start. She wasn't even sure she knew this woman, the one who had come home covered in another person's blood.

Clenching her jaw hard, Jerry stepped into the washroom. Arloa soaked in the tub of water, running a soapy cloth over her stained skin. Her heart raced to the point it was hard to breathe, even hard to speak. They locked gazes.

"It's Riley's, isn't it?"

Arloa's lips parted, her gaze boring directly into Jerry's. "Yes."

"You *killed* him?" The accusation rang clearly through the small room.

Arloa stayed quiet for another second. She finished cleaning herself and wrung out the cloth before resting it on the edge of the tub. "Hand me the towel and robe please."

Jerry hesitated for a moment as Arloa stood up and stepped out. She grabbed the towel and handed it over and held onto the robe while Arloa dried herself off. Once she was wrapped up, Jerry crossed her arms and held her ground. She wanted a damn answer already.

"Yes."

"Yes, it's Riley's?"

Arloa nodded sharply.

"Where is he now?"

"The sea took him. Well, most of him." Arloa walked through the bedroom and out into the living area. She grabbed the leather bag she had dropped by the door and handed it to Jerry. "I thought you might be able to use this."

Furrowing her brow, Jerry locked her gaze on Arloa's impassive face. She undid the ties slowly on the bag and opened it, her stomach churning at the brain settled inside. As soon as the scent hit her, she knew she wanted to eat some. Cursing, she dropped the bag right where Arloa had picked it up from.

"What the hell is this?"

"You need it, don't you? To keep your crew alive? To stay alive yourself. Take it."

"Fuck." Jerry reached up and slid her hands into her hair, pulling at the roots. "What did you do?"

"There was no end to it, Jer. I tried every legal way possible to get him out of power, and nothing was working. I had no other choice."

Jerry's breathing came rapidly, her heart once again racing because she couldn't figure out what to say or do. "You killed him. How many more have you killed? Fudala? Caprese? The entire Melora family?"

Arloa had the decency to look guilty.

"What the fuck?" Jerry spun around, turning toward the open windows. She strode wildly to them and back again, the energy running through her nerves uncontainable. She didn't know what to do or what to say. "And this is how you were going to tell me?"

"No, I didn't plan to tell you. Not this way."

"Then what happened?"

"He nearly escaped. I'm usually…usually it's a lot cleaner than this, but he tried to escape and nearly managed it, so I didn't have a choice. I had to do it this way."

"This way." Jerry's heart shattered. "You planned this? You plan it every time. That's why you weren't worried about the kidnappings—because you're the one doing them! Fuck, Arloa, who are you?"

"I'm the same person you met in the bar nearly two years ago."

Jerry shook her head wildly. "You're not her."

"I am!" Arloa's voice rose loudly. "I haven't changed. I was there that night to meet with Miriam, not to kill her but to use her to get into power. I needed help getting into my position. No one would elect a Kauket into office. Do you know what my family has done?"

"Yes!" Jerry screamed. "I know exactly what they've done!" Jerry breathed heavily, the air rushing from her lungs as she stared wide-eyed at Arloa. "I've been the victim of their methods for years, and you're exactly like them. Fuck, I should have known better."

"Riley was a sadistic asshole. He got what he deserved."

Jerry couldn't fault the logic there. She'd had the thought before, had hoped it would happen even, but to be standing in front of his murderer who had no remorse about what she'd just done was not something she had imagined possible. "And the others? How many have you kidnapped and killed?"

"Twenty-seven."

Jerry's heart sank. Arloa didn't even have to think about it, and that was way more than Jerry had thought it would be. She sat down on the sofa and covered her face with her hands, her head hanging. What the hell was she supposed to do with this? Her shoulders were tight, her heart was broken, and if Arloa took one more step toward her, she was likely to jump out the window after breaking it out. "You're a monster."

"No," Arloa defended. "Each of the people I've killed deserved it."

"You deserve it."

"Jer, let me ask you this."

Jerry nearly snorted at the use of the nickname. It wasn't anything she wanted to hear now.

"How many people have you killed?"

"That's different. I'm a pirate. I kill to survive."

"Do you?" Arloa raised an eyebrow as she sat next to Jerry on the sofa, her hand landing on Jerry's knee. "Because Damon wasn't just to survive. Blaise Lotchski wasn't just to survive. His crew wasn't just for that."

Jerry clenched her jaw. "How do you know about that?"

"I know what happens in my city. I don't set my sights on someone, someone I became obsessed with quickly, without doing my research into who she is."

Knocking her chin up, Jerry eyed Arloa carefully. "You know everything about me, don't you?"

"Yes," Arloa answered.

"I'm so fucking naive." Standing sharply, Jerry stalked back to the window. Her head pounded relentlessly, and she couldn't make sense of what was happening. She had missed so many signs that were there. The extra time between dates in the beginning, the way Arloa knew exactly where to find her when she'd been marooned, how to get her out of Joab without being detected. She should have questioned it more. This wasn't just love, doing this out of the kindness of her heart. This was practiced, methodical, an obsession.

Arloa finally came over to her, pressing a hand to Jerry's shoulder. "You're not naive. You didn't want to see it, but it was there all along. You ignored it because you put your heart first, and that is what I love about you, Jer."

Spinning sharply, Jerry glared. "I don't know you. I thought I did, but I don't know who you are anymore."

"I am the same person I always was." Arloa straightened up. "I haven't changed, but now you know everything."

"Do I?" Jerry charged back. "Because I feel like I know nothing. You have been lying to me for months."

"Not lying," Arloa cooed. "I just didn't tell you everything, but if you're taking over the underground, then you should know everything."

Jerry's stomach dropped. She'd seen most of the records that Miriam had kept, most of the files and Arloa's name hadn't really come up. "You're selling Miriam the brains for the market that I created."

"I am, to keep people alive."

"That's not why you're killing them, though."

Arloa had the audacity to give Jerry a demure look. "It's an added benefit, but it's not the sole reason, no. This world needs to change, and there needs to actually be an equal balance of power. That won't happen while they're in charge."

"So just blow up the government building while they're all in session!" Jerry threw her hands up in the air, unwilling to make a compromise on this.

"That would throw Raegina into chaos and anarchy."

"What about the rest of the world, huh? Potelia is one of the more progressive countries, but you know that we can't control them."

"They'll follow suit."

Jerry paused, the weight of what Arloa said hitting her full force. "You've planned a world-wide coup?"

Arloa's head canted to the side. "The start of one, yes. There are factions working across Penum to take back what is rightfully ours."

"Nothing is yours, and nothing is mine. We occupy a planet that we have destroyed."

"So let's stop destroying it."

"You can't do that by murdering all of the politicians you don't like!" Jerry had reached screaming level again, heat and fire burning in her cheeks. She couldn't even begin to fathom where Arloa might think this was a good idea in any sense of that word. "Look, I'm all for change. I'm all for improving this piece-of-shit rock we live on, but you can't do that the way you want to."

"And how are you managing to work on that problem?"

She wasn't. They both knew it. Jerry hadn't had a moment to breathe beyond survival since she had been born. She'd grown up with the problems that the world perpetuated, and she'd found her way through it but that was it. She'd never stood up for what needed to change.

"We can do this, Jer." Arloa stepped forward and grabbed Jerry's hands, lacing their fingers together. "You and I can change Raegina for the better. All we have to do is get the right people into power."

"You don't need me for that."

"I do. Believe me that I do, and that's part of the burden you're taking on with the underground."

"So you wanted me to do that so you could manipulate me?"

"No, not at all. I want you to do it because it's where you belong. What we can accomplish together with that amount of influence will be astounding. You're not afraid to get your hands dirty, and that's exactly what Raegina needs."

"You want me to join your coup."

"I want you, first and foremost. I love you. But yes, I want you to join me to fight against the oppressive governmental control." Arloa's eyes had lost their wild look, but that didn't mean that she was ready to jump on board with this lunatic idea.

"No. I can't do this." Jerry's mind spun. She had no idea what to think or where to go with this information. Her heart ached at the thought of Arloa committing atrocities, and if she worked hard enough, she could see Riley's face as she killed him.

"There is no other choice. We either fight or we give in to what they want."

"I just... I need some time to think about this." Jerry moved toward the front door. "I need some time." Escaping, she slipped from Arloa's clutches and sucked in a deep breath as soon as she made it outside. "What the fuck?"

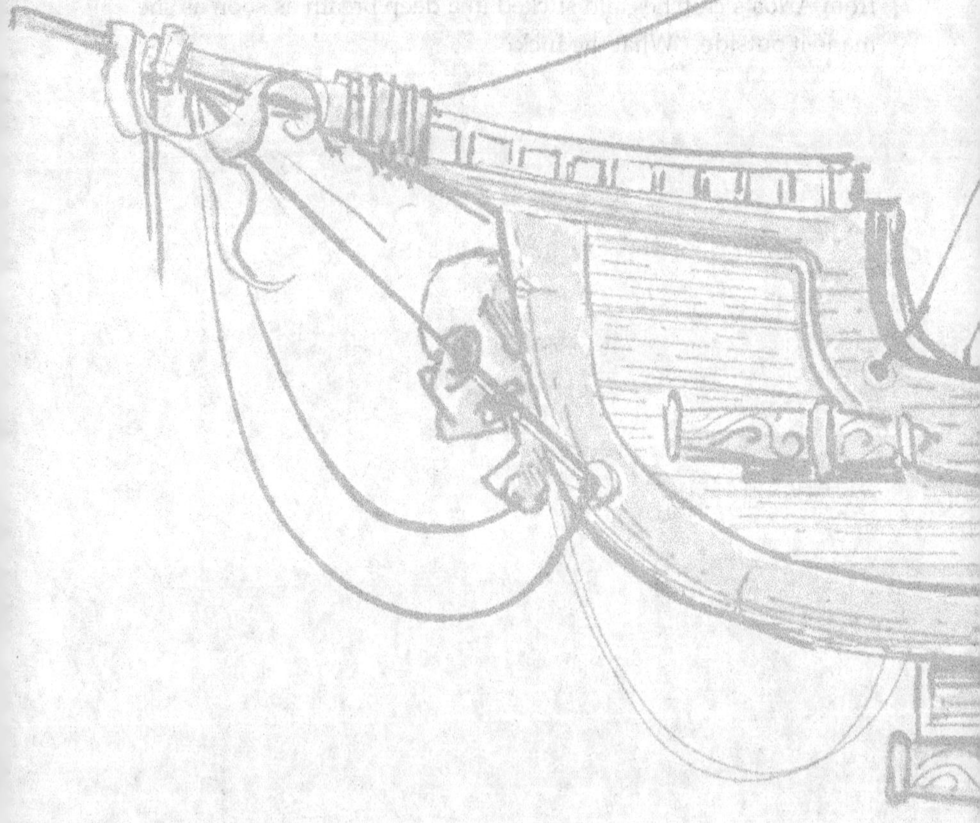

CHAPTER 24

Jerry made it back to *Yarrow*, shutting the exterior door and leaning against the interior one as she breathed heavily. Everything in her life was falling apart. She should have seen it. She wanted nothing more in that moment than to jump off the edge of the dock and never have to deal with it. Jerry clenched her fists against the metal of the door and shut her eyes tight.

What the fuck was happening?

Who the hell was Arloa?

What had she gotten herself tangled up in?

She didn't know absolutely everything that Miriam was involved in, but nothing she had discovered so far was completely out of the realm of the ordinary, and it wasn't anything Jerry hadn't expected to find. But this…Arloa had insinuated that Miriam had a hand in everything, but Jerry wasn't sure she did. Surely, she would have mentioned it, right?

"Cap?" Yafe called through the interior door as it slid open.

Jerry cringed. She didn't need any witnesses to her mental breakdown, not again. Jerry straightened her back and bolstered herself to come face-to-face with Yafe, the one person she knew she could trust.

"What happened?"

Jerry shook her head, bewildered. How would she even begin to explain this? No words could encapsulate the conversation she'd just abandoned. Yafe stood in front of her, blocking the entrance to the ship. Her face softened, and she canted her head to the side. In an instant, her arms were open, and Jerry slid into them, wrapping herself in the embrace.

Tears prickled at her eyes, her throat clogging up with snot. She couldn't breathe. What had she gotten herself into? What was she going to do? Yafe squeezed a little tighter, and Jerry melted into her. She couldn't let go. She needed the lifeline that Yafe was giving her. For the last few months, she had been on her own, surrounded by no one other than Arloa. She'd been ensconced in Arloa's lies and manipulations for so long that she couldn't even see straight.

"What happened, Cap?"

Jerry shook her head, taking a deep steadying breath. She pulled back slightly, her lips parted just as she was about to speak when the alarm on the exterior door resounded through the entryway. Jerry cringed.

"Is that her?" Yafe whispered.

"More than likely," Jerry muttered and stepped away from Yafe. "I don't want to talk to her."

"I don't think you can avoid whatever this is."

Sighing, Jerry knew Yafe was right. She couldn't avoid Arloa, not if the plans with Miriam were going to go through, not if anything was going to continue from there on out. Jerry squared her shoulders as the alarm sounded again.

"Whatever it is, Cap, I know you can handle it. You always do."

Jerry said nothing, thinking that Yafe had way more confidence in her abilities than she did. She was barely out of Joab again, she had barely helped them survive, and now she was going to plummet them into another world where they would all be on the run. None of them would have a chance of normal lives after this.

Jerry put her hand to the sensor and opened the main door. Yafe stepped out of the entrance and closed the interior door. Guess they would be having the conversation here, which was probably a good thing. Jerry didn't need to try and figure out how to get Arloa off the ship.

As soon as the door lowered down to connect with the pier, Jerry's heart clenched. Arloa's hair was still around her shoulders, the curls blowing in the breeze off the harbor. Her face was shadowed, but the stare was direct. Jerry was taken aback by it. Her heart pattered as Arloa stood still, her dress loose around her body, the jacket tight around her waist. She hadn't even taken the time to get dressed properly.

"Are you coming in here or not?" Jerry stated, her voice low and confused.

"I didn't know if I'd be invited in."

"Pointless to talk with you out there." Jerry waited patiently. It was going to be Arloa's decision to come and talk to her. Jerry waited, their gazes locked across the distance.

Finally, Arloa stepped forward, the heel of her boot clacking on the wooden door. Jerry straightened her shoulders and waited. She was going to leave the door open just in case. "I'm sorry I didn't tell you sooner."

Jerry snorted. "Because that's a conversation starter. Oh, hello, Jer, did you know I murdered someone today and fed you their brains?"

Arloa frowned and sighed, shifting the jacket tighter around her middle. "You knew I'd done it before."

"When we were desperate," Jerry hissed. "Not because of any other reason. It was the survival of my crew."

"It was, and this isn't just about your crew." Arloa stepped right up to Jerry, their bodies nearly touching. "I need you to listen to me because this isn't about murdering someone. It's about making a damn difference in order to save lives. This is war."

"What war?" Jerry shook her head.

"Look, this war has been brewing for decades. It's time for us to stand up and take action. It's all part of the plan."

"I don't know if I want to be part of that plan." Jerry held her ground, not moving as Arloa looked up at her. "I'm not a soldier."

"None of us are." Arloa took a deep breath. "Look, I've known this was coming my entire life. I grew up in that world, and I'm not willing to keep it the same. It needs to change. We have to make them see what they're doing wrong."

Jerry cocked her head to the side. "What you're doing is also wrong."

"There are always casualties in war."

"This isn't a war!" Jerry snorted. "This is you trying to make something out of nothing. Do you want to fight back? Then fight back, but you don't kidnap and kill people who don't even know what they're in the middle of."

"It's a tactic."

"It's asinine!"

"Listen to me, please." Arloa made a move to touch Jerry's hands but stopped herself. "You have been caught up in this from the start, but now you have the footing to take a stand if you want to. I don't want to force you to do anything you don't want, but you knew this was coming. We need a revolution."

"So you want to be at the start of it?"

"It's already started." Arloa locked her gaze on Jerry. "It started years ago, but Jer, I want you in this with me. I want to stop hiding it."

"I don't want to be a part of it."

Arloa nodded slowly, but she didn't move away. Cold air from the coming winter whipped through the open entry and surrounded them. Arloa shivered. "I thought you might feel that way."

"You killed someone."

"So have you, and we both had our reasons for it. You can't

keep putting that on me like I'm the only person in the world to take a life."

Jerry clenched her jaw, knowing that Arloa had a point even if she didn't want to admit it. She just thought that Arloa wouldn't get her hands dirty—not like that. It shouldn't surprise her, truthfully. Jerry pressed her lips together hard, staring into Arloa's steel-blue eyes. This was Arloa, passionate to her core about helping the underdog. Moving in swiftly, Jerry pressed their mouths together hard.

She turned Arloa into the wall, pushing her against it and holding her there as their tongues tangled furiously. She smelled so clean, her skin freshly scrubbed. Jerry clenched her eyes shut against the onslaught of the image of Arloa covered in blood.

"Why do you do this to me?" Jerry whispered against Arloa's ear, pressing their chests together.

"You're not the only one." Arloa reached up, skimming her fingers down Jerry's neck to the front of her tunic. "Ever since I met you, I haven't been able to stop thinking about you."

Arloa's fingers brushed Jerry's breast, her nipple hardening. Jerry hummed as she nipped a trail down Arloa's neck to the top of her dress. She splayed her fingers along her hip, pushing her even more into the wall.

"Jer..." Arloa breathed, her voice hitching. "Just touch me already."

Jerry grunted and palmed Arloa's breast, squeezing a little harder than she normally would. She pressed her thigh between Arloa's legs and pushed in. Arloa ground down against her, her eyes fluttering shut as her head tilted back into the wall.

"You're insane," Jerry murmured. "This will never work."

"It has to." Arloa gasped. "There's no other option."

Jerry snorted and bit hard on the top of Arloa's breast, sucking her skin and swirling her tongue until she knew there would be a mark left.

"We can't lose," Arloa murmured, her voice sounding far

away as if she was struggling to string the words together. "I want to do this with you."

Jerry wasn't sure there was ever another option. Ever since she had met Arloa, her world had revolved around her. Jerry lifted Arloa's skirts, pulling the material up to her hips and settling her thigh right against her. "This is going to fail."

"Not with you it won't." Arloa gasped, her nipples hard as she pushed her chest out. "Fuck, with you we'll succeed."

"What's the plan?" Jerry moved her mouth back to Arloa's chest, swirling her tongue in salacious circles.

Arloa moaned, her hips rutting against Jerry's thigh. "We take Raegina first."

"How?"

"I can't..." Arloa gasped. "I can't concentrate right now."

"You better." Jerry stilled every movement but kept the pressure against Arloa. "I need to know before I agree to this."

"But this way?" Arloa whined, running her fingers over Jerry's front, no doubt trying to distract her and entice her to answer. "I just want you to fuck me."

Jerry laughed, low and seductive. "Answers will get you fucked."

"Fuck." Arloa dragged in a deep breath. "Elections are in a few months, and with Riley dead there will be an emergency election for Senate Leader."

"Which you'll run for?"

Arloa shook her head. "No, I won't win that."

"You deserve it." Jerry leaned in and nipped at Arloa's neck. Despite what she'd thought when Arloa had come home, she knew that Arloa could handle that position with flying colors. "Watching you take them all to task would be sexy as hell."

Arloa whimpered and rubbed herself against Jerry again. "Please, don't stop."

Jerry laughed and pressed their mouths together in a passionate kiss. She wasn't going to give this one up. They both needed this release, for the pent-up emotions of the last few days to break through the drama of their lives. "Answer me."

"What was…the question?"

"What is the plan?"

"Fuck. Right." Arloa bit her lip, concentrating. "We'll take the Senate Leader position. Not me, but Burkhart." Arloa groaned when Jerry added counter-pressure. "I…I need to lie low."

"I'm not sure that's possible for you." Jerry kissed her again. "You stand out in a crowd."

"Not to everyone. Jer…" Arloa swallowed hard. "I'm so close."

"Then come already."

Arloa's rutting increased, her breathing got shallower, and her nails dug into the back of Jerry's arms as she held on tightly. Arloa's voice echoed in the entryway, and Jerry was filled with satisfaction that she was the cause. This woman was wild against her.

"What happens after you take Senate Leader?"

Arloa gasped, her face scrunched as she moved faster.

"What happens next?" Jerry pressed, adding in a counter motion to Arloa's movements to give her even more friction, exactly what she needed.

"Jer, I can't…" Arloa dragged in a breath. "I…I can't stop."

"Then don't," Jerry whispered, pressing their mouths together. Arloa shattered against her. Her groans reverberated through the room, her hands tightening their grip on her arms. Jerry held Arloa tight against her until she calmed, pressing gentle kisses to her neck, chest, and cheeks. "How did you find me in Joab?"

"I'll always find you, Jer. Always."

Jerry dragged in a deep breath and kissed her lightly. "What happens after we gain control of the Senate?"

Arloa smiled, her lips curling upward but her eyes still closed. In an instant, Jerry was flipped around, pressed against the wall with Arloa against her. "We change everything."

"Where do we start?"

"The authorities. We change everything about them, putting in new laws, new leaders." Arloa pulled at the ties of Jerry's pants and pushed them over her hips. She pressed their mouths together, sensually kissing Jerry.

Moaning, Jerry held onto Arloa's hips, moving their mouths together slowly. She would follow Arloa no matter what—there was no doubt about it. She had followed Arloa every moment since she'd shown up in her life. Jerry held Arloa close, her heart filling with love and adoration.

Arloa broke the embrace, giving Jerry a wicked grin as she lowered herself to her knees in front of her. Jerry threaded her fingers into Arloa's hair, holding on tight as Arloa used her tongue against the inside of her thighs.

"Join me, Jer. I need you."

Fuck. Jerry wasn't going to be able to hold back with this one. Arloa used her hands against Jerry's knees, spreading her legs until her pants stopped the movement.

"May I?"

Fuck. Fuck. Fuck. Jerry wasn't going to say no. She tightened her grasp in Arloa's hair, moving her hips toward Arloa's waiting mouth. "Fuck, yes."

Arloa took her time, pressing gentle kisses to Jerry's thighs, to the crease of her leg and hip. She nuzzled her way through the hair between Jerry's legs, her breath hot. Jerry pushed against Arloa's head, trying to get her exactly where she wanted.

"Join me, Jer," Arloa whispered. "I need you to join us."

Jerry bit the inside of her cheek, holding herself firm. She wanted to know exactly how much Arloa would beg, how far she would take it.

"Help me make this a better planet." Arloa dove in, her lips encapsulating Jerry's clit with a deep suck and swirl of her tongue.

Jerry groaned, scraping her nails across Arloa's scalp. Her mind whirled with everything that could happen in seconds if she allowed it. Jerry held her ground, undulating her hips against Arloa's mouth.

"Help me…" Arloa licked her full up "…make a…" Arloa sucked her hard, flicking her tongue rapidly over her clit "…difference."

Jerry grunted. She had never thought Arloa would beg, not like this. In her wildest dreams, she had dared to let her mind travel this direction, but she'd never thought it would actually happen.

"Let's work…" Arloa flicked her hard again "…together on this…"

Jerry clenched her jaw hard, grinding her teeth together. She was putty in Arloa's hands, unable to hold her own.

"Jer…" Arloa whispered, barely stopping the pattern long enough to speak "…I love you…" she thrusted two fingers into Jerry, curling her fingers slightly "…be with me."

"Yes…" Jerry hissed, her hips thrusting forward as waves of pleasure washed through her. She had needed this more than she could have imagined. It was the ultimate surrender, not just on her part, but on Arloa's. They were finally together without any secrets, without any barriers, without any lies. Jerry collapsed onto the floor, Arloa against her in an instant. Her lips were so soft, tender, as they kissed. Jerry held Arloa to her, deepening the embrace as she lingered. "You know I'll go with you wherever you need me."

"I love you," Arloa whispered.

"I love you, too." Jerry nipped Arloa's lower lip. "Let's take on the world."

CHAPTER 25

FOUR MONTHS LATER

Jerry stood at the helm of *Astilbe*, having left *Yarrow* out of Raegina's borders. It had been months since she'd been back, and she longed to see those curls blowing in the breeze and the smile on Arloa's face as soon as they docked. She turned the wheel slightly, pulling down on the thruster to slow their momentum.

As soon as she docked and lowered the door, Jerry made her way down to the pier. She met up with Arloa, snagged her hand, and dragged her in for a long kiss. Grinning, Jerry pecked her lips again. "Fuck, I miss fucking you."

Arloa chuckled, but her cheeks pinked. "Tonight, if there's time."

"Sure, make me wait for it."

"Never." Arloa laced their fingers together.

They walked to the small bar where they had met, sliding into their preferred seats. Jerry ordered herself a malt, something she had also missed in all the time she had been at sea. Living at sea was the best decision for her, though. She didn't want to live in Raegina proper again.

"How is *work* going?" Arloa asked.

Jerry's lips quirked at the slight intonation in her voice. They both knew what her *work* was, but they weren't willing to say it in a way anyone else might hear. "Well, you know that."

"I do, but I'm trying to make small talk."

"Then tell me what laws you're working on. That's far more interesting than the captain's job. All I do is stay in the wheelhouse and break up arguments between crewmates."

"Nonsense. You do far more than that."

"Not at all." Jerry checked the radio when the sound came through the speakers announcing the time. They had another hour before they could move, and they had timed everything perfectly. "Vivian said she wanted to meet with you, by the way. Something about some file or another that she found."

"What file?"

Jerry shrugged. "I don't know."

"Is she doing well? I know the transition—"

"She is. She'll be moving back to Raegina when the time is right, which is soon. I'm going to miss her, that's for sure." The stab to Jerry's heart was expected. She and Vivian had grown close over the past few months, but there was no denying that being out at sea that long was a struggle for her. In the end, it would be easier for Jerry to keep control of what was happening with someone like Vivian living in the city.

Jerry reached forward and rested her hand on Arloa's knee. "About tonight..."

"Everything is ready."

"I know." Jerry gave her a slight smile. "But will you come with me for a few days? I miss you."

Arloa's lips turned upward. "I thought you'd never ask."

Jerry kissed her fully then, using the moment to center herself before they went into the next big adventure of the night. They had spent the last three months planning this, and the goal was to take exactly what they needed in order to survive. Arloa was working on it on the political front and not getting anywhere, even with the Senate Leader Burkhart on their side. They hadn't managed to push through to attain the patent or the money to formulate more vestigen.

This was their backup plan, and they finally had to take action on it.

As the hour passed and Jerry finished her second malt, she paid for their drinks and held her hand out to Arloa. "Shall we?"

"Always." Arloa giggled, leaning into Jerry's side. She knew it was to play off the image that they were a couple in love, that they weren't going to steal highly classified information, that no one would suspect them when they left. But still, Jerry warmed at the thought that all of that was true.

They walked together down the cobblestone road, making their way to the building right on the edge of the inner part of the city. Arloa unlocked and pushed open the door, holding it for Jerry to step inside. She'd kept her appearance distinctly masculine since she'd come back from Joab, finding it suited her much better than the feminine expectations.

Jerry didn't hesitate as soon as they were inside the building with the door shut and locked. She pushed Arloa by the shoulder into the wall and covered her completely. Even though she knew she wasn't going to be able to get what they both wanted in the short window of time they had, the least they could manage was this. Their mouths connected, tongues tangling as Jerry sucked in a deep breath and held Arloa as still as she possibly could.

"Jer, we don't have time."

"There's always time," Jerry mumbled before giving Arloa one long last kiss. "There. Now…where are we going?"

"You're insatiable." Arloa snagged Jerry's hand and pulled her down the hallway.

Jerry followed, her stance hardening the closer they got to where they needed to end up. Arloa slipped down the stairs into a basement, then moved into a small room. Behind a picture was a door, and she pulled a key on a chain out from between her breasts and unlocked it.

"Ready?"

"Never," Jerry muttered. She followed quickly in the dark. It smelled of stale air and dankness. Jerry scrunched her nose against it, so used to the clean air of the seas by that point. She shivered as they went forward, sliding through the tunnel underneath the city. Arloa pressed her palm against the wall to guide their way.

By the time they made the correct turns and came up to the door where they needed to break in, she stepped aside and let Jerry take control of the situation. She winked at Arloa, pulling one of the pins from her hair. Blowing on her knuckles, she knelt down and maneuvered the pin into the lock. Pressing her ear close to it, Jerry listened for the distinct click that would allow them inside.

Keeping quiet, Jerry stood up and pocketed the pin. She was going to take every chance she got to steal those from Arloa while they were on this excursion. They moved in silence as they walked through the door and into the bowels of the government house. Arloa took the lead this time, ducking her chin and covering her head with a dark scarf as soon as they were in a hallway to hide herself from the recordings.

They kept completely silent as they slipped into the archives room. Arloa moved swiftly to the back corner of the room, but Jerry took her time wandering around. Flexing her fingers against the leather gloves, Jerry skimmed the boxes of files in front of her.

They were looking for a Hail Mary, but it was their last chance to find something that could turn the tide of the revolution. They needed people, but the people they kept finding usually died swiftly from the virus. Jerry stopped short at one box. The lid was on tightly, but the writing on the edge of it had been rubbed off throughout the years.

Reaching forward, she ran her glove-clad fingers over it. On instinct, Jerry pulled the box out and settled it onto the floor. She moved through the old papers carefully, afraid that they would break if she touched them too roughly. They were ancient, definitely left over from the old times. Rubbing her lips together, Jerry narrowed her gaze in the dim light of the room to read the fading ink on the dry paper.

Jerry stood up immediately and raced to the corner of the room to find Arloa. She said nothing as she shoved the paper in front of her. Arloa hissed but took the paper and read it, her eyes widening and her fingers digging into Jerry's forearm.

"This is it. Where'd you find it?"

"Nowhere near here."

"Clean up." Arloa bent down after handing the paper back to Jerry and started to put the box she had been rifling through back together.

Jerry moved down the rows of shelves and stopped short as soon as she rounded the corner. A portly man stood with his chin down, staring at the box in question. Jerry swallowed the curse down and backed up slowly. She made her boots as silent as possible on the floor as she went back to Arloa.

"We need to go now," Jerry whispered into her ear. "We've been made."

Arloa dropped the papers she was holding and gripped Jerry's hand. They said nothing as they snuck back toward the door they'd come in, but it was blocked by two other people. They had to get Arloa out of there unseen. Her position in the senate was vital to their plans, and she couldn't handle the scandal. Not when they were getting closer to the goals.

Jerry swallowed hard and squeezed Arloa's fingers, slipping the folded piece of paper into her hand. These authorities looked to be the second-rate ones, and she knew she could take them. She knew she could trust that if they took her Arloa would find her and get her out. Jerry squared her shoulders and let go of Arloa. She stepped forward, right into the light with her head tilted down.

"Excuse me," Jerry said, her voice low.

The pudgy one jerked toward her. "Oy!"

Jerry smirked, bringing her elbow up into his chin and pushing hard against his throat. She swung her foot out behind his ankle and knocked him to the ground in a matter of seconds. The second one came at her, and Jerry ducked down. She shoved her shoulder into his gut and held her ground, forcing him to fall with his companion. She then looked up at the third one, a smile on her lips and a glint in her eyes.

"Are you all who's left?" she taunted.

"You'll pay for this."

"Will I?" Jerry laughed as she turned on her toes and ran right in the direction she'd left Arloa. She had to trust that Arloa would have snuck around and hidden herself, and that when Jerry moved and they followed, the door would be wide open. She said nothing as she moved, diving between the stacks to get away from the authorities but not too far ahead.

Their boots were heavy on the ground, the chains at their waists jingling as they went. Jerry laughed to draw their attention to her. She caught sight of Arloa's skirts as she turned down one of the stacks and Jerry slowed her pace and took the one right before it. She wove her way around and stopped again three-quarters of the way down the aisle.

"What do you say, boys? Tired yet?"

"You're under arrest for—"

"Nope. I'm not." Jerry put her hands against the shelves and pushed herself up, landing both her feet squarely into the third one's stomach. She knocked him down and ran over top of him while the other two came at her from the front of the room. This time, Jerry didn't wait or slow her pace.

She ran as fast as she could down another aisle of shelves and straight for the only exit the room had. She gripped the door-frame and spun herself to the side and back toward the office they had come in from—Bert Riley's old office. Arloa's skirts vanished at the end of the hall, and Jerry moved as fast as she could to catch up.

She slid her way through the door and locked it behind them after pulling the picture back in front of it. She held her breath as the loud claps of boots against marble reached the room. Arloa gripped her hand tightly, nails digging into her skin as they waited. If they made too much noise trying to escape, then they would no doubt be heard by the authorities as they went. They couldn't have that. They waited as the three authorities cursed and searched through the office, their boots casting shadows under the doorway.

Jerry held her breath, her knees aching from the position she found herself in, but she wasn't about to move—not until they were free and clear. It took too long for them to give up and leave. Jerry's heart thundered when Arloa pulled her down the dark, dank tunnel they'd used to get in there. By the time they got back to the small building on the outside of the city center, Jerry's paranoia was truly justified.

"Did they follow us?"

"No," Arloa mustered. "Vivian took care of the recordings, right?"

"She was supposed to."

"Then we're fine. Come on."

Arloa led the way, walking at a leisurely pace that Jerry had to struggle to slow down and match. They walked through the city streets, arm in arm, and saying absolutely nothing to each other. When Jerry looked up, she found that they were in front of Arloa's shared living space.

"Is this safe?" Jerry murmured.

"Best place as any."

"But *Astilbe*…"

"Will still be there when we leave in the morning."

"You're still coming?"

"Always."

"Even with that paper?"

Arloa slid Jerry a look as she pressed her hand to the sensor on the door. They made their way up to her apartment, and as soon as they were inside, Arloa stopped her with a hand on her arm. "Jer, this paper makes no difference in who we are to each other. You know that. I can work from your ship as easily as you can work from here."

"Yeah, but if that's what I think it is—"

"It is. And all I have to do is get this formula in the hands of my scientists, and we'll be back to making vestigen in a few short months. Think about it—no more killing in order to survive."

Jerry breathed a sigh of relief. "If only we could find a damn cure."

"One step at a time, love. One step at a time." Arloa moved in, wrapping her arms around Jerry's neck and pressing their mouths together. "For now, we have this. Tomorrow is a new day and a new part of the plan."

"And tonight?" Jerry asked, cupping Arloa's cheek.

"Tonight is ours….well, as soon as I get this to my scientists."

"You never take a break." Jerry laughed and rested her head on Arloa's shoulder. "Fine, do your work. Then I get you all to myself."

"Yes, ma'am." Arloa winked as she flounced away.

ABOUT THE AUTHOR

Adrian J. Smith has been publishing since 2013 but has been writing nearly her entire life. With a focus on women loving women fiction, AJ jumps genres from action-packed police procedurals to the seedier life of vampires and witches to sweet romances with a May-December twist. She loves writing and reading about women in the midst of the ordinariness of life.

AJ currently lives in Cheyenne, WY, although she moves often and has lived all over the United States. She loves to travel to different countries and places. She currently plays the roles of author, wife, and mother to two rambunctious youngsters, occasional handy-woman. Connect with her on Facebook, Twitter, or her blog.

facebook.com/adrianjsmithbooks

twitter.com/adrianajsmith

instagram.com/adrianjsmithbooks

tiktok.com/@sapphicbookmaker

ALSO BY ADRIAN J. SMITH

<u>**Romance**</u>

Memoir in the Making

OBlique

Love Burns

About Time

Eira

Admissible Affair

Daring Truth

Indigo: Blues (Indigo B&B #1)

Indigo: Nights (Indigo B&B #2)

Indigo: Three (Indigo B&B #3)

Indigo: Storm (Indigo B&B #4)

Indigo: Law (Indigo B&B #5)

When the Past Finds You

Don't Quit Your Daydream

<u>**Crime/Mystery/Thriller**</u>

For by Grace (Spirit of Grace #1)

Fallen from Grace (Spirit of Grace #2)

Grace through Redemption (Spirit of Grace #3)

Lost & Forsaken (Missing Persons #1)

Broken & Weary (Missing Persons #2)

Young & Old (Missing Persons #3)

Alone & Lonely (Missing Persons #4)

Stone's Mistake (Agent Morgan Stone #1)

Stone's Homefront (Agent Morgan Stone #2)

Urban Fantasy/Science Fiction

Forever Burn (James Matthews #1)

Dying Embers (James Matthews #2)

Ashes Fall (James Matthews #3)

Unbound (Quarter Life #1)

De-Termination (Quarter Life #2)

Release (Quarter Life #3)

Beware (Quarter Life #4)

Dead Women Don't Tell Tales (Tales of the Undead & Depraved #.5)

Thieving Women Always Lose (Tales of the Undead & Depraved #1)

Scheming Women Seek Revenge (Tales of the Undead & Depraved #2)

Broken Women Fight Back (Tales of the Undead & Depraved #3)